SUCCESS STORIES

—Discover how television lured veteran stage and screen actress Angela Lansbury back to the small screen after a thirty-year absence to star in *Murder, She Wrote*.

—Learn how dynamic producer Steven Bochco put together an off-beat ensemble of talented professionals for his highly successful program *Hill Street Blues*.

—Follow the trail-blazing career of *Cagney and Lacey* director Karen Arthur, who went from Broadway dancer to independent filmmaker to featured director on one of TV's hottest shows.

—Meet independent producer Aaron Spelling, whose innovative story ideas have led him to create such popular programs as *Dallas, Dynasty* and *Hotel,* plus the hit feature film *Mr. Mom*.

—And be encouraged by the many agents, writers and other well-known professionals who tell their wonderfully inspiring stories of how they broke into TV—and reveal how you can too.

OFF CAMERA

Born in Philadelphia, RICHARD LEVINSON and WILLIAM LINK now live in Los Angeles. They have created over a dozen TV series, including *Columbo* and *Murder, She Wrote*, winning two Golden Globes, three Edgar Awards for mystery writing, the Peabody, the Writers Guild of America Award and numerous other prizes for film and television work. They are the authors of a memoir of their TV career, *Stay Tuned*, and two fiction works, *Fineman* and *The Playhouse*.

OFF CAMERA

Conversations with the Makers of Prime-Time Television

by
Richard Levinson

and
William Link

A PLUME BOOK

NEW AMERICAN LIBRARY

NEW YORK AND SCARBOROUGH, ONTARIO

PLUME TRADEMARK REG. U.S. PAT. OFF. AND FOREIGN COUNTRIES
REG. TRADEMARK—MARCA REGISTRADA
HECHO EN HARRISONBURG, VA., U.S.A.

SIGNET, SIGNET CLASSIC, MENTOR, ONYX, PLUME, MERIDIAN AND
NAL BOOKS are published *in the United States* by New American Library,
1633 Broadway, New York, New York 10019, *in Canada* by
The New American Library of Canada Limited,
81 Mack Avenue, Scarborough, Ontario M1L 1M8

Library of Congress Cataloging-in-Publication Data

Levinson, Richard.
  Off camera.

  Includes index.
  1. Television broadcasting—Vocational guidance.
2. Television industry—Vocational guidance.   I. Link,
William.   II. Title.
HE8700.4.L48 1986   384.55′023′73   86-18089
ISBN 0-452-25873-1

First Printing, October, 1986

1 2 3 4 5 6 7 8 9

PRINTED IN THE UNITED STATES OF AMERICA

for Christine

CONTENTS

INTRODUCTION

This is a book about American television as it is—not as it should be, might be, can be, or will be.

The men and women that we interviewed function and often flourish within a system they may or may not condone, a system so institutionalized that it has existed, with relatively minor changes, for almost four decades.* Lamentations about its influence, however justified, are very much beside the point. It has affected—some would say infected—generations of Americans, and it is likely to continue doing so, shaping habits and attitudes in ways that are not yet fully understood.

If there is a genesis to this collection, it lies in a book we wrote about our personal experiences on the other side of the looking glass (*Stay Tuned*, St. Martin's Press, 1981). In the aftermath of publication we were invited to sit on panels, participate in seminars, speak for attribution, and, like seemingly everyone else on the planet, appear on television.

To prepare ourselves for this unaccustomed—and pleasantly seductive—public exposure, we cast around to widen our perspective by seeking the views of our colleagues. Much to our surprise, we found that there was little we could unearth, aside from the occasional Sunday supplement interview or an article in *TV Guide*, in the way of

---

*An exception was the shift from advertiser control to network control in the fifties.

practical information. It simply didn't exist, at least between covers.

This may not appear to be the greatest of unmet needs until one considers that the average family watches television (or at least has the set turned on) for almost seven hours a day. America seems to be a nation of observers, with television as its most popular spectator sport.

And yet, as we discovered, little has been written about the techniques, motives, and opinions of the professionals who actually make television on a day-to-day basis—the writers, actors, producers, and directors, and their support structure, who are responsible for providing so many of our collective fantasies and role models.

Given this vacuum, as well as our fascination—sometimes affectionate, sometimes less so—with the medium in which we earn our daily bread, we decided to conduct a series of interviews on our own.

It was, perhaps, a misguided impulse, since what falls under the generic heading of "television" are dozens of categories and subcategories. The motion picture industry, as it exists today, is manageable; one can get a handle on it. But television is like dropped mercury; it shatters into fragments and rolls into corners.

Of necessity—and to preserve our sanity—we imposed arbitrary parameters. TV news and sports, for example, are massive fiefdoms unto themselves; to deal with them, either separately or together, would have resulted in a work of encyclopedic length, and so we have left them to the scrutiny of others.

We also eliminated daytime and late-night programming, as well as game shows, talk shows, documentaries, music videos, PBS, and cable. Instead we chose to explore that aspect of television with which we're most familiar, the evening hours between eight and eleven Monday through Saturday, and seven to eleven P.M. on Sunday, known as "prime time," the most criticized (and the most watched) segment of the average viewer's daily diet.

Curiously, given the fact that they take up so much of the nation's time, most of the people we interviewed are not well-known. Aside from an occasional Aaron Spelling or Brandon Tartikoff, who for various reasons may catch the fancy of the press, the public at large is generally unaware of those behind the scenes, however influential.

David Greene, for example, directed parts of *Roots*, which reached an audience, at times, in excess of fifty million. He also directed such acclaimed television films as *Friendly Fire* and *Fatal Vision*. Yet his name is not recognized beyond the borders of the television industry; journalists would rather seek out the new-young-film-director-of-the-week for an interview.

Robert Papazian produced *The Day After*, a TV movie about the aftermath of a nuclear exchange, which engendered debate on an international scale, but the press didn't beat a path to his door. Nor did they spend any time in depth with Edward Hume, the author of the teleplay.

Like Hume, most TV writers work in near total anonymity. Only diehard "Trekkies" and sophisticated viewers know that *Star Trek* was conceived by Gene Roddenberry, and although *M*A*S*H* was one of the great success stories of the popular arts in recent years, the general public is unfamiliar with the creative contributions made by Larry Gelbart. Names such as Loring Mandel, James Costigan, and Ernest Kinoy may not ring many bells, yet in their medium they are arguably on a par with such far better-known screenwriters as William Goldman and Robert Towne.

The same tunnel vision even applied to Steven Spielberg, who directed a breathtaking Movie of the Week called *Duel*, but who had to wait until he "graduated" into motion pictures before he was discovered.

Part of the reason for this neglect is that television is comfortable, familiar, and endlessly available. It lacks the vestigial glamour of the movie business, and though it has the power to make reputations overnight, those who benefit are usually actors. It is also perceived by sections of the public as junk food. Viewers will settle in to watch *Dynasty* or *Dallas,* sometimes even refusing to answer their phones, but they do so, one suspects, with a faint air of condescension. When they stand in line for a prestigious motion picture they do not have a slippers-off attitude; they are paying good money, and what they are about to see has been validated by the critics (many of whom, ironically, appear on and owe their influence to television), so it deserves respectful attention.

Our purpose in this book is not to redress any imbalances, nor raise up unknown Lazaruses and expose them to the limelight. Rather, it is to examine the work habits, methods, backgrounds, and attitudes of members of the television community. We have attempted to select a cross section of interview subjects, from veterans who began their careers in theater, radio, or motion pictures, to relative newcomers who grew up with television.

Our choices may seem to be arbitrary, and in truth they are highly subjective. We asked Steven Bochco, for example, to talk about the problems and satisfactions of producing a weekly dramatic series (*Hill Street Blues*). We might just as easily have spoken with Barney Rosenzweig of *Cagney and Lacey* or Peter Fischer of *Murder, She Wrote.* Instead of Karen Arthur, whom we chose to represent the dramatic series director, we could have talked to Seymour Robbie, Charles Dubin, or any one of a dozen others.

When it was time to interview the head of the television division of a major studio, we decided against those we felt would take a corporate stance, so we asked Barbara Corday to talk with us. As a writer, as well as someone new to the job, she seemed less likely to dispense packaged opinions. And Brandon Tartikoff, representing the network point of view, promised to be—and was—an articulate and sometimes controversial spokesman for his vision of the way things are.

In some cases we have worked with the people we

interviewed. Bochco was our story editor on *Columbo*, David Greene directed seven of our television movies, Angela Lansbury is the star of a series we co-created, and Aaron Spelling gave us our first assignment when we came to Hollywood. The advantage of talking with friends is obvious: The interview is comfortable and candid, more a conversation than an inquisition. But there are others in this book whom we never met before the interview, and their generous cooperation is much appreciated.

It should be noted that the opinions expressed by the subjects are not necessarily shared by us—nor, for that matter, by each other. Still, in spite of the contradictions that are normal to any group of disparate individuals, there seem to be four common threads running through the interviews. One is that of frustration engendered by the daily battles against the restrictions of time. The second is the almost unanimous feeling that television, unlike motion pictures or the theater, is a producer's medium. The third is the fact that the ability to write is the most useful talent in terms of getting a toehold in what must seem to the outsider to be a closed industry.

The fourth factor became vividly apparent, at least to us, as we prepared these interviews for publication: the element of change. Like streaks of light in a cloud chamber, the men and women who work in prime-time television are constantly in motion. Steven Bochco is no longer with *Hill Street Blues*; shortly after our interview, he left MTM for 20th Century–Fox. Schiller and Weiskopf left Fox for Universal. Gary Goldberg talked to us about his plans for *Sara,* but it was canceled at the end of the 1984–85 season.

It is more than probable that others in this book will no longer be where they were at the time of their interviews. Hot shows will have cooled. Executives will continue with their endless game of musical chairmen. And any given season's schedule will be, as James Agee wrote in another context, a "preview of a period piece." Eternity, by TV standards, is measured in months. All one can hope to do is fix an extremely fluid medium at a moment in time.

Finally, most of our subjects, either during the formal interview or in preliminary conversations, seemed to agree on one very significant point—that television, give or take a fourth or fifth network, will more than likely remain much the same for the rest of the century. This despite satellite dishes, cable hookups, VCRs, or any of the new technologies presently on the horizon.

For critics of the medium, this is not encouraging news. For many in the audience, the viewers who use television as time-killer, baby-sitter, entertainment vehicle, pacifier, companion, and/or window on the world, it may well be a matter of supreme indifference. But for the people in this book, and others like them, speculation is all too often little more than a luxury. Most of them, of necessity, deal in the here and now, and their concerns are immediate and parochial: meeting air dates; selling a series; coping with malevolent weather on location sites; grappling with escalating costs; and—always—coming up with ideas. In an environment that is far from ideal, excellence is rarely a first priority.

Like it or not, this is the nature of the beast. The internal workings of the industry seem locked in, almost immutable, with scant likelihood of meaningful change. Improvement can only come through individual effort and, as idealistic as it may seem, the desire to make things better as an end in itself.

Some years ago the Writers Guild of America held a panel discussion on, of all things, "How to Improve the Quality of Television." One of the writers who attended listened very carefully to the combined wisdom of those assembled and then drove back to the studio where he was under contract.

He settled in for lunch at the writers' table in the commissary, surrounded by his fellow craftsmen. One of them engaged him in conversation, ascertained that he had indeed spent the morning speculating on ways to upgrade the medium, and asked, "Well, what's the solution?"

The writer pondered for a moment, wondering how to summarize three hours of philosophical dancing on the head of a pin. Finally he said, "Write better. Pass it on."

PART ONE
THE TELEVISION SERIES

PREFACE

For better or worse—a useful phrase when discussing commercial television—the weekly series is the bread-and-butter staple of prime-time TV. Whether drama or comedy, the hour and half-hour program is the basic building block of each network's nightly schedule.

Although the length may vary (there have been half-hour and ninety-minute dramas and, on occasion, hour-long comedies), the viewer is deemed to require a daily dose of both laughter and emotional adrenaline. Game shows may flicker in and out of fashion, variety may surface one season and submerge the next, but the episodic series has remained a constant.

There are, of course, changes of content within the form to accommodate the vagaries of public taste. Situation comedy has evolved over the years from *Dobie Gillis, The Munsters,* and *Gilligan's Island* to the socially relevant shows of Norman Lear and the gentle humor of Mary Tyler Moore, *Cheers,* and *The Cosby Show.*

In drama, action-adventure has been the mother's milk of the medium, but along with the private eye and the cop, the audience has also embraced, with varying degrees of affection, the sheriff, the doctor, the lawyer, the reporter, the comic book superhero, the mystery writer (*Murder, She Wrote, Ellery Queen*), the soldier of fortune (*The A-Team*), and members of the family unit, whether on

Family and *Call to Glory* or on such nighttime soaps as *Peyton Place, Dallas,* and *Dynasty.*

For economic reasons—everything on television exists for economic reasons—the number of episodes produced each season for a given series has dwindled from a high of thirty-nine to somewhere in the low twenties, and since the advent of the so-called "second season" and "third season," many programs are given what is known as a "short order," i.e., a commitment from a network to underwrite from four to six segments. This is the television equivalent of an out-of-town tryout, a way of assessing new (or not so new) concepts to see if they will meet with the viewer's approval.

Even with the reduction in the number of episodes, the staff of a series will be at the mercy of the clock and the calendar—there is never enough time. Networks delay "locking in" their final schedules for the upcoming season for as long as possible, seeking a competitive edge; then, having decided (at one time in March, at present in late April or early May), they expect their gardens to bloom instantaneously with scripts and final versions for an early September debut.

Since most writers and directors are transients—hired usually for no more than a handful of episodes and then moving on to other shows—the producing function has become preeminent. As Horace Newcomb and Robert S. Alley note in their book, *The Producer's Medium*:

> *Given the structure of the industry's economic organization the producer is often assigned legal and financial responsibility for the final television product. . . . He is involved from beginning to end, sees to it that continuity is maintained, that peace is kept between other members of the team, and, most important, that the series concept remains secure.**

*Newcomb, Horace and Robert S. Alley, *The Producer's Medium*. New York: Oxford University Press, 1983. p. xii.

This is one of the fundamental differences between television and the motion picture industry. Initially theatrical films were controlled by the studios, by the much-reviled "front office," presided over by the Harry Cohns, Irving Thalbergs, and Louis B. Mayers. But with the downgrading of the studio system over the years, creative authority has tended to flow to bankable star actors and top-rank directors.

In television the producer, and particularly the writer-producer (known as a *"hyphenate"*) calls the shots—subject to much backseat driving from an ever-expanding bureaucracy of network executives who march under a banner that reads: "It's our money."

The payment of that money is made in the form of a "license fee," a negotiated sum-per-episode that entitles the network to two on-air usages: a first run during the season and a rerun, usually during the summer. Since the supplier tends to spend more money on each segment than he receives from the network, he often finds himself in a deficit position. His one hope to recoup these overages, as well as make a profit, is to sell the series into syndication. There is little "back-end" interest in a series, however, unless there are more than sixty episodes available, which is why it is more important for a supplier to have an existing series renewed than to place a new one on the air.*

Television series are manufactured (a word connoting an assembly-line process, in many ways sadly appropriate) by two main entities: the majors (Universal, Fox, Columbia, Paramount, MGM); and the independents (Lorimar, Embassy, MTM, etc.). The networks will occasionally pro-

---

*At this writing, there are clouds on the syndication horizon. For a variety of reasons (large inventories, cost, shows coming into the pipeline, and competition from the likes of *Wheel of Fortune* and *The People's Court*), syndicators have all but lost interest in buying hour series. At the same time, the networks are holding fast on license fees. Suppliers are beginning to ask themselves why they should go deep into deficit on programs if they can no longer recoup on the back end.

duce a show "in house," but the number they are permitted to make is limited by currently existing consent judgments. It is also possible for a network to enter into a special relationship with a supplier; for years Aaron Spelling has had an exclusive contract with ABC.

When a series sells, the supplier will hire a producer (unless one has been involved from the beginning, in which case he may have a creative and/or financial interest). That producer will staff the show, move into a suite of offices, surround himself with framed photographs of his wife and children, and hit the ground running. In his mind's eye he will have a vision of Sisyphus standing at the bottom of a mountain with a giant stone waiting to be rolled uphill.

To help him in this time of need he will have at his disposal— assuming that he works at a studio—a production department, an art department, wardrobe and makeup departments, full legal services, secretaries, soundstages, editing and projection rooms, a print shop, a music contractor, a casting department, free coffee, and his own (albeit sometimes temporary) parking spot. Everyone in each of these departments will tell him that he is spending too much money.

Within the constraints of his budget he will hire an associate producer; a story editor; staff writers (particularly if he is doing a comedy show); a director of photography; and then, for each weekly episode, free-lance writers, directors, and actors.

A curious fact about the pool of talent available is that it is divided, as if by an invisible San Andreas fault, into the field of comedy and the field of drama, and rarely do the twain meet, at least professionally. There are comedy writers (usually teams) and dramatic writers; comedy directors and dramatic directors; comedy producers and dramatic producers. Actors may venture back and forth between these separate-but-equal worlds, but generally those in other job categories tend to remain within their own specialties.

Part of this phenomenon may be a carryover from the traditions of radio, and part is typecasting. Certainly much of it has to do with the differences between film and tape techniques. Many situation comedies are performed in front of an audience and recorded on videotape with several television cameras in constant motion. The director will sit in a control booth, deal with relatively few actors and a limited number of sets, and edit electronically in front of a TV monitor.

The dramatic episode, by contrast, is almost always on 35mm film and is shot like a motion picture with one camera, many actors, frequently "practical" (real) locations, and a seven-or eight-day shooting schedule. The footage is edited on a Moviola or a Kem, each piece being spliced together to form the final cut.

Other than the technical differences, there is also a "mystique" of comedy, and particularly the writing of comedy; it is an article of faith that some people know what is "funny" and some people do not.

The hapless writer of episodic drama has no such cachet; he (seldom she, since women seem to gravitate to—or are more welcome in—the field of comedy) is considered a mere workaday craftsman, someone who will be handed a set of characters and an already established format. His function is to provide a story line and dialogue, and he will frequently be rewritten by the staff. For whatever reason, he will often be paid less than his opposite number in comedy.

In both fields a writer "steps up" when he is asked to do the script for a pilot, which is the prototype for a new series. If the pilot results in an on-air commitment, he may suddenly find himself with a multiple script assignment; from there it's entirely possible that he may become story editor and eventually producer or executive producer, all within a season or two.

Since America puts a premium on entertainment, the men and women who fashion prime-time series are well paid, and no tears need be shed on their behalf. Nevertheless, it should be noted (if only because their efforts occupy so much of our waking hours) that they work under conditions that are antithetical to quality. Deadlines prevail. Stress is endemic. The whim of the viewer and the ferocious competitiveness of the marketplace create a climate that leads to blandness and a tendency to imitate what has already seen successful. Excellence is not always rewarded, nor are good intentions.

Moreover, even those who strive to do their best are constantly frustrated by the ramifications of a system that exists to deliver an audience to an advertiser at the lowest cost per thousand. Many actors, writers, directors, and producers hope to break loose into motion pictures where, presumably, they will breathe the heady air of creative freedom.

Others continue to stay in the trenches, grinding out their weekly quotient of film and tape; caring or not caring according to individual temperament; engaging in a dialogue each evening—again, for better or worse—with tens of millions of their fellow citizens.

THE TV SERIES: DRAMA

The Producer
STEVEN BOCHCO

Steven Bochco was born in New York in 1943 and graduated from Carnegie Tech (now Carnegie–Mellon). From 1969 until the present he has functioned in a broad range of capacities in the television industry: writer, story editor, producer, and creator and/or co-creator of nine series. Coauthor of the screenplay for the motion picture Silent Running *(1971), he is also cocreator and, until the summer of 1985, when he moved to 20th Century–Fox, the executive producer of* Hill Street Blues, *perhaps the most honored series in the history of the medium.*

What was your major in college?

BOCHCO: I was a Theater Arts major, and I graduated with a Bachelor of Fine Arts degree. My reasons for going to Carnegie Tech were, probably in this order of importance, to get out of my house, to go to a college I thought I could survive for four years, and to learn something about the theater in general and writing in particular. Television, film—neither of these was a factor. To be perfectly honest, I was an eighteen-year-old kid, unconscious about my motives; I was looking to leave home and live in an environment I thought might be supportive of talents that I had but which I felt were unformed.

Did you always see yourself as a writer?

BOCHCO: Yes. I wrote all my life, at least from the time I was seven. Short stories, poems, whatever. I always had teachers telling me I had a talent for writing, so very early on I formed an image of myself as a writer. Not as an actor, and I had no interest in directing. None. To this day.

It's quite a journey from Pittsburgh to Los Angeles, from a college campus to employment at a major film studio. How did it happen?

BOCHCO: During the sixties MCA gave writing grants to theater departments around the country. The purpose was to fund young writers who were in need of financial aid. I received one of those grants through Carnegie Tech. Also, my then-wife's stepfather was an attorney in Los Angeles, and he knew people at Universal Studios. It was really through his auspices that I was able to get a summer job there between my junior and senior years. I became an assistant to the head of the story department, a wonderful man named Mike Ludmer. He had me read material, synopsize it, things like that. He also used me as a link between the grant program and the studio. At the end of the summer he said to me, "If you like, when you graduate next June, I'll give you a job here." So I had that rarest of opportunities, a chance to go back to my last year of college knowing I had a job waiting for me in an extremely unstable industry. I took my last final, I got in my car and drove day and night, and two days later I was in Los Angeles, and the day after that I went to work for Universal. I stayed there for over twelve years.

Initially doing what?

BOCHCO: Writing. Mike Ludmer took me under his wing and made me available to producers all over the lot. Now, you have to understand something. I was twenty-two years old, I was probably not a terribly good writer, and for sure I was very young and inexperienced. There was very little of practical value to my work at that time. Nevertheless, Mike would send me around to meet people at the studio.

My first writing credit, believe it or not, was a shared

credit with Rod Serling. Universal would take unsold pilots and episodes of *Chrysler Theater* and they'd get writers to add an additional forty-five minutes on an hour's worth of material. They'd film the new material, splice it into the existing picture, and sell it in a movie package overseas. And make a lot of money, one would assume, because they certainly did a lot of them. As a kid, under that umbrella—I think I started out at one hundred fifty dollars a week, and happy to have it—I was thrilled to be actually writing something.

They put me with a man named Harry Tatelman, and the first thing I worked on was a *Chrysler Theater* called "A Slow Fade to Black," by Serling. At that time I didn't know anything about credits; I didn't know anything about anything. I just wanted to write, and Harry was very patient and very kind to me; he worked with me and I wrote all this added material and they filmed it. Suddenly I had a writing credit. I never met Rod Serling. Never met him, never spoke to him, and suddenly my name was up on this movie.

I did that kind of work for several years. Then, through a series of circumstances, I became a story editor on the Robert Stack segments of *The Name of the Game.* I worked on that show for two seasons. Then I moved over to *Columbo* as story editor. After that I did *Griff*—the ill-fated *Griff*—and *McMillan and Wife.* During *McMillan* I did some pilots, including *The Invisible Man.* My first producing credit was a Movie of the Week for ABC called *Lt. Shuster's Wife,* starring Lee Grant.

Having been a writer for all of your professional career, what did you discover when you finally produced your own film?

BOCHCO: I discovered that I knew absolutely nothing about producing—and that Universal didn't care.

Was that because the various departments could make a picture without a producer if necessary?

BOCHCO: Absolutely. The more producing credits I acquired, the more I realized that Universal's willingness to allow writers to produce was simply a result of their need to maintain a writing continuity on their television series. I didn't really learn how to produce until I left Universal.

One of your final projects there was a police drama series called Delvecchio *starring Judd Hirsch. Both Michael Conrad and Charles Haid, later of* Hill Street Blues, *were regulars. Was that your training ground for* Hill Street?

BOCHCO: Yes. I was coproducer of the series, under Bill Sackheim, and I wrote eight scripts out of the twenty segments that were made. I didn't do any formal research into police work, in the sense of taking books out of the library, but I did spend a lot of time talking to cops, ex-cops, and lawyers. Boy, I learned a lot. There was also the fact that I grew up in New York City, and I had some feeling about city life, and inner-city life in particular.

Michael Kozoll, who later cocreated Hill Street Blues *with you, was one of the writers on* Delvecchio, *wasn't he?*

BOCHCO: That's right. That's where we met.

When you moved from Universal to MTM, Kozoll collaborated with you on a script for a Movie of the Week called Vampire. *Why that particular project?*

BOCHCO: I was looking to justify my position at a new place, and for whatever reason, I've always been interested in that kind of mythology—vampires and all that stuff. Bram Stoker's *Dracula* is still one of my all-time favorites. I can't wait for my kids to read it. Also, I was looking forward to working with Mike again, and *Vampire* served to bring him over to MTM and expose him to the company.

After Vampire *you created and executive-produced a short-lived series called* Paris, *starring James Earl Jones. Still another police show.*

BOCHO: Yes. It had certain fundamental flaws, but it was nicely intentioned, and it fed into what *Hill Street* finally became, because what I began to do in *Paris,* to an even greater degree than what we had done on *Delvecchio,* was to try and frame the thing in the context of a man's personal life. Woody Paris was a police captain with an enormous amount of responsibility and very little authority. He was a true kind of middle-management guy. He had a wife; she was the one he exposed his anxiety to about the world in which he lived and the kind of work that he engaged in. She was supportive at times, and at other times she wasn't because of her own unmet needs.

So Woody Paris was a step closer from Delvecchio to Frank Furillo of Hill *Street.*

BOCHCO: Yes, I'd say so. A shaky step in many ways.

Since the concept for Hill Street Blues *originated with Fred Silverman, at that time the president of NBC, how did you and Kozoll get involved?*

BOCHO: In January of 1980, NBC asked MTM if I would do a pilot for a police series. Kozoll had been with the company for a year; his contract was running out and he was planning to leave. Since MTM wanted to maintain a relationship with him, they asked if I'd mind if he and I worked together on the NBC commitment. I had just come off *Paris,* and I was very tired. Quite honestly, I didn't like the experience of being solely responsible for the burdens of writing and producing. So I said, "Gee, I'd like to do a pilot with Mike. I think it would be great fun." But we were both reluctant to do a cop show, a fact that we communicated to NBC. They said, well, why don't you come up with some ideas that you want to do and we'll have lunch and talk about it?

Ironically, the idea we liked the best, and the one we took with us to the lunch, is now being done by Aaron Spelling, the hugely successful *Hotel.* We wanted to do *Hotel.* We thought it would be a wonderful venue for stories, and we could get away from what we had been doing for years, which was working on cop shows. We didn't have any particular interest in doing another one, and we didn't feel we had anything fresh to contribute to the genre. So we go to have lunch and we tell them we want to do *Hotel* and they listen politely, stifling yawns over their veal scaloppine.

"They"?

BOCHCO: Brandon Tartikoff, NBC's head of programming; Michael Zinberg, also of NBC; Stu Erwin of MTM; and Mike Kozoll and myself. When we finished, they told us that Fred Silverman wanted a cop show. And we said, gee, no, we don't want to do that. And they said, well, Fred wants *Fort Apache, the Bronx*. It was a movie that was currently in production, and there was a lot of talk about it. And that's what Fred wanted. And we said, well, we don't know, we don't know.

They tried to make it a more attractive proposition, telling us that unlike other cop shows, where you have your typical hero and his sidekick, this one could be done with an ensemble. We could have a lot of cops. Fred wanted to focus on aspects of their private lives. That did ring a bell. So Mike and I spent a day or two talking about it, not with one hundred percent enthusiasm, but with some growing sense that maybe we could do something that was fresh and unusual. We finally agreed to do the pilot on two conditions. The first was that they had to give us creative autonomy. Much to our surprise, they said okay. The second condition was that they set up a meeting for us with Broadcast Standards. We wanted to discuss our needs, since our show was not going to be typical of the average television series. I felt very strongly that if we couldn't get some rhythm from Broadcast Standards on the kind of show we had in mind, there was no point in doing it. We didn't want to spend three or four months of our lives in an intense involvement with something, only to have it shot down by a bunch of guys worried about offending special-interest groups. So we have this bizarre meeting at NBC with the Broadcast Standards people, fighting, arguing, yelling about something that didn't even exist—probably to the embarrassment of Grant Tinker, who was at the meeting.

The truth is that I have never liked Broadcast Standards. I've always fought them. I think that what *Hill Street* started out to be—and evolved into—was partially a result of my almost daily warfare with network Broadcast Standards.

When you conceptualized Hill Street, *you and Kozoll made certain creative decisions that are still part of the fabric of the series: the use of overlapping dialogue; a down-and-dirty quality to the cinematography; a moving, hand-held camera; almost surreal humor butting up against hard drama; and a heavily populated environment. How much of this was the writers and how much the director?*

BOCHCO: With all due respect to the enormous contributions—and they were astonishing—made by Bob Butler, the director, and Greg Hoblit, the producer, everything that was on the screen in that pilot was on the page. And the joy of that pilot, and the miracle of that pilot, was that Bob Butler knew how to translate what we had written into film. We had dialogue running down both sides of the page; every bit of background conversation was scripted. So you had to read that script and be imaginative and open to what we had done. Instead of saying, "Guys, you can't do this," Butler looked at it and said, "You know something? We'll just have people talking at the same time because that's the way you've written it. I'm going to use a lot of hand-held camera because that's what seems called for."

What was the substance of your discussions with the art director?

BOCHCO: The substance was twofold. One, to make the

set look really old and gritty and filthy and run-down and broken; and two, to use the existing *Paris* set so we could save some money.

What about the cinematographer? Did you have discussions with him about the look of the picture?

BOCHCO: Michael and I communicated our needs to Bill Cronjager, our director of photography on the pilot and for the first season, through the director and the producer.

Did Cronjager resist the kind of sloppy, messy, ragged look you wanted?

BOCHCO: To some degree he did. Not because he wasn't fully capable of it, and brilliant in its execution, but because he had probably been fired a few times for doing that. I remember two producers at Universal who fired a DP—he was really quite remarkable—for not giving them the kind of brightly lit, clean-looking film that they wanted, and that Universal required for all of its series. I mean, a guy would get fired for that.

Who selected Mike Post to do the music?

BOCHCO: Mike Post was my choice. He worked with Steve Cannell; they were good friends. I met Mike through Steve and worked with him on several other projects, dating back to *Richie Brockelman, Private Eye.* I just felt that he was the one to do *Hill Street.* He read the script and liked it a lot. I remember having a conversation with him in which I said, "You know, my instinct here is that whatever we do musically should play against what we see." And literally—everything happened so fast on *Hill Street* in the beginning—literally three days after that conversation he called me up and asked me to come over to his house. I said sure. He lives just five minutes from me, and I went into his little studio behind his house, and he sat down and played me this fragment of a theme, which was the *Hill Street* theme, and I fell in love. Everything about it seemed right to me. He gave me a cassette that he had recorded off the piano, and I brought it to the office. Nobody liked it. Kozoll was nervous about it, Greg didn't like it. I took it home, and my wife didn't think very much of it. I kept playing it for people, and they would look at me and say, what are you, nuts? I suppose I was hearing something they weren't hearing. But I guess I got a little stubborn about it, and the more everybody began to listen, the more they began to like it. I should also add that I think that piece of music is a substantial reason for the series' ultimate success.

Is television, in your view, a producer's medium?

BOCHCO: Television is a writer's medium, which is why writers become producers. Most of the really successful television producers are writers, or at least started out as writers. It gives—I'm talking specifically about series television—a creative continuity, a textual continuity. It just makes absolute sense to have the person who wrote the pilot, conceived the characters, executed the template, if you will; it makes sense to have that person responsible for the week-after duplication—or variation—of that basic theme.

What is the difference between an executive producer, a producer, and a supervising producer?

BOCHCO: I don't mean to sound cynical about this, because I'm not, but the fragmentation of the producer's credit comes from a number of things. It comes from the need to define among equals who is more equal. It comes from the need to give writers credits that are important enough to validate substantial salaries. And it comes from the fact that there is no particular job description for a producer. What you hope is that if you have an executive producer, a co-executive producer, a supervising producer, a producer—in that mix of creative energies and strengths and weaknesses you're going to have a total package of individuals who can execute the enormously complex task of writing and producing a weekly television series.

Over the years we've added titles to accommodate our need to promote people. When we started, Mike Kozoll and I were the executive producers and Greg Hoblit was the producer. That was it. Then David Anspaugh became the associate producer. The following year Kozoll withdrew, I became sole executive producer, Greg became supervising producer, and Anspaugh and Tony Yerkovitch became coproducers. And so on and so on as we brought in more people who could contribute.

What's a typical day for you as a man who runs an ongoing television series?

BOCHCO: Let me give you a busier typical day because it makes me sound more important. I'll get up between six and six-thirty, make myself a cup of coffee, and grab the newspaper. I'll usually spend an hour to an hour and a half working at home. Either I'm reading a script—because I'll have a meeting about that script as soon as I come in to the office—or I'll be looking at a tape cassette of *Hill Street* in some current stage of post-production. It will either be an assembly, or a first or second cut, and I'll look at it and make my notes so I can give them to an editor and send him on his way to effect the changes. This saves me from having to carve out screening-room time and frees up at least two hours a day for me to work with the writers, which I still consider to be the overwhelming brunt of my labors. After this homework I'll usually come in and spend the bulk of my day in my office with two to four writers. We'll either be in the process of creating a story for the next episode, or else several episodes down the line, depending on when this is during the season. As the day goes on I'll be interrupted by a hundred things, like dealing with the set, the ongoing problems that arise on a functioning series set, whether it's questions arising from the material, or an actor having a spasm of some kind. Or I might have a meeting with the MTM executives. Very often you're dealing day-to-day with network concerns. What episode are you going to air on what date? When are you going to be preempted? Can you give them a certain show for their May sweeps or their February sweeps? Plus there's always casting; you may have to run down the hall and see an actor read. Not to mention the guy coming in at ten-thirty in the morning to take everybody's lunch order, which can get to be a very funny little respite from the work.

Does this day ever end?

BOCHCO: Up until the fifth year of the show I wouldn't finish until seven or seven-thirty. Then I'd go home, have dinner, and spend some time with my family. Maybe Barbara and I would have dinner out; we'd catch up with each other and deal with whatever unique problems we had as a husband and wife working in different capacities on the same project. Then I'd get into bed and read a script, look at a tape, whatever.

The series has a remarkable acting ensemble. How were they chosen?

BOCHCO: To a substantial degree the initial casting came out of my previous relationships. It also came from Mike Kozoll's relationships, but to a much lesser extent because Mike had not been producing as long as I had. Over the years I've formed all kinds of relationships, both in Los Angeles and from my days in college. I also learned to do something that is generally not recommended in this industry, and that is to hire friends. If they're good, the fact that they're your friends shouldn't be held against them. Working with them creates a sense of community that I think is very important, even though there's a downside to it, namely the problems of redefining a relationship in employment terms, boss-worker terms. Nevertheless, it's worth it. Charlie Haid, Bruce Weitz, and I were classmates at Carnegie Tech, so they were friends of almost twenty years' standing when they did the *Hill Street* pilot. My wife went to Carnegie Tech, though not at the same time I did, although I met her briefly while I was there. Jim Sikking, who plays Lieutenant Hunter, is an old friend; our kids went to school together and our friendship predated *Hill Street* by many years. I had worked in the past with Kiel Martin, with Mike Warren, and with Joe Spano, who came to us through Greg Hoblit. And I got to know Mike Conrad and became very close to him when we were working on *Delvecchio*. So there really was a nucleus. It was like a repertory company that I was able to put together—over, I might add, the unbelievably strenuous objections of the casting people at NBC. Interestingly, the two actors whom I had never met in my life were Daniel J. Travanti and Veronica Hammel.

Daniel was absolutely the first actor to walk in the door and read for the role of Furillo. How many times has that ever happened? And Veronica was the absolute last actress we read for the role of Joyce Davenport. We didn't meet her until two days before we were due to start shooting. In fact, we may have already been filming when she came in. And she was very reluctant to do a series. She'd never done one, and she had turned several down. I remember walking in the hallway with her right outside my office before she came in to read. She expressed her anxiety about doing a series, and one of the things she said to me that I'll never forget was, "If I get this part and this series sells, are you going to stay with the show?" And I said, "I'll tell you what: If you get this part and the series sells, I'll never leave it as long as you're there."*

The weekly casting on Hill Street, *including the smallest parts, is excellent, considerably above the level of casting on most television series. Why?*

BOCHCO: We were very fortunate. The casting director who helped us with the pilot was Lori Openden. She did a wonderful job finding really fresh faces—blacks, Puerto

---

*Bochco was unable to keep his commitment. At the request of MTM he left the series at the end of its fifth season.

Ricans, ethnics of all kinds. We were able to avoid that tired television look. But at the time the pilot was accepted, Lori was committed to *The White Shadow,* another MTM series, so we couldn't have her for *Hill Street.* Once again I imposed on an old friendship—a casting director named Geri Windsor. I knew her when we were both at Universal, so I brought her over to MTM, and she did our casting for the first season. She did a remarkable job—so remarkable that the company quickly yanked her away from us and made her the head of MTM's casting department. Then Lori came back and cast the show for the next three years. And lest that not sound like a particularly difficult task, keep in mind that the average episode of *Hill Street Blues,* aside from what were then thirteen or fourteen regulars, had a half dozen floaters, semiregulars, whose deals had to be made on a week-to-week basis. Plus anywhere from twenty to thirty-five speaking parts every single week. And we had a policy that we've only recently begun to break a bit, which was not to bring actors back who had already been on the show.

Given the fact that you've used so many different directors, how do you maintain a consistency of style?

BOCHCO: I'll preface this by hoping that nobody feels we are being arrogant or patronizing—but Greg Hoblit takes directors to school on this show. When a new director comes to us, we sit him down and give him a crash course on our needs. Within a few days he'll probably see fifteen hours of *Hill Street.* He'll steep himself in the visual style of the show. As he begins to prepare, Greg will translate things into director's terms. Greg has probably directed more episodes of *Hill Street* than anybody, and he's a wonderful teacher. He can look at a director's plan for one day and then say, "I think it would be better if you do it this way or that way, or you don't need to cover this scene, you can do it in a one-shot, you can hand-hold here and use two cameras there," all based on his own directing experience, and from watching every other director who has worked the show. Greg has the ability to put into a director's head, in a very short period of time, an enormous amount of data about how we work. What he does is remarkable. And he, in effect, inherited the stylistic approach from Bob Butler.

The quality of the writing on Hill Street *remains high, year in and year out. Is that because it's a staff-written show?*

BOCHCO: Yes. *Hill Street* is as much of an ensemble writing effort as it is an acting effort. The way it works under me is that we have a writing staff of five or six. There are three primary story resources: me, Jeff Lewis, and David Milch. We're responsible for about ninety to ninety-five percent of all story material that you see in a given season.

Do you buy from outside sources or free-lance writers?

BOCHCO: Almost never. We have, on rare occasions, but it's almost always unsuccessful. I don't know whether that's a result of our inability to bring along outside writers or whether it's more a result of the kind of show this is—a serial melodrama. It quickly evolved into a staff-written show for obvious reasons. You try to arc a season's worth of complex storytelling involving fifteen to seventeen regular characters. We probably use up more material in a single season than most series use in five years. In a given episode there are two or three separate little stories going on, as well as another two or three big stories.

Many of these stories continue for weeks.

BOCHCO: Sometimes two or three weeks, sometimes four, and sometimes they ripple beyond that and echo in subsequent episodes, then die out, only to resurface ten to twelve weeks later.

Can you describe the writing process, given the fact that so many people are involved?

BOCHCO: Basically Jeffrey Lewis, David Milch, and I will collect all kinds of material, things that we know will function well as purely modular stories within an hour. Each segment has one story that has a beginning, a middle, and an end, along with other story lines that we may weave through three, four, six, or ten hours. We come up with the single stories as well as the ones that will carry us through a number of episodes.

The way it generally works is that David and Jeffrey and I will sit down and structure an hour show, scene by scene. We'll talk it through, and I'm usually sitting at the desk with a pad and a pencil. I'll take all of the stories within an episode and weave them into a four-act structure. Or Jeffrey will do it. We eventually come up with a four- or five-page step outline for internal purposes. Then we decide who's going to write the teleplay. Usually it's divided among three or four writers. Sometimes it's divided into acts, or even scenes. Then one of the writers has to assume primary responsibility for the sections where we bring stories from the outside into the squad room. That's where all kinds of things overlap, and someone has to take all of those elements and weave them so that things crisscross in the appropriate fashion.

For instance, we sent Joyce Davenport over to the District Attorney's office and we brought in a new public defender by the name of Chapman. Female. And over the course of six or seven episodes, in and around all of our other story lines, we began to show her as a rather frantic, wired individual. After a while we focus on her in a two- or three-part story as we expose her addiction to cocaine.

Has there been much in the way of interference from the network on Hill Street?

BOCHCO: Yes and no. Relative to other shows and other producers, no. I've had far less. But has there been network interference on any sort of chronic level over the years? Of course. For instance, we did a story about a guy who's found dead in a hotel room having clearly been involved in a meaningful relationship with a sheep. Ain't no way to get around the fact that this guy was having a relationship with this creature. Well, NBC was beside itself. We suddenly found ourselves in negotiations as to just how far we could go in implying that this man actually had carnal knowledge of this beast. NBC wanted the thing out to begin with. The battle you fight is to establish your right to have something as a story line, and your secondary battle is how far you go, scene by scene, in making it clear to your audience that this is what was going on. In this case we wound up doing it. We made a few compromises, but the story went on.

Not all network suggestions are necessarily obstructionist. Didn't NBC ask you to complete at least one story line in any given episode?

BOCHCO: Yes. During the first year they had a lot of distress over the way the show tended to serialize. And they had a very valid point. We made a fundamental alteration in the series between year one and year two—in the second season we put one story in each episode that actually completed itself within the hour. In that way the casual viewer, even though he was tuning into an episode in which four other story lines were ongoing, could latch on to at least one story that had a beginning, a middle, and an end. The network had a valid complaint, and we responded with great pleasure. We were creating our form as we went along, and that was something we hadn't anticipated.

You cocreated a series about a minor-league baseball team called Bay City Blues, *which went on the air during the fourth season of* Hill Street. *What was it like doing two television series at once?*

BOCHCO: It was unimaginably gruesome. I hated it. I don't know how Steve Cannell, or Aaron Spelling, or Glen Larsen, or any of the other multiple series producers survive. I simply hated every moment of it. It was a nightmare. Not only for me, but also a nightmare for Jeff Lewis and David Milch, because the three of us were spread over both shows. As was Greg Hoblit. I don't ever want to do that again. To try and produce two television series simultaneously—each requiring one hundred percent of your time, which is the only way I know how to do it, is impossible, at least for me. Having said that, I should add that I loved *Bay City*. I thought it was an interesting experiment, a lovely concept. I don't think we anticipated the problems of doing that kind of show week-to-week. We had difficulties at the production level, and some of the casting wasn't right. But even if everything had been perfect, if we had resolved all of those problems, I still think the show finally would have failed because of the subject matter and because of the way we chose to treat it. We did it as the really small drama that it was, as opposed to artificially adrenalizing the series. I tend to believe that series television is adrenaline-addictive and that you can't make an hour series successful unless you provide, in the body of the show, a certain number of life-and-death situations; situations that give the kind of adrenaline charge that people have come to expect. Minor-league lives in a minor-league town playing minor-league baseball, compounded by the fact that the people who do that are usually in their late teens and early twenties, just does not provide the kind of melodramatic base that I think is required for a successful hour television series.

What kind of mail do you get?

BOCHCO: It's remarkable. We get the standard kind of fan mail—I love your show and could I please have a picture of your cast?—but once you get past that you're into a whole other world. The audience—and by the way, we're not a top-ten show, we're not even a top-twenty show—the audience that is fanatical about *Hill Street Blues* is generally well educated, upwardly mobile, younger, and genuinely concerned about the environment in which they live. They go out of their way to watch us every week. They have a rather passionate interest in what we do, and they express that interest in letters that are alternately furious with us—I mean, really angry; not lunatic, just angry—or else thoughtful, moving, and always interesting to read.

You're a rather ribald and raunchy show. Do you get many letters from the Bible Belt, or from various pressure groups?

BOCHCO: Some. Nothing particularly organized. I try to answer as much of the mail as I can. It may take me several months, but I answer hundreds of letters every year. And one of the things I've said to people is that we are equal-opportunity offenders. We're as apt to take a shot at homosexuals as we are at blacks, Hispanics, or Bible Belters. I mean, we just take as many cheap shots as we can at every living, walking, breathing thing on this planet. On the assumption that we will also, by the same token, occasionally please people affiliated with any given interest. But we never set out to either please or displease anybody. It's of little concern to me what you think, philosophically, of what we do. What is important to me is that I engage your attention, and having done that, that I engage your feelings. Whatever those feelings are, you'll take them to bed with you and maybe you'll be moved to sit down and write me a letter, pro or con. And we pay attention. I love that communication. We live in Los Angeles, we live in New York. That's not America.

Do you feel any responsibility to the millions of people who watch your show?

BOCHCO: I used to say, as a blanket statement, that I don't. I used to feel my only responsibility was to myself, to the advancement of my craft. But I've modified that. Now I think I have a responsibility to be responsible—if that makes any sense. I have a responsibility not to violate my audience's expectation of a certain standard of excellence that *Hill Street* has established for itself. And I monitor that very carefully.

I don't feel I have a responsibility to present a balanced point of view. That's propaganda, not entertainment. I don't like being told that something I do offends some kind of arbitrary standard. At this moment you have many people, people who could do interesting and innovative work, who simply won't come near television because of its restrictions. On the other hand, I'm a realist. I know that I function in a medium that is not an art medium. It's not even fundamentally an entertainment medium. It's basically a selling medium. So in spite of the medium that I'm in, I always feel, with no particular resentment, that I'm blessed in doing what I do.

The obligatory question: How do people get into the business?

BOCHCO: Talent, hard work, luck, and knowing somebody who can give you a job. Probably in reverse order.

THE TV SERIES: DRAMA

The Writer
STEPHEN KANDEL

Stephen Kandel was born in New York City in 1927 and graduated from Dartmouth with a degree in History. After a brief career as a journalist he went on to become perhaps the most prolific writer in television. He has written over a dozen theatrical features, a novel, television movies and pilots, and countless episodes for television series, from Mannix, Mike Hammer, Trapper John, *and* Kojak *to* Dynasty, Charlie's Angels, Paper Chase, Hart to Hart, *and* Mission Impossible. *He has been both a producer and a story editor, and he has won, among other awards, two Christopher Medals, an Edgar from the Mystery Writers of America, a Writers Guild Award, and the Humanitas Award.*

Since television wasn't all-pervasive when you were in college, it obviously wasn't your first career choice.

KANDEL: No. I was trying to decide between teaching classes after getting a graduate degree or working as a journalist. I supported myself through my senior year by writing theses illegally for inept students and doing a lot of tutoring, but I also worked as a stringer for six small New Hampshire newspapers, so I became a newspaperman of sorts. I moved to New York and began doing a little article writing.

My father was a screenwriter, so therefore the last thing

I wanted to be was a screenwriter. Television never occurred to me. Then he was given an assignment to write a television script for a series called *Hollywood Detective,* starring Melvyn Douglas. This was the Stone Age of television. I saw one of those scripts, read it, and said, with the wisdom and maturity of my years, "This is really a piece of shit." My father said that if I thought it was so bad, I should write one myself. So I sat down that afternoon and knocked one out, just for the fun of it. And they bought it. They paid me two hundred dollars. I said, "This is incredible! It's finding money. This is it!" Eighteen months later I sold a second one to a series called *Harbor Patrol.* And went on from there.

How did you get from New York to California?

KANDEL: I met a man named Ivan Tors, an entrepreneur in television and films. I wrote a section of a screenplay for him based on John Gunther's book, *Inside Africa.* The picture was never made. But Ivan said—Ivan being Hungarian—"Steef, if you come to Hollywood, I will guarantee you a script." He didn't mention price, but whatever it was, it was more than I was making.

I had just gotten married. I packed my wife, an Electrolux vacuum cleaner, and all the rest of our household belongings into a Volkswagen beetle and we bumped our way across the country, arrived in Los Angeles, and in due course Ivan gave me a *Sea Hunt* to write. I got paid seven hundred and fifty dollars for that, and I thought it was wonderful; riches beyond imagining. Then I went into a panic, wondering if I'd ever write another. I ended up doing twenty-six of them.

What I was writing for was syndicated television, TV that was made directly for the resale market rather than for prime-time network broadcasting. Those days were my introduction to what I regard as the essential quality of television. And that is, simply, that it's a method for selling toilet paper, and writing is a very minor adjunct.

Because for one of those shows, a Western called *Tucson Trail,* I wrote a really moving and powerful story about a Catholic priest in the West at the turn of the century who lost his calling when he discovered that he had strong homosexual tendencies. Being ambivalent about his sexuality, he decided to test it with a love affair with a woman.

Well, of course they didn't want to make it, but in order to let me down easily, they said they'd submit it to the Catholic diocese for approval. To everybody's horror, the Catholic diocese thought it was a sensitive story that should be told. Two days before principal photography commenced, the producer called me in and said, "Steve, we've just had a bit of luck. The company has a commitment to a collie—a trained dog—and we can get the dog for nothing because they've already paid for the commitment. So we're scrubbing the female lead and replacing it with a collie. Would you mind doing a quick rewrite?" That's when I realized what television was. A love affair between a homosexual priest and a straight collie.

Let's let that just lie there. As a specialist in the episodic form, what do you think constitutes a typical dramatic episode from the writer's point of view?

KANDEL: An hour dramatic script consists of four acts, preceded by a teaser. The teaser is some small piece of action or drama that hooks an audience's attention and causes them to continue watching after the first commercial break. The first act usually establishes character and situation and gives the outline of the plot. The second act develops the plot and ends with a major action or dramatic sequence. The third act proceeds to solve the plot problems and then introduces a twist or surprise, and the fourth act solves whatever problems remain, usually in terms of melodramatic action.

When a writer wants to do a given TV series, the first requirement is that he or she should know the general parameters of the show. If possible, an episode of the show should be seen. Either that or the pilot, if the show hasn't been aired yet. It helps to read one or two already existing scripts to get an idea of the main characters, the general style of the show, the balance between drama and melodrama, action and comedy. Given that, and speaking for myself, I prepare three or four brief story springboards— in other words, action, plot, and character, with an emphasis on *character*. I like to come up with somebody very interesting who can become involved with the running characters.

You go into an office and there are the usual preliminary social niceties and then you tap-dance. That is, you begin to pitch like a salesman selling roofing and siding. You try to convince them of three things. One: that you understand the requirements of this particular series well enough to write it. Two: that the story is reasonably fresh and rooted in some dramatic truth; that the characters to some degree have real problems that a mass audience can emphathize with. And three: that you'll be able to deliver this particular piece within time and roughly within budget. You won't start with the sinking of the *Titanic* because they can't afford to sink the *Titanic,* even with stock footage.

If they like the first idea you tell them *stop!* You're ahead, don't fight it. If not, the thing to do is to keep pitching until something catches fire. Then a mutual process will occur that I always enjoy. They'll say, "Wait a minute, there's something there." You say to yourself, "What?" They say, "Let's kick it around a little." And you kick it around a little. Then comes a mutual rap session, out of which emerges a crystalized agreement on what the story will be. Hopefully you'll have a deal. That is, a deal to write a story.

The story will be ten or fifteen pages which outline the basic script you are going to write. You go in with that story and there are further discussions. Now there's something tangible on the table. It's further refined and occasionally rewritten. Then you go home and do the teleplay, which is usually sixty pages long. You deliver that and there's another meeting, a major one, in which you get coherent or incoherent replies to all of your questions. Then you do either a rewrite or a polish, depending on how close you were the first time around. Then it's filmed. Your script may be modified, but normally that's just in terms of whatever physical and financial necessities the show dictates. So that's the procedure in the best of all possible worlds.

In the *less* than best of all possible worlds, you come in with a story, they like the story, you write the story, they like the story you wrote, and you go forth and write the teleplay. Then you come back, and there are two new producers, and the network is suddenly involved, and everyone wants the idea they bought except they want it changed slightly—to an entirely different idea. You write it again, and when you come back, the two new producers are now at loggerheads, having a cat fight right in front of you, and you're writing for two people who are diametrically opposed as to what you should do. When you finish, there are a welter of pages and nobody is happy. Maybe it will get shot and maybe it won't, but you'll never recognize your bastard child on the screen.

What kind of relationships does the free-lance writer have with the usual cast of characters: the producer, the director, the story editor, and the network?

KANDEL: A free-lance writer almost never has a relationship with the network. In episodic TV you have a working relationship with the producer and/or story editor. You seldom have an opportunity to interact with the director, and that's a shame because such a relationship can be very valuable. On some shows the producer has enough of a sense of self to allow you to talk to the director, and you often find that the director has misread something you've written or that you've misunderstood something the director wanted. When you have the opportunity to discuss things, you can change the script to accommodate him.

You've been an executive story consultant, a story editor, and a story consultant. Do these differing titles describe differing functions?

KANDEL: Absolutely not. For two and a half years I was the jack-of-all-trades for Quinn Martin Productions. He had four and sometimes five shows on the air at the same time, and I did scripts and rewrites for all of them. I was a roving troubleshooter. Quinn had a very strong sense of job titles. He and my agent got into a huge squabble about what my title should be, and I suggested Utility Infielder. That remark tainted my relationship with Quinn permanently; he didn't think I took things seriously. Which was true.

At that point I wrote scripts for *Cannon, Barnaby Jones,* and *Streets of San Francisco.* I also acted as story editor for *Cannon,* I developed a show called *Caribe* and wrote some scripts for it, and at the same time I did polishing and rewriting for all of his other series—whatever they threw on my desk. My deal, however, was nonexclusive, which drove Quinn crazy because I could also write for outside series. He would come into my office—a cubicle— and he'd chat with me, and I could see him craning to see what was in my typewriter. Quinn is a rather plump fellow, and there he was, craning to get a look at what I was writing. Was it somebody else's script? Was it a Movie of the Week? Was it one of his? And so I'd go to tremendous lengths, of course, to find out when he was coming so I could put something in my typewriter that would drive him crazy.

The important thing to know about being a story editor is that what you do depends on your relationship with the producer. In some cases, when that relationship has been good, I've listened to writers make their pitch, worked with them to develop what I thought was a viable story, and then told the producer at the end of the day, ''I've met with four writers, and out of it I've got two good working ideas. Here they are and I think they can handle it.'' And the producer will simply validate my judgment. At times I've even worked with producers who will let me make the assignments myself, although that's relatively rare.

Aside from meeting with writers, isn't a story editor also expected to write scripts?

KANDEL: Yes, as well as doing a great deal of rewriting. He'll often change a free-lance writer's script so that it fits the parameters of an episode of the series. That may only require minor polishing—the hero wouldn't say this, or he'd do something in a different way. But sometimes a complete rewrite is needed to salvage a good idea that was done in an unacceptable way. Often it's a mix of the two. The story editor may rewrite act one because it doesn't work and act two, three, and four are okay except for an action sequence that's too complicated and needs some character modifications. There's a tremendous range of work.

Does the story editor have any contact with the actors on a series?

KANDEL: Yes. What actors usually want is not a staggering script but a staggering part, and they go by length. They sit there and count the lines. So as a story editor I've occasionally rewritten to the star's demands. And in the case of one blessed show twenty-odd years ago, to the stars' artistic standards, which were very high. A show called *The Rogues*. The cast was David Niven, Charles Boyer, Gig Young, Gladys Cooper, and Robert Coote. They were all extraordinary actors. If they couldn't say a line, it was the line's fault. If the scene didn't work, they'd stop production. I'd chase my tail down to the set and we'd have a discussion about what was wrong. I'd rewrite on the spot to make the scene work for them because they all had perfect pitch. If they told you something wasn't happening properly, it wasn't ego—it *was* ego, but it was informed ego. The problem was always with the script, not them.

You could do things with that cast that you couldn't do anywhere else. I wrote a show that opened with Gladys Cooper delivering a two-and-a-half-page monologue. Unheard of. I mean, the audience has got to go to sleep. Well, when she finished the first take, the crew applauded. It was just marvelous. It was the British National Theater on television. I thought that was the way things were going to be. The series lasted for a year. Still in reruns. Thank God. Black and white. One year.

At various times during your career you were a producer. Did you enjoy it?

KANDEL: I liked it very much, but my first day as producer I got to the studio around seven-thirty in the morning and got home around eleven at night. I woke up my wife, delivered a half-hour tirade on the problems of the day and the idiots I had to deal with, and for some reason she wasn't particularly interested. In fact, after a while she began getting pretty testy. My children would shy away from me because their mother told them not to talk to strangers. It got to be a problem, so I quit. When I was a free-lance writer, I was always home. I have four children, and I spent a lot of time with them. It was wonderful. Eventually I get tired of showing up at an office. That's been a continual pattern with me: Stay at a studio as a producer or a story editor for a year or two and then go back to free-lance writing out of my own home because I like the relative freedom.

When my children were very young, by the way, they were baffled by what I did for a living because they were under the fairly common misapprehension that the actors invented their own dialogue, and what did anyone need a writer for? Then, as they grew older, all of them at one time or another tried writing television scripts. They were curious about it. My son worked quite diligently and came to the intelligent conclusion that it was harder than it looked. They appreciated the amount of flexible time—not free time but flexible time—that I had. As a free-lance writer, I was able to be with them a good deal. They thought it was really quite a coup that I got paid for having the leisure to play tennis in the afternoons, and take them out to breakfast, and go away with them on trips. Of course, they weren't usually up at night when I was doing the work.

Over the years you haven't seemed to gravitate toward any particular genre. You've written Westerns, medical shows, mysteries, social drama, cartoony shows like Wonder Woman . . .

KANDEL: Cartoon shows.

You mean Wonder Woman?

KANDEL: No. I mean cartoons. Literal cartoons. I have no shame. I see a writer as a craftsman who should be able to function in every genre. I've written nonfiction books, I've written a novel—two novels actually, but one's not finished—I've written radio drama, science fiction, half-hour comedy sitcoms. Why not? Whatever turns you on. What I'd *like* to do is to write better drama than most of the time I'm able to. By that I mean that there's not a lot of room to write relatively serious drama on television. In addition, if you write for episodic TV, it's sometimes difficult to shift gears and write something of a more complex nature. You have to take a long breath and pull yourself back from the craft to the art. And the craft—which, given talent, is learnable—consists of applying workable and adequate solutions to dramatic problems, usually with the use of melodrama. Quick and easy. It becomes second-nature, an automatic response. Here we are, I know how to get out of this problem. But then, if you take a little time off and you look at it, you say, of course I know how to get out of that problem, so does everybody else, it's the predictable way out. But what if I dealt with these people a little more carefully, a little more closely. *Then* how would this problem be resolved? Not necessarily happily, not necessarily neatly, but somewhat more truthfully and perhaps more dramatically.

But this is hard to do in series television because nobody wants it. Well, I shouldn't say nobody wants it, because I've written some serious drama. But it's difficult because you're working in a form that's rigid and demanding. And the form has an audience that's equally demanding in its own way. To write serious drama means to deny the audience what most of that audience wants, which is relaxation, relatively painless entertainment. If you give them a knotty social problem, they're not always pleased. I'm talking about the hour episode now, because the audience rearranges its expectations when they're watching a longer form, the two-hour TV movie, for example. And there has been an occasional series that the audience expects more from, such as *The Defenders* or *The Law*. But most of the television series that were rooted in serious drama died very young. I've received awards over the bleeding corpses of high-quality series. They run three shows, they run five, they run seven shows. But it's rare that they survive.

You are, to say the least, extraordinarily prolific. How do you avoid the writer's dilemma of the occasional block, the dry spell?

KANDEL: Writers have many areas of vulnerability, and one of them is the fear of blocking. You say to yourself, "What happens if I can't do this thing, because so much of it is done on an unconscious level and the unconscious mind is an untrustworthy workman?" I'm fortunate because I don't block very often, but when I do, I have two methods of dealing with it. One is mildly psychotic and the other very practical. I do a lot of writing at night, and if I get hung up or temporarily blocked, I create a condition of deliberate schizophrenia and I lecture my unconscious. I say, "All right, we're sitting here, sleepy, two o'clock in the morning; you want to stay up all night, you're going to feel like shit. But this is where we stay until you come up with something." It works. The practical method is this: I divorce art from craft in what I'm doing. I tell myself that I know how to do this because I've done it and because I know the technical demands of the medium. I remind myself that I really enjoy doing reasonably good cabinetry or even reasonably good carpentry. I like to come up with a neat solution, a well-built piece of television writing. And that usually does it for me.

What's your relationship with your agent?

KANDEL: A friendly one. I've had the same agent for almost thirty years. Ideally he performs three functions. One: He has a much wider perspective on what's happening in the business than I do. Two: He negotiates for me. That's very important because he's a better negotiator than I am, just as I'm a better writer than he is. And third: He's somebody I can talk to, who has, to some degree, my best interests at heart. I can get an honest response from him; he'll tell me the truth. Not in terms of material, since I don't regard him as a massive maven on creativity, but he might say, "Somebody at X studio doesn't like your work. He thinks you write too fast and too much." I've heard that a lot—I can't be any good because I'm writing five shows at the same time. My agent can also fill me in on the politics of the industry. Or he can say, "Look, they're doing more half-hour comedies. I know you haven't written half-hour comedy for a while, but why don't I set up some meetings and you can talk to these people because it'd be another area for you?" Finally he keeps me in touch with the business aspects of a complicated business. I don't count on my agent to get me work, because an agent can't get you work.

What's happened to the free-lance television market in the past decade?

KANDEL: To a great degree it's vanished. There was a time when a TV series consisted of thirty-nine episodes per year. In order to make that many episodes, a great deal of autonomy had to be vested in the actual production unit. Now, for many reasons, TV makes only twenty-two episodes a year—twenty-two more expensive episodes and twenty-two episodes that are overlaid with a great many more executives. So each segment is given much more intensive scrutiny; there are many more cooks spoiling that particular broth.

There's also much less sheer physical writing required. More rewriting but much less original writing. A staff system has emerged that I think is a response to that overlay of executive observation and the fact that there are only twenty-two episodes. A staff used to be designed to facilitate the work of free-lance writers. Now a staff *replaces* the work of free-lance writers. As a result, you get a considerably more homogenous product. You don't get the occasional miracles, the script that somebody wrote in the darkness of his or her mind. Because a staff has very fixed and specific ideas of what the series should be. Scripts may be better crafted, more polished, but I think you lose a certain amount of spontaneity, a certain amount of chance and risk and quality.

What's happened as a practical matter is that it's very, very hard to make a living as a free-lance writer. It's a tragic situation. When I started, I was paid very little for a script. But now, when they're paying sixteen thousand dollars for an hour script, everyone's very nervous about giving that kind of money to someone they don't trust in advance. So fewer and fewer writers are writing for the fewer and fewer available openings.

This business has changed radically from the free-lance writer's point of view. When I broke in, I was doing syndicated television—it didn't pay very much, demanded less, and employed a lot of writers who didn't have to be terribly good. Then, between one year and the next, syndicated TV died, fell apart, vanished. Because it was discovered that they could rerun network television, which was already made and therefore cheaper. As a result, the standard for employability rose, and a lot of writers who had been able to make quite a good living were suddenly out of the business. They were totally and completely unemployable.

Then, about ten or twelve years after that, the shows began to put on staffs, and there was a corresponding sharp diminution in the amount of assignments available for free-lance writers. There was also a move toward giving free-lancers multiple deals. If somebody wrote an acceptable script, they'd give him three script commitments. That limited the free-lance market—didn't eliminate it, but limited it—and again narrowed the number of writers who could get work. Then, about five years ago, shows became staff-written to an even greater degree. So the free-lance market now is a dying animal. And I might add that it's much more difficult to break into a staff than it is to be hired to write one script.

In the light of that grim assessment, is there anything you'd suggest for the would-be free-lancer?

KANDEL: Yes. Write a script. The only thing that will still catch attention is a written script. I know of a number of occasions where people have broken into television simply by writing a script. There's a very good writer named Larry Hertzog, for example. I think he was living in Indiana and he liked the show *Hart to Hart*. He wrote a script and sent it in. They sent it back and said thank you very much. He wrote another script and sent it in. Somebody said, "Hey, this isn't bad," and wrote him an encouraging letter. By the time he did his fourth script, they bought it. The fifth script they hired him. He then became the key writer, and he's now producing *Hardcastle and McCormick*.

Another example: I'm doing a show now called *McGyver*; I think I'm the executive script consultant. A writer I know, who shall be nameless but who's had trouble getting work for a few years, said the hell with it and wrote a sample script. Now he's working for the show. It was a good script—he had a calling card. However, a lot of writers I've tried to encourage over the years haven't been willing to do the work. They'll come up with wild, funny, wonderful ideas, but they won't take those ideas and harness them into actual teleplays, into sixty or sixty-five pages. Somebody who does that much work gets attention. I don't know any other way.

What are your personal feelings, as a writer, a parent, and a citizen, about violence on television?

KANDEL: Violence is the cheapest solution to a problem. I'm rarely offended by films, and I take an absolutist approach to the First Amendment, but I was offended by *Rambo*. I will defend to the death its right to be made, but it offended me. Not because of its political implications but because it asserted clearly and loudly that the best solution to a vexing problem is mass murder. And I don't think that's healthy for a culture.

Oddly enough, television doesn't do *real* violence. Television does television violence, which is a slight variation on Road Runner comic-strip violence. And it's becoming acceptable on an unconscious level, I think, to a large percentage of the population, and that's damaging. In my own work I try to find better creative solutions than the use of violence. First of all, I don't think violence is dramatically effective anymore. A car chase is a cliché and a boring one. You can't do a good car chase on television, and who would want to? I try to write violence that is rooted in dramatic reality, and there shouldn't be much of it. You should care about the people and what drives them so that the incident of violence is the final explosion of a brew of real and recognizable human emotions. Then you don't need to have fifty anonymous and faceless figures being blown away with a machine gun; you can have a kick, a slap, a scream. That kind of violence, I think, is much more effective.

But let's be honest. I do this for a living, I do it within the requirements of this particular commercial form, and if violence is required, I deliver it. I may try to excuse myself privately by delivering it with as much taste—and *there's* an odd word in this context—as I can, but I have written violence into scripts and I've even written car chases. As for my feelings as a parent, none of my children are overtly violent. Well, one of them played football, so I suppose you can't say that. But I think he was more affected by sportscasting than melodrama on episodic television.

Do you watch much television?

KANDEL: No. I watch the new season to a limited degree every year, and that's about it. I'm very fond of opera, I appreciate ballet, I'm a founding member of the L.A. Chamber Orchestra, I like serious music, I like drama, I go to New York and spend every night at the theater, and I also go to the theater here in L.A. In other words, I like to watch somewhat more serious drama or musical drama than I write. I also read a great deal, fiction and nonfiction. History, government, psychology, sociology. As for magazines, I subscribe to everything, from the *New England Journal of Medicine* to *The Nation*, the *New Republic*, *Atlas*, and *Foreign Affairs*. And I'm very rigid with myself—when they come in, I read them, no matter how late it is. Because otherwise they accumulate in stacks.

You've done a number of long-form television movies, you've written feature films, but now you've seemed to settle in as a specialist in hour-long dramatic television. Why?

KANDEL: Economics. I like the long form, I like it a lot. I've written quite a few of them. There's more room and usually an allowance for better writing. It's much more satisfactory to write and much more satisfactory to see done than an hour episode. But it doesn't pay as well. It takes longer to write, longer to produce, and the amount of time between getting an assignment and seeing the picture made is a long haul. Also, the TV movies don't seem to rerun that often. An hour episode, on the other hand, includes a payment of an additional fee every time it's aired. And the cumulative amount of money you receive, while the initial payment is lower, is almost equivalent, or even more in some cases, than the total amount received for a two- or three-hour Movie of the Week. Plus, as a practical matter, it takes much less time to write. I'm a very fast writer. I can write an hour show in a couple of days, no problem. So for me the pay per hour is very good. Also, it's steady.

As for theatrical features, I'd love to do more of them. I sit out in the sun and the rain waiting for people to come by, seize me, and say, "We've been looking for you to do a feature film." The last time I did a theatrical picture was about ten years ago. I wrote a terrific script, he said. I say it was a terrific script because two studios were bidding for it. I wasn't hired to write it; I just wrote it. And then I went through a year and a half of hell in the process of making a really terrible movie. A year and a half. It turned out to be a butchered, bad movie, and I had a lousy experience; I had very little control and I felt that this was not a good way to go.

If I had more fortitude and less children, I might have sat down and started from scratch again. But I simply haven't tried. It's a very limited market. There are very few writers, comparatively speaking, who make a reasonably good living writing theatrical motion pictures. And they have to have a lot of patience; it takes a great deal of time and effort. I don't think it's for me. And if somebody asks me, I'll do one like a shot.

You've taught several courses in television writing. How did you go about it?

KANDEL: I took a fairly rigorous attitude. In one of the courses I required the students to write a full teleplay or screenplay during the semester. We took the hour as a basic standard, although people could write different things. I tried to replicate, in the classroom, the actual procedure. Students had to pitch me an idea, then they had to write and rewrite a story. I took them through the process of writing a scene and how to balance the dramatic progression of an hour-long piece. I also tried to make clear to them that writers had to read, that writers had to know a lot, and that writing was hard work. I was rather hard on them. I applied real standards. If they were seriously interested in learning what commercial writing was, terrific. But if they only wanted to indulge themselves and play discussion games, no.

As a result, I usually had thirty-five students come to my first lecture, and when they heard what I was up to, I was lucky to have fifteen left. I even flunked students, although I never flunked anyone who finished a script. In the course of teaching them I tried to spend a lot of time working with each student one-on-one. And I also tried to explain something that's very painful for would-be writers to hear—that there is an intangible, indefinable necessity called talent. I mean, not everyone can extrapolate totally different characters from his or her own experience. Take a nineteen-year-old male college student and ask him to write a sixty-year-old woman who is just going through menopause. And write that woman so that others can believe he's really been inside her. Some people can do that and some people can't. And the damnedest people can and the damnedest people can't.

On top of everything else, I tried to make clear to my students that there's a tremendous amount of self-discipline involved, that talent isn't enough. That disturbed them; they resented the discipline. I had reactions that ranged from black students telling me I wasn't fit to discuss the black experience because they needed the sense of something unique of their own, to students who said they had no intention of writing for money. They'd say, "We don't want to write an hour, we want to write an hour and fifteen minutes." And I told them fine—but then they should realize that they weren't talking about commercial writing. Because the ability to write within a given set of boundaries is one of the problems they'd have to deal with. They found that very difficult to accept. Nobody becomes a writer, I think, in order to write commercially. I don't think you can become a successful commercial writer without having once desired to be a writer on your own unique terms. But the necessity for channeling that unique ability, that unique vision, is part of being a writer. *King Lear,* I believe, was written in fourteen days. As a commercial enterprise. By a man who had problems with his wife, and rent to pay, and an acting company saying, we've got a deadline and would you for God's sake get the pages down here. And he didn't even have a word processor. But there he was. He knocked it out.

Could all of this be taken as a rationale for not doing good work?

KANDEL: No, it's a rationale for doing the best possible work, but within what are certain given frameworks. You want to write a novel, fine. I loved writing a novel. I really did. I had absolute freedom—and then I met my editor. And there we go. And it was okay, because the limits don't have to hurt. They can sometimes help.

Speaking of the limits, what troubles you the most about the business—let's take a major jump and call it the profession—that you're in?

KANDEL: I don't like the way the networks—and by the networks I mean most network executives—misperceive the audience. They establish a low common denominator and attempt to order writing aimed beneath it. I think that's unfortunate. These executives are essentially bureaucrats, but most of them had ambitions or have ambitions to function in a more creative area of the business. They want to produce, write, direct. And these desires are sometimes failed desires and sometimes nascent desires, but as a result they attempt to maneuver into a position of control over the people who are doing what they'd really like to do. They try to control the creative and the production processes, and I think that's a terrible limitation of the system. They don't like to let go. One of the problems this creates is self-censorship on all levels, by the writer, by the director, and by the actor.

Actors in television are mostly very competent but rarely more than that. And yet you see the same actors doing little theater and they're terrific. They're different people. Because they say to themselves, hey, wait a minute, here I can really let go. And they do. And you see *performances*. The nature of television inhibits good performances. It inhibits good writing, and good performances feed on good writing.

We don't have rehearsals, and that's a killer. I've written live TV, and in live TV you had a run-through. That was wonderful for the writer. You wrote a script and everybody said fine. Then the cast read it. And you shot yourself. Because you said, my God, this scene is false, the lines don't work, and you went back and rewrote it completely to fit the actors. You never do that in television anymore.

Yet you continue to write for the medium.

KANDEL: It would be easy to say—and fairly accurate to say—that my reasons are economic. I'm well paid. Another reason, however, is that I get a certain amount of ego gratification from building something to specifications—and building it well, within those specifications. But you have to recognize the fact that the specifications are there. The system has placed them there and they must be abided by. If you're in the business of making iron ingots and you say, I don't like the shape of an ingot, I want them in curlicues, then you're out of business. They want stackable, oblong ingots.

You've spoken of television's underestimation of its audience. But shortly before this interview Death of a Salesman *was aired opposite a rerun—a rerun—of a female cop show called* Lady Blue. *And* Lady Blue *won the time period by a substantial margin. How do you feel about that?*

KANDEL: Well, we don't have a single audience, we have a vast mass of audiences. And the fact is that in order to attract the largest possible number of people—which is what television is all about—you write, direct, produce, edit, and release a piece of film that will demand the least of an audience that doesn't want very much demanded of it. If we ever get to airing things for specific segments of the audience, then there will be a much wider variation in the work.

Also, audiences tend to change with the times. The audience in the 1960s and the early seventies, in a period of relative economic prosperity, was an audience that was prepared to deal with treatments of serious personal and social problems. I don't think that audience exists now. We live in troubled times. We have troubled audiences. A steelworker who has just seen half of his friends laid off for life is not someone who wants to go home and deal with serious sociopolitical problems. He doesn't want to see *Death of a Salesman*. The last thing he wants to see is *Death of a Salesman*. Because he's just been living *Death of a Steelworker*. He wants to watch a half-hour sitcom. He wants to watch *Lady Blue*. He wants to watch fantasy.

The Director
KAREN ARTHUR

Karen Arthur was born in Omaha, Nebraska, in 1941. She was raised in Palm Beach, Florida. After a career as a ballet dancer and an actress, and after making two independent films, Legacy *and* The Mafu Cage, *she became a television director on such episodic series as* Cagney and Lacey, Two Marriages, Boone, Remington Steele, *and* Hart to Hart. *Currently under contract to ABC, she has directed such two-hour Movies of the Week as* Victims for Victims, A Bunny's Tale, *and* The Rape of Richard Beck. *For her work on* Cagney and Lacey *she received an Emmy Award in 1985.*

Many directors begin their careers as actors. You took a different route.

ARTHUR: At a very early age I got involved in dance. When I was sixteen, I went to London with a ballet company. Never went to college. Instead I went to New York and did a short stint with Joffrey. Then I decided I didn't want to be a ballet dancer, although I choreographed several ballets—my first step behind a camera, so to speak. From there I became interested in musical comedy. I was what they called a soubrette in those days, a dancer, singer, and comedienne. I did shows like *High Spirits*—I took over for Tammy Grimes in that—and I did *Sweet Charity* and *Irma La Douce*. I also went out on the road with shows like *Damn Yankees*. I played all the great

Gwen Verdon and Chita Rivera roles on the road. Then I decided to take my acting more seriously, and I went into regional theater. "Straight" theater, you might say. I did some directing and choreographing, mostly musical comedy, in various places around the country, and I also directed some nonmusical theater.

Why did you come to Los Angeles?

ARTHUR: To be an actress in film and TV. I was still in my early twenties, and I thought, Well, now is the time, while you still have a young face and body, to go to California. So I came to L.A. and acted in television and a few feature films.

Did you turn to directing because you weren't getting enough work as an actress?

ARTHUR: Absolutely. I was bored to tears sitting at home waiting for the phone to ring. As an actress you're not able to initiate things, you feel impotent. So I decided to direct in the theater. I did workshops and whatever I could get. I directed some original plays, and then I did pieces like Genet's *The Balcony* and *The Little Prince*, subjects that I could turn into experimental theater by using my dance background. Friends of mine, actors, would look at me and say, "What are you doing—this is a film town! If you're going to direct, why aren't you making movies?" So I went to UCLA and took one of those six-week summer crash courses in filmmaking. I learned about camera, sound, editing. And I made my own film. I shot it myself, I did my own sound, cut it together—and I just fell passionately in love with the whole film process and decided everything I had been doing up to that point had been a preparation for directing films.

Thousands of young people take courses in the mechanics of filmmaking. How did you manage to break through?

ARTHUR: I began showing people my UCLA movie. It was eighteen minutes long, very masturbatory as most first films are, very surreal and artsy-fartsy, but I took it around to some of the producers I had met as an actress. They all just patted me on the head, and I began to realize that nobody was taking me seriously.

I decided that since what I wanted to do was direct feature films, maybe I should just go out and make one. I saw a one-act play in the theater called *Legacy,* by Joan Hotchkis. It was essentially a monologue, and it spoke to me. There was room in it for me to make a directorial contribution. So I acquired it and started to raise money. I began to intern with various directors so that I could actually be on a set observing. They were mostly film directors, although I spent some time with Jerry Thorpe when he was first doing the *Kung Fu* series. Through the American Film Institute program I also sat with Arthur Penn and Peter Hyams. I got to meet grips, gaffers, different crew members.

When I decided to do my feature film, I went to these people and said to the then focus-puller, now the cameraman, John Bailey, will you be my cameraman, and talked to a woman who was cutting commercials, Carol Littleton, and asked her to be my editor. I finally raised the money and made *Legacy.* It was ninety-four minutes long and cost $46,000. That was in 1974, and that was the beginning.

Who distributed the film?

ARTHUR: I did. I four-walled it, I took it to film festivals around the world, and I spent almost two years learning what distribution and marketing is about. When I came home to Hollywood, I had my own feature film under my arm, and I went around to the same producers again.

Did you have a different reception?

ARTHUR: Not really. They patted me on the head again and said, "How do we know you made it in twelve days and how do we know it really cost only $46,000?" At the time I didn't even have a Directors Guild card.

Finally a very dear friend from my musical comedy

days, Michael Gleason, was made the producer of a TV series based on the miniseries *Rich Man, Poor Man*. He said to me, "You're talented, I'll give you a shot." This was at Universal, and the executives said, "Fuck her, don't hire her." And he said, "You don't understand. I don't want to fuck her, I want to *hire* her." He put his job on the line. I was the first woman to get a DGA card and work on the Universal lot since Ida Lupino.

Today a woman director is not unusual, but when you began, you were pretty much standing alone. How were you treated?

ARTHUR: With curiosity. People would stop by the set just to watch a woman directing. And the men on the crew tested me to see if I knew what I was doing. After the shoot they came up to me and said they'd never worked with a woman before, and that I had reversed some of their expectations.

My only real problem was with one of the lead actors, and that was because I told him that he was very talented but that he was posturing; he was falling into the habits that can be developed after someone plays a character for a long time. He wasn't struggling to make it fresh. After that we didn't get along. But the crew was okay. Like every other crew, they can tell in ten minutes if you know what you're doing. The truth is, it was my first experience in episodic television, and I was scared. A studio lot and soundstages, all those people and equipment—it can be awesome. Fortunately I wasn't a total novice. I'd made a feature film and three other grant films, so there was some feeling of confidence.

Also, during the time I'd spent interning on other directors' sets I made it a point to learn as much as I could. For instance, one week I'd decide to learn about dollies. I'd go to the library and read everything I could find about dollies until I knew the vocabulary backward and forward. And then, on the set, I'd spend the entire week with the dolly grip, watching to see when he'd lay track or pipe and when he wouldn't. I'd ask him questions, and he was thrilled to give me the answers. The next week I'd spend with the electricians, and the week after that I'd spend my time in the lab trying to understand timing a print, and what's a CRI. And, of course, having done independent films, I already had a prior education. I'd actually recorded my own sound and mixed it; I even learned how to thread the machines.

Once, when I couldn't make a dent as a director, I figured I'd get in through the camera department, so I spent six weeks at Universal loading film. I loaded every magazine in the joint from three A.M. in the morning until eight A.M. It was the graveyard shift, cleaning clapper boards and loading film. So I had done everything—poorly, terribly, horribly—but I had at least done it.

When you come in to direct a Remington Steele, *a* Hart to Hart, *or a* Cagney and Lacey, *all of them very different from each other, do you vary your approach?*

ARTHUR: No, at least not in terms of my preparation. The research, the interaction with the actors—all of that is pretty similar, whatever the show.

Normally you have seven days of prep time. That's standard for a director in episodic television. In the beginning, when I wasn't working much, I'd try to go in a couple of weeks early, especially if it was a show I hadn't done before. I tried to screen as many segments of the series as the producers would like me to see, usually shows they felt were their better efforts. They'd also tell me where they wanted the series to go during that particular year, be it the first season, the second, whatever. I studied the film and then, armed with my script, I went on the set and began to smell what the chemistry was between the actors and the crew. I watched how the cameraman worked and just got the general lay of the land. When my prep time started, I went in and talked with the actors about script problems and some of the ideas I might have had. One difference between *Cagney and Lacey* and most other shows, by the way, is that they have a read-through. That's very unusual in episodic TV. Everyone takes an extra half hour at lunchtime, and there's an hour's reading. It gives an advance opportunity for work.

My first step in every show, even before dealing with the actors, is to sit down with the producers—most of the time they're also the writers—and discuss what they want from the script, as well as what I'd like to do. So that before I talk to the actors I've already solidified the way in which the producers would like to move the script and the way I'd like to move it. Sometimes these discussions are harmonious, sometimes they're not.

If the writers weren't also the producers, if they were free-lancers, would you ever meet them?

ARTHUR: Oh, yes. On *Hart to Hart* and *Remington Steele* I worked very closely with several of the writers. This may not be typical, but on the shows that I did, many of the scripts were written by nonproducing entities and then finished by the producing entities.

During casting are the producers open to your suggestions?

ARTHUR: They're certainly open to see people. When we sit in the room, and push comes to shove, I've never had an actor forced on me by a producer. If I say, "Guys, no way, I've worked with this person and he or she's just not up to it," they'll go with my decision.

Has a network ever forced you to use a particular actor?

ARTHUR: Yes. Many times. Unfortunately.

How else do you prepare, other than screening film, talking to the actors, and hanging out on the set?

ARTHUR: I always do research. If the genre is Ninja warfare, I get into the martial arts, I spend time reading, interviewing knowledgeable people, and looking at as many movies and videos as I can get my hands on. I have to try to bring some reality to something I don't know anything about. *Cagney and Lacey* had a sequence about autopsies, so I went to view several autopsies so that I could bring truth to that moment. I did a circus episode for *Remington Steele*, and I spent weeks working with circus people, the high-wire acts, animal trainers, things like that.

Once I'm assigned to a show, I keep bugging the producers. I tell them to give me at least the genre. They'll say, well, you're scheduled to do an underwater show. And I explore that world, whatever world it is.

Do you notate your script before you go in to shoot?

ARTHUR: My scripts are infamous. I do floor plans on all locations. And I do storyboards on everything. On the location floor plan I draw in various colors. Cagney may be red and Lacey blue. The camera is always yellow. I'll block number one where they start, number two where they move, and so forth. I draw in arrows of different colors to represent actors on the move, and they're color-coded with the camera and the direction it's moving in.

If something unexpected comes up, do you make changes on the set?

ARTHUR: Absolutely. All it is, is a plan. And as I've become more experienced I'm notating less. When I didn't work a lot, I'd have weeks to prepare, so I'd ask for a script as early as possible, even if it was only a rudimentary sketch, even if scenes I worked on would get thrown out. But when I began prepping one week and filming the next, when I got really busy, I found that I didn't have time to floor-plan as well as storyboard. I opted for one or the other. If I wanted to deal with the cameraman in terms of lighting or mood, I found I could do it better with storyboards.

Did you draw them yourself?

ARTHUR: Yes. When I was a kid, I studied art. I always thought I might be an artist someday.

What about photography? Was it ever a hobby of yours?

ARTHUR: No. I've never had any photographic experience.

When you're working on an episode, what is your relationship with the director of photography, given the fact that you didn't select him?

ARTHUR: It's very close. I've watched him, I've seen how he deals with his crew. I've also seen some of his shows, so I know what's happening stylistically from his point of view.

Do you think that your work as a director has been influenced by your experience as a choreographer?

ARTHUR: No question. When I understood the concept that if I took a stage and stood it on its end it became a frame, I realized that what I knew about choreography— the emotions of an audience being triggered by a dancer's movement—could be very useful. For example, a diagonal movement has far more emotion than a straight-on movement. A straight-on movement has more power. The right side of the stage is the major side, the left is the minor side. If you want something to be more off-key, you play the actor on stage left. Stage right is more direct. So I've incorporated the things I've learned as a choreographer into the staging of actors on film.

This is somewhat technical, but most directors break up a scene into rather simple elements. They usually shoot a rather static "master," which covers the scene, or at least a part of it, and then they take various close-ups and over-the-shoulder shots. The editor cuts all of this film together, going from wide, to close, to over-the-shoulder, in an attempt to give the scene pace and variety. You, on the other hand, seem to enjoy shooting only master shots, very long takes in which the actors and the camera move continuously in complex patterns, delivering wide shots and close-ups without cutting. Is this approach a conscious choice?

ARTHUR: Definitely conscious. It's part of my style. And it's a dangerous technique when you're doing episodic television. There are very few producers who will allow it, and even fewer networks. They feel safer with a lot of coverage. I used to fight them in the beginning because I didn't understand that. And I'll admit that I've gotten myself in trouble. I mean, when you're in one long master, and it doesn't work, there's no way to get out of it.

Fortunately for me, it's worked more often than not. And when it does, it gives a sense of movement, drive, and energy that the scene might not otherwise have. But it is a risk. I've done as many as ten pages with no coverage. Not only are the actors involved with a ten-minute take, but so are the members of the crew. That means that nobody can mess up anywhere—or else we have to go back to the top again. It's taken three hours for a cameraman to light a difficult master, and I've needed thirty takes to finally get it. But it's wonderful when it works. The actors adore it. They feel like they're in the theater, as if they're acting from A to Z.

Eventually I've modified this style somewhat because I began to realize that one of my reasons for attempting to do such long masters was the challenge. I wanted to set something up to be done all in one and have everybody rise to the occasion. We would have accomplished something as a unit that would really bind us all together. But every so often a cameraman would say, "You've got the actress walking into a close-up and she needs to look good, but we're seeing three hundred and sixty degrees and there's no place for me to put a light." So I began to feel that I could do the same thing in two pieces instead of one. I could cut from a master that has a stronger beginning to a master that has a better ending. And that would permit the producers, who have the responsibility for the final cut, to get out their scissors if the scene really wasn't working. It gave them an alternative.

Do you take an interest in lenses?

ARTHUR: Oh, I'm fascinated by them, yes. One of the things I think is so valuable about episodic television, particularly for a newcomer, is that on every show you can learn with a new toy. It gives you a chance to experiment. Of course, the script has to warrant it. I wanted to get on a crane, for example, because in small independent features you can't afford one. So when I was assigned to an episode that needed scope, I ordered up a crane and used it. And learned. The same with lenses. After my crane episode I'd do my 400mm lens episode because we worked on a location that we wanted to disguise—we're always making L.A. a substitute for Cairo or New York—and long lens shots help impact everything. They also give a feeling of urgency and emotion. Then maybe I'd do a whole show on a 25mm lens.

For what effect?

ARTHUR: You get more objectivity. The actors can move more freely because the focus is not nearly as important since you have a much larger depth of field.

What are some of the traps for a director in episodic television?

ARTHUR: Getting too ambitious for every sequence. Not finding the moments in the film where you can get in and get out quickly. If you have a very important scene, you want to spend time on it, so you might have to sacrifice another scene that may only be a minor one. You should let everybody know what the money scenes are. And it helps to schedule those scenes at the right time of day. Your crew may be a better crew in the afternoon than it is in the morning. And your actors may be better in the morning. So you decide what kind of scene it is, technically difficult or more difficult in terms of the acting, and you try to schedule it accordingly. You don't want to do your major scenes when you're tired and your judgment might not be the best.

When the episode is finished filming, do you do a first cut?

ARTHUR: I try to, although that's not always expected of you in episodic. For me a film doesn't end until it's on the air, and the recent DGA contract has given episodic directors some protection in this area. In all of my earlier films I was always there every minute of the day, but I'll never forget what happened on *Rich Man, Poor Man* when I showed up for the edit. I got there at eight in the morning, and the editor looked around and asked me what I was doing there. I said, "Well, we're editing now, aren't we?" And he said, "You mean, you're going to sit here the whole time?" I said, "Yes, isn't that what we do?"

What happened when you started working on shows back-to-back? You obviously didn't have the luxury, in terms of time, to sit down with an editor when you were preparing another episode.

ARTHUR: Then I'd beg him or her to come in late and stay a few extra hours at night so I could look at the cut, or work on a difficult sequence. Or I'd ask if we could get together on weekends. I mean, I'd do whatever I could to maintain my participation in the cut.

Are you involved at all with the composer when you do episodic television?

ARTHUR: The only place I've ever been able to have any input in terms of music was on *Cagney and Lacey,* and that's because Barney Rosenzweig, the executive producer, is very supportive toward the directors he believes in. He was the first one in episodic who told me, "Go ahead, do those masters, make your little features, I'll stand behind you." And I can't tell you how helpful that is, because one of the pitfalls of episodic is that you get so much flak from so many producers that pretty soon you start to say, well, if nobody's going to care if I work all night long to design this magnificent shot, or if they're going to cut it to shreds, or if, as in the hands of certain producers, it gets chopped into insert shots, then what's the point? But Barney let me get involved with the music, and given my background, it's something I like to do.

After all, I know where my movie needs help. I know where it's dangerous to get too sappy or melodramatic or too pointed—the old pointer that tells the audience where to be afraid or where to be sad. Now that I'm doing two-hour television movies instead of episodes, I work with the composer all the time. Sometimes even before the film is finished.

Did you ever have any dealings with the networks?

ARTHUR: Not as an episodic director, no. Everything filtered down through the producers. I'd hear that "they" didn't like this, or "they" didn't like that.

As you became established, you began to work more often. Did you take any time off?

ARTHUR: No. I went from show to show. I did two years like that. Back-to-back.

Why? Money?

ARTHUR: No. I'm not really interested in money. But it's so hard to get work in the first place that when something comes up, how can you say no? *I* can't. I mean, wow!—I get to do this this week, and that next week, and I'm at Fox two weeks from now, and Paramount a few weeks after that. It's exciting.

Do you think that kind of heavy workload can have a negative effect on a director's performance?

ARTHUR: No question. I began to see it on *Cagney and Lacey*. Barney came up with a great idea. He has a family over there, and he wanted that family to be more extensive. So he hired me to do every other show for the season that was coming up. And he hired another director to do the rest. There would be two directors who would alternate and do a season's worth of episodes. The other director and I were very excited, as were all the actors, because it was going to be something unique.

As it happens, the other director fell out due to a feature commitment, but I still did every other show. And that came at the tail end of a year where I had been directing episodes back-to-back. So during the last period on *Cagney,* I began to realize that I was repeating myself and falling into some bad habits. The few people who have managed to maintain their artistic integrity and have done nothing but episodic television for most of their careers—well, I don't know how they do it. And there are not many of them.

They burn themselves out.

ARTHUR: Yeah, and I understand it. I totally understand it. You begin to see the easy way, you become facile. And you're tired. You don't have the energy to stay up that extra night and design shots, or rehearse late with the actors, or walk that location again on weekends.

When I started, I'd take actors who were trying to break in, actors who wanted to work, and I used them to film pieces of *Hart to Hart* on my videotape. We'd go on a weekend to all of the locations and I'd work out what lenses I wanted to use and I'd get some of my staging in mind for the filming of the actual show. I don't do that anymore; it was partially a result of inexperience and the desire to protect myself. I'm more skilled now.

But all the skill in the world—knowing how to best use a room by looking at it, knowing whether to keep the actors still or do a walk-and-talk—all of that isn't much good if you never allow yourself to stop, get off the treadmill and take a breath.

When you're directing someone like Tyne Daley, who plays Lacey on Cagney and Lacey, *what is your function? She's lived with her character long before you arrived.*

ARTHUR: The biggest help I can be to Tyne, who brings immense thought and work to every moment, is to catch her at repetitive habits. Directors fall into certain comfortable patterns, and so do actors. I might ask her to stretch for something else as opposed to brushing the hair from her face, which might be a mannerism she's unaware of.

Is she more receptive to you when you're directing your fifth show than she was when you directed your first?

ARTHUR: Not necessarily. I think that being an actor is such a vulnerable place to be that most actors really appreciate the fact that someone is watching closely enough to catch moments that are not working or are emotionally shallow.

Are most series regulars open to suggestions?

ARTHUR: Oh, yes. At least in my experience. And I'll tell you something: They want to rehearse. They'll give you nights and weekends. Some of them, of course, are more difficult than others, but even then they'll surprise you.

On one particular series, while I was observing a few weeks before I was scheduled to come in and direct, I watched the lead actress absolutely ream out several directors. She was taking enormous liberties, really letting her ego out, and she mutilated not one, but four, directors. They just went to their knees. It was frightening. I remember standing there asking myself if I wanted to be the next one up on the firing line, whether the job was worth it. When my turn came to direct, I decided that either I'd have my head cut off or I wouldn't, so I took a deep breath and made a suggestion. Maybe it was the chemistry, but she was very responsive. And in ways that I didn't even expect.

Would you advise young filmmakers, directors in particular, to consider television? Or should they ignore it?

ARTHUR: Well, I came out of features. My way was to become an independent filmmaker. But I began to realize that it takes me a year to develop a project, a year to raise the money, a year to get it shot and edited, and then another year to see it through distribution. That's four years of my life during which I may have said "Action!" for twenty-two days. Coming from features, I had a high hat on my head about doing episodic television. But I finally reached a point where I understood that a director directs. There were many, many things that I knew nothing about, and I'd never learn them if I stayed with the independent feature route, or at least it would take me until I was my grandmother. So I made the decision, went to my agent, and told him I wanted to work in television. I said I wanted to do episodic because I'd have an opportunity to come up against different experiences every single week, new challanges every week. Good, bad, or indifferent. And I'm thrilled that I did it.

As for advice, the best thing I can tell young filmmakers is that they should learn the business. When they hear I'm getting ready to do a project, they'll call me and ask to be involved. And I'll say, "What do you do?" And they'll say, "I want to direct and I want to produce." And I'll say, "But—what do you *do*? Are you a grip, are you a gaffer, are you a sound mixer, are you a cameraman?" Half the time they don't know what I'm talking about. I mean, they don't even understand the possibilities of employment or even the semantics. That's what befuddles me the most. I think that because this business has an aura to it, people don't realize that it can be approached systematically. There's a language involved, a vocabulary. Also, it seems as if they don't want to get down to the brass tacks of making movies. They all want to start at the top.

What they should really do, for example, is learn exactly what a gaffer does. Even if they live in Nebraska and it's difficult to watch a gaffer at work, they can certainly find books on the subject. They should understand what the components are and learn the vocabulary, so when they write that letter to try to get an introduction, or when they make that journey to Los Angeles or New York or Chicago, at least they're armed with an understanding of the process.

THE TV SERIES: DRAMA

The Actor
ANGELA LANSBURY

Angela Lansbury was born in London in 1925 and came to America while still in her teens. Her first two motion picture roles, in Gaslight *and* The Picture of Dorian Gray, *won her Oscar nominations, and she received a third nomination for* The Manchurian Candidate. *Among her other films are* National Velvet *and* State of the Union. *After her Broadway debut in* Hotel Paradiso *she won the first of her four Tony Awards in the title role of the musical,* Mame. *In television she was nominated for an Emmy for the miniseries,* Little Gloria, Happy at Last, *and was awarded a Golden Globe by the Hollywood Foreign Press Association for her work in* Murder, She Wrote.

Your series, Murder, She Wrote, *was hardly your first brush with television.*

LANSBURY: No. I did quite a bit of television in the 1950s. Live, anthological shows such as *The Hallmark Hall of Fame, Studio One, Philco Playhouse, Showcase Theater.* I was living in California at the time, and in those days they used to hire you and pay you about a thousand dollars and your airfare. You'd go to New York, you'd rehearse for two weeks, and then you'd do the show.

You had a wide range of live television experience, but you'd never done a series. Why, then, after a long and successful career in motion pictures and on the stage, did you decide to do a weekly television show?

LANSBURY: This may not be statistically accurate, but it seemed to me in 1984 that, at least in America, television was the largest source of employment for actors. Broadway was shrinking in the opportunities it offered. Movies had also shrunk immeasurably since the days when I started out and was under contract to a major studio. I believe that actors now look to television not only for monetary reasons—to be employed as opposed to not working—but also artistically because it affords opportunities to play roles that one might never have a chance to do.

I certainly avoided television for years. I felt it would burn one out as a performer, that this vast audience you play to would become bored with the sight of your face if you did too much and wouldn't pay to go and see you in a movie or in the theater. Which we have discovered is, with some exceptions, true. For instance, Carroll O'Connor is a good example of an enormous television star who went to Broadway and failed—twice. Now the first play he did may not have been the greatest. But in the second play, which was not well reviewed, he got ace reviews. But it didn't help the play to run. In other words, his name on a Broadway marquee didn't mean anything, as compared to what it means in *TV Guide*.

In spite of all your trepidations, you decided to take the plunge.

LANSBURY: Yes. I'd just finished a two-year stint with *Sweeney Todd*, and I was sick of being out on the road. I wanted to stay put in one place. I was also of an age when I thought that if I ever intended to go and do television, if I was going to take the bull by the horns and reach out and hit that enormous audience which is the television audience, then I had better do it. I was healthy, I was strong, I felt energetic, and I decided to have a try. I didn't know what the subject matter was going to be, but I just pointed myself in the direction of a series.

Did you have any concerns about leaving Broadway?

LANSBURY: I felt secure enough about my career in the theater that I could safely put it "on hold" at that particular time in my life. Not that Broadway wasn't important to me. It got its grip around my ankle in 1957. And thank goodness it did, because it came at the end of a very low period in my career when the film studios were pulling in their horns and television was rearing its head in a big way. Adjustments had to be made by actors who'd been nurtured by the studios. This was in the fifties, and we suddenly had to go out and get work in live television. And I did that. We all did, those of us who could.

As I mentioned before, the work took me to New York, and I began to get the smell of Broadway. I liked it and I didn't like it. It was a pull-me push-me feeling between the New York theater and California. I adored living in California. It was very hard for me to live in New York. But finally, of course, I had a great success with *Mame* in 1965 and my whole life changed. I moved to New York and stayed there.

Until you accepted the role of Jessica Fletcher, the mystery novelist from Cabot Cove, Maine, in Murder, She Wrote.

LANSBURY: Yes. I'd had a chance to try many facets of the business. I'd done movies, theater—regional theater, Broadway, London theater, national theater, RSC—as well as live television and radio. But one thing I hadn't done was a weekly series, so when the offer came, I accepted.

Were there any surprises when you began working, any aspects of the process that you hadn't anticipated?

LANSBURY: Oh, a lot of things, yes. Where to begin? The speed at which everything is done. The last-minute approach to deciding details—very, very important details such as who's going to play which part, and is the script as good as it can be, and is the director going to help or hinder? I was just astonished at the speed that was required to make an hour show in seven days. We now do them in eight, but when I started, it was seven—and that meant working sixteen hours a day to get enough film to edit down to one hour's worth. You have to do so many setups, generally around a hundred, for the average episode.

Most weekly series have several lead actors, or else actors in continuing supporting roles. Your series is atypical: You're in almost every scene and there is only one star. Since you're the only continuing character, what is your workload like?

LANSBURY: Well, most weekday mornings I get up at half past five. I leave the house at six-fifteen. I have breakfast before I go because I find that if I don't, I'll feel light-headed and woozy driving in the car—and it's important that I don't feel light-headed and woozy because I study my words as I'm going to the studio. I work on them. I usually study them the night before in bed before I put the light out, but I also go over them in the car. I'm driven to the studio, so I sit in the back with the light on and learn my lines.

When I arrive at the studio, I go straight to my trailer. It's generally warmed up. I'm met by my assistant, who is also my dresser, and she has the place heated up and the kettle on. I sit down at my dressing table and start to put on the base of my makeup.

You do your own makeup? Most actors don't.

LANSBURY: It gives me a little bit of time. If I didn't put it on myself, I'd have to go into a smoke-filled makeup trailer that's usually a mass of activity, with male and female actors all in the same room. There's so much noise and clatter that it's almost impossible to think, or study lines, or get things together about what you're going to do in the first scene. I prefer that quiet time to myself. Fortunately I have a big motor home that's like an apartment, and therefore it's like going into my own piece of ground.

Then, about fifteen minutes after I've started to put on my base, my hairdresser arrives and begins to curl my hair on the iron. It takes me about an hour and a quarter to get my hair and makeup done and put my clothes on. The dresser is getting my wardrobe ready and the set costume lady is in attendance, and she brings whatever is necessary. I may also, during that hour or so, get a visit from the designer, who's worrying about the clothes that I'll wear in the next episode. One of the biggest single things I have to deal with is what I'm going to put on my back in every scene.

We have our first rehearsal at about a quarter to eight. The assistant director will come to the door and say they'd like to get a rehearsal for the camera and would I please come to the set. If we're using a new director, chances are I'll have met him briefly during the previous week. So I walk out onto the set and greet all of my fellow actors who are there—some I know, some I don't—and I'll also greet the director, who proceeds to outline to me how he sees the scene to be played, where the camera is, and what the action is going to be. At that point it's more or less a traffic problem. We haven't really had time to go over what the scene's about, but as we start to rehearse, we'll begin to discuss it. I'll certainly put forth my two pennies' worth if I feel that he's handling Jessica wrong, because I know how she walks into a room or how she approaches a situation. The other thing I have to deal with is that we'll often start at the end of the script. For various reasons we rarely shoot in sequence. And since we're doing a mystery, we very often have to address the problem of finding out where we are in the plot. Do I know what I think I know at this point or don't I?

And then the day begins. We usually start shooting about eight-thirty, after rehearsals and lighting. If the crew call is at seven, we'll film for six hours, until one o'clock. At one we have our forty-five-minute lunch, the idea being that we'll all have our makeup and hair refurbished and be ready to shoot again exactly one hour later. Then we shoot all afternoon, nonstop. Of course, I have a few free minutes here and there.

When I began the series, we filmed until we finished the allotted day's work, which was anywhere from eight to nine at night. Now I only film for twelve hours. I start at the studio at six forty-five, and I finish at six forty-five in the evening. Then I go home and my husband Peter hands me a drink, a Perrier with lime. I have a small dinner and then, depending on how tired I am, I will look at the pages for the following day and go to bed.

And you do this five days a week?
LANSBURY: Yes, for eight months.

Since a variety of writers do the scripts for the series, how do you keep the character of Jessica Fletcher consistent?
LANSBURY: It's not easy. I often run into inconsistencies and I don't have time to vet every script, to say that I, Jessica, would not react to another character in a certain way or that I would not use that particular set of words or respond in a certain manner. Therefore I often have to make the words incidental to what my inner thought is. A look in my eyes, not necessarily what you hear, is what keeps Jessica consistent.

You've said that acting is done with the eyes. Obviously this would be more true of television, which tends to be a close-up medium, than the stage.
LANSBURY: Absolutely. Absolutely.

Do you feel, as some television actors do, that you're not the master of your fate, that you have to rely on others? Particularly in the matter of scripts?
LANSBURY: Well, scripts are not my function, are they? So I do have to rely on others. I can't do it. I'm not a writer. I can't tell them what to write. I do make suggestions to try to get them to keep Jessica within certain lines

and maintain her credibility. I get upset when her credibility is a little thin at times, because that's when I have to do a lot of eye work to overcome situations where I find myself doing something as the character that I don't buy. And I also get upset when I feel that Jessica isn't involved enough in the story, when she's on the sidelines and not really making a proper contribution.

It's in the nature of series television not only to have revolving-door writers, but also a constant stream of directors passing through. When new directors come on the show, would you say they're intimidated by you?

LANSBURY: Yes, I think some of them are. They feel that I'm there every week and therefore I have a certain control over what I'm going to do. And they're right. What they don't understand, unfortunately, is that I really like to work with directors. I enjoy working with them. But I do object when a director comes in and tries to impose something on the character of Jessica that I feel is out of place and doesn't fit. I feel like saying to him, "Look, I've played this role X number of times and I know how I want to react to this moment." If they want to say to me, let's sharpen up the moment because it's a story point that I have overlooked, then I'm thrilled and excited. I respond when a director wants to sharpen things and make a moment more acute and interesting because it makes Jessica more interesting in that particular situation. I'm always listening and I'm always open to direction. Actually, a director has his work cut out for him in series TV just getting the nine or ten-odd pages shot in the period allowed.

Since you're a constant on the show, many directors will leave you to your own devices. Do they then focus their attention on the other actors?

LANSBURY: Some do, but in the main they don't pay enough attention to the *performance* of the other actors. And that annoys me very much. Because I think that actors often need help, they need to be told. They're frequently on the wrong track and they should be put on the right track. But, as I said, there's no time; there's certainly not enough time to rehearse. You know, if you're playing a scene with two or three people, it takes more than just reading it through and then shooting it. But that's what we sometimes end up doing. If we all get the words correct and don't bump into the furniture, we'll hear, "Cut. Print!"

Would it be fair to say, in terms of weekly television, that actors are asked to give a "result" performance?

LANSBURY: Yes. I call it "instant acting." You have to know your craft awfully well, and you have to know your character very well, to give a credible performance under those circumstances.

Now, I'm not in favor of opening up deep character analysis and motivations. Basic motivations, yes, but those are self-evident. You don't need to go into a long, five-hour character analysis to know how to play a scene. But you *do* have to know your words. And many actors don't know their words well enough to "play" the scene. You have to be glib, and fast, and be able to get them out, to speak with conviction or, if you're playing a villain, to be able to absolutely wipe up the floor with your adversary. You have to know your words backwards. And most actors have great difficulty knowing their words without rehearsing them a few times. Only by practicing with your fellow actors can you learn to speak the lines with energy, accuracy, and conviction.

Unfortunately time is the enemy, and unless the actors get together on their own, which I try to arrange often between setups, this valuable practice is never accomplished. It's difficult to learn a line by rote and then just spill it out and hope to get any kind of dramatic rise and fall in a scene. I mean, as I'm talking to you now it's the emotional climate in me at this moment that's driving these words out. But if an actor doesn't know the words well enough to have that emotional drive behind them, he's never going to be really able to play a scene.

On the first take are the guest stars and the others actors usually groping for their dialogue?

LANSBURY: No question about it. I was watching a well-known actor on a television movie the other night. There was a scene he played where he didn't know his words. And I knew it. He was just sort of winging his way through the scene. Quite obvious. With the ''ers'' and the ''hms.'' It was an unimportant scene, so he really hadn't bothered to learn it very well. Later on he had a very important scene, and there he really knew his dialogue. He drove the scene and it came alive and it was exciting.

Each week you're exposed to a new cast of actors, dozens and dozens over the course of a season. Many of them are young and have only been doing television for a few years. How do you feel about their skills and training?

LANSBURY: I was driving along in Hollywood the other day and I noticed a huge sign that said ''Television School of Acting.'' I thought to myself, that's interesting, I wonder what they teach there. I thought about it quite a bit, and having worked with many young television actors I now understand that there is a style of acting that seems to have been devised by teachers and schools to prepare young would-be actors for their television tests, readings, and what have you.

There's nothing wrong with it, but it leads to what I call ''skin-deep'' acting. It just doesn't go any deeper than a very surface sketch. You get a sketchy kind of performance. It's effective, it'll fool you sometimes, and some of the kids are very good at it. But I don't believe it has much longevity to it. It wouldn't work on the stage, and it's too lightweight to really work in motion pictures. But it does work in television, in sitcoms and in a miniseries, although in a miniseries it may not be able to be sustained. It's so thin, this little veneer of acting ability, that you see through it very quickly because there's no real substance underneath. It's all visual, it's all facial, it's tears in the eyes and gleaming smiles, and it's just surface stuff. But as I say, it's effective and there's nothing wrong with it. You just can't expect too much of it. It only holds for short periods. Couldn't carry a huge, long scene. Wouldn't know how to take a big dramatic scene and build it, starting at the beginning. But they can do the short, swift stuff.

Apparently you wouldn't advise young actors to begin their careers on television.

LANSBURY: No. It's not a good foundation. You build bad habits. I'd recommend a background in theater, because some of the requirements of the stage deal with your instrument, your vocal instrument, your ability to get the message across the footlights to the back of the house. Although so many theaters these days have amplification that I suppose having the vocal equipment is hardly a prerequisite anymore. But many young actors don't know about energy, and that's something you have to have in the theater.

But do you need it on television? A major difference between stage acting and TV acting is a matter of scaling down.

LANSBURY: Yes, but if you're not coming from anywhere, you're not scaling down, you're starting at the least. So if you're asked to give the most, many young actors simply don't have the equipment.

The theater gives you that extra set of muscles. It's rather like running a mile in four. Take my experience with *Sweeney Todd,* for instance. It's a great role, and it called upon all of my strength and my ability as an actress, as a singer, to create an enormous character for a couple of hours every night. A role that the audience is seeing for the first time. The theater asks a very great deal from the actor; it has a whole group of different requirements.

On stage, over the years, you've tended to play roles that were quite flamboyant. Mame, the lady major in Anyone Can Whistle, *Mama Rose in* Gypsy, *and, of course, Mrs. Lovett in* Sweeney Todd. *The same is true of your film characterizations, especially the evil mother in* The Manchurian Candidate. *Now you're playing a nice lady with few eccentricities or quirks. Is that more difficult than undertaking something that's larger than life?*

LANSBURY: Much more difficult. During the course of my career, and I've been in the business for almost forty years, I've always said the most difficult thing for me would be to play myself. It was always easy for me to cover myself with layers of characterization, physical quirks and attributes, tics, heavy makeup, and wigs. The accoutrements of the actor appeal to me greatly because they make my job more fun. Being a theater actress, I love the theatricality of the things that I can lay on.

On the other hand, occasionally I played very simple roles where I did practically nothing. I wasn't playing myself, I was just playing very simple, straightforward women, and to my amazement I found I was actually very successful doing this. I didn't get many opportunities, but when I did, I found the results were very telling. So I've played the simple person before—although I've never played the *interesting* simple person.

And that's what you're trying to do with Jessica Fletcher?

LANSBURY: Yes. I try to bring to her as many interesting facets as I can without tricking her up. I don't want to make her quick and tricky; I want her to be an all-rounder. Do you know what I mean by that? A very broad person who is almost like Everywoman. I want her to have a bit of every woman in her.

Now you could say that's a very easy way to play a character because you know you're going to appeal to somebody all the way across the board. Well, that's okay. I think that a person like Jessica can be fruitful and satisfying to a lot of women. I know that women have said to me, "My gosh, you've become an absolute role model for us." And to me that's exciting and thrilling. I like to feel that the sky's the limit for women. And just because you're fifty-nine or sixty or sixty-four or eighty-four doesn't mean you can't be a vital, interesting, alive, energetic person. An inquisitive individual who can relate to all kinds of people and have an active interest in many things that aren't necessarily on the menu of the average woman, such as industry, commerce, money, farming. I mean anything, just anything. You name it. Women can be involved in these things without being dull, without being necessarily "feminist," but simply by being alive and vital individuals. I'd like Jessica to fall into that category. She takes and gives back all the time. She gives as much as she gets, and there's more to her than being a substitute English teacher or a writer. She's a pretty special piece of feminine goods as far as I'm concerned.

Before you did your series, you appeared in several miniseries. Is there much of a difference for the actor between a miniseries and weekly show?

LANSBURY: Not really, no. There still isn't any time. You come in and they expect you to know who you're playing and how you're going to play it. Nobody ever tells you what to do, nobody suggests anything. They just assume you know. At least they assume I'm going to come in and know exactly what to do. I suppose it's one of the things about being an old war-horse—nobody thinks for a minute you might want a bit of help.

What do you expect of the director of photography?

LANSBURY: (*laughs*) I expect him to make me look like a million dollars. I do expect him to take care for the simple reason that if an audience is being asked to watch somebody for an hour, then they should have the benefit of seeing a pleasant picture and not have to look at a woman who is in pain because the lighting is so bad. A face like mine, given its years, needs to be treated with care and consideration by a cameraman. It doesn't take much time. Once they get the key to it, it's very straightforward. Key light, fill and mix. It's automatic and quite mechanical.

You seem to attach a great deal of importance to wardrobe.

LANSBURY: What I have to deal with is keeping the clothes consistent with the character. I have to justify what Jessica is wearing in every scene. I say to myself, well, why did she buy this? Why is she wearing this smart a suit at this point, and why is she in this old shirt here?

When we first started out, Jessica was a pretty down-home kind of person. Not only down East but down home. She dressed nicely, but she came from a small town. That's how we introduced her in the pilot, and then we saw her going to New York and finding her first success with her first novel. But since that time she's published many books and she's probably made a good deal of money. She's not rich, but she's certainly well enough off and has enough taste to be able to buy some nice clothes which she wears from time to time. And sometimes she looks quite glamorous. Well, why not? She's been on talk shows and she's visiting big cities; she's doing press conferences. So she has to dress better than when we first started. But I always have to keep up a look that's proper, that doesn't impose anything that's wrong for the character. I have to handpick everything I put on my back very carefully.

Are choices brought to you?

LANSBURY: Yes. They have to be. I have no time to shop. I've refused to spend my Saturdays putting wardrobe together—I just have that one day to myself. I talk to the costume designer and give him a general idea of what I want, and he also tells me what he feels. I rely on people to help me in these areas. I'd be delighted if someone would say, "Angela, I've picked you out so-and-so for that scene. I think it would be fine if you were wearing a blouse and slacks, and in the next scene we'll get a jacket.'' That's what I'm always looking for, that kind of help. I've had some wonderful designers and costumers helping me. And it's not the easiest thing in the world, because I need somebody who thinks just like me. Often a designer with the best intentions will bring me something and I'll think, are you mad? Do you really think I'm going to wear that?

Do you go to dailies?
LANSBURY: No. I watch the show when it's on the air. Sometimes I watch it before it airs because they give me a tape. But I like to watch it during prime time. I like to see it with the commercials, to see it as the viewers see it.

As of now you're just completing the first season of Murder, She Wrote. *Have you been too busy to get a sense of the public impact of the series?*
LANSBURY: Just beginning to. Just beginning to get it. I know we found a large audience right away, but it's taken this long for me to understand just how far-reaching the show has become. Right now, when I'm out and about, people come up to me and tell me how much they enjoy the show. They tell me that they love it, and that's very important to me, because when I first started, and I didn't know what the reaction was, it was like playing to an empty house week after week after week.

Other than the public visibility and the financial rewards, are there any other satisfactions for you as an actress in doing a weekly series?
LANSBURY: None whatsoever. No. There really are not. Although I shouldn't say none—occasionally, when the chemistry's right, I'll get together with a group of actors that I enjoy. If we get a good piece of material in our teeth, we'll have fun playing it. We're like kids. Maybe once in every five shows that will happen, and I'll enjoy

every minute that I'm working. It happened just recently with a show that we did—I felt it had punch, it was interesting, and it had energy. It was fun to do, I liked it.

As a theatrical art form, however, series television could never satisfy me. But there's something to be said for winters in California. And let's be honest—it's damn nice to be wanted at sixty.

The Producer
GARY GOLDBERG

Gary David Goldberg was born in Brooklyn, New York, in 1944. In 1965, he dropped out of Brandeis University and eventually returned to college at San Diego State, where he received a B.A. in 1975. He began his career as a television writer on the first Bob Newhart series, then became story editor and eventually producer on The Tony Randall Show. *After that he coproduced* Lou Grant *and then created and produced a number of his own comedy series, including* The Last Resort, Making the Grade, Family Ties, *and* Sara. *Goldberg has won most of television's major awards, including the Humanitas, the Peabody, and the Emmy.*

Is it true that a little over fifteen years ago you were living in a cave in Greece?

GOLDBERG: It's true. In 1970, Diana Meehan and I—Diana is the woman with whom I've shared my life—took off for about fourteen months, and we spent four of those months living in a cave on the island of Mikonos. It's since become a very trendy place, but at that time there was nobody there.

When Diana decided to go after her master's degree in communications at San Diego State, I more or less went along to help out—to take care of our baby and watch the dog. As long as I was there, I thought I'd see about getting a B.A. In the spring of '74, at San Diego State, I did the first writing that I had ever done.

No previous ambition to be a writer?

GOLDBERG: I had no ambitions at all at that point. Sports was the only thing that I was interested in. When I became a parent, and I suddenly realized that I couldn't make a living at sports, it took me a long time to find something else that I wanted to do.

As it turned out, I was very fortunate. Nate Monaster, a past president of the Writers Guild, was the Distinguished Visiting Lecturer that year at San Diego. When I started writing, I got encouragement from a teacher who advised me to show some of my stuff to Nate. So I gave him the first thing I had ever written. It was kind of autobiographical, about some time I'd spent as a waiter at the Village Gate in New York, and he really liked it. Then I wrote a script for *The Mary Tyler Moore Show* that he thought was terrific. He introduced me to agents and sent the material up to Los Angeles, and everyone was very encouraging.

One of the agents, Mike Wise, said to me, "What are your favorite television shows, because you could be a television writer." And I said, "Well, I don't know, I don't have a television set." And he said, "Well, I think you should get one." So I found this motel that was going out of business and selling its TV sets. A friend of ours had a truck, and he drove us over and we got one of those old black-and-white sets from the motel—it cost twenty-five dollars—and we brought it home and I plugged it in. That was the season of *Get Christie Love*. When the show came on, I watched a few minutes of it, and then I turned to Diana and said, "I can do that, I can definitely do that." And when I started writing, I loved it. I loved the process of doing it. I mean, no one knew that I had made the decision to become a writer, so no one cared about it, but I was getting tremendous enjoyment from sitting down and writing. And I was doing it sixteen, eighteen hours a day.

What was the first show you sold material to?

GOLDBERG: I wrote one script for *The Dumplings*, a short-lived series from Norman Lear's company. That led to the first Bob Newhart show, where I wrote some episodes. Tom Patchett and Jay Tarses, who produced the Newhart show, were beginning a new series for Tony Randall, and they offered me the job of story editor on that. The following year I produced *The Tony Randall Show* and then I moved on to *Lou Grant* as a producer. Or, rather, coproducer with Seth Freeman. Gene Reynolds and Allan Burns were the executive producers.

How did you like producing?

GOLDBERG: I really welcomed it, because early on, as I was feeling my way in the television business, it became clear to me that you could write something, but it wasn't necessarily going to end up the way you wrote it on the screen. I think I made a decision that I had to become a producer to protect my vision. I began to realize that many of the choices I made as a producer were just as important as the writing itself. Getting the right actors, getting the right director, costumes—the decisions you make as a producer are vital. It was actually thrilling for me to see how my writing could be enhanced by my producing decisions.

After Lou Grant *you created and produced your own comedy series,* The Last Resort. *Suddenly, in a very real sense, you were out on your own.*

GOLDBERG: First I have to say that when I had executive producers over me, I was very fortunate that they were Tom Patchett and Jay Tarses and then Gene Reynolds and Allan Burns. They're all very dedicated, and they only work on projects for which they have tremendous passion. So when I left *Lou Grant,* it wasn't because I wanted to get a yoke off my neck. On the other hand, as I gained confidence I wanted to test my own ideas to see if they would work. *The Last Resort* was basically a biographical piece, so I was glad to be the one with more or less the final say.

It was about a group of college students who came to the Catskill Mountains to work in a hotel for the summer. The maitre d' was a guy who had never been through high school, so there was a clash between two generations and two different points of view. The comedy was very physical. There was a big dining room and a big kitchen. Lots of activity. I like physical comedy very much, although I don't think I practice it as well as others do. As a writer, I'm more comfortable dealing in smaller, more intimate comedy. *The Last Resort* wasn't successful. We ran for sixteen episodes and had very marginal ratings. It was a great experience, and I learned a lot from it.

Your next series was Making the Grade. *It seemed to be less physical and dealt more with social commentary.*

GOLDBERG: *Making the Grade* was an attempt to do *M*A*S*H* in a high school. It was about teachers trying to cope in a ghetto school. We chose a one-camera technique as opposed to using multiple cameras because we wanted a fast-paced show with many stories, and we tried to get a sense of the whole building going at once.

What are your options when filming or taping a situation comedy show—what are the advantages and disadvantages of these different techniques?

GOLDBERG: Well, I've done both in a variety of ways. *Making the Grade* used one camera, a film camera, and there was no audience. *The Last Resort* used three film cameras and was shot live in front of an audience. *Family Ties* is shot on tape by four cameras, live in front of an audience, and for me that's the only way I'd now do a half-hour situation comedy. Having an audience present, which you don't on a one-camera film show, is a great advantage. It gives a tremendous amount of energy to the actors, and you get a very strong, and hopefully legitimate, laugh track. The audience creates immeasurable excitement and enthusiasm, and it helps with comedy timing.

The drawbacks are that you're limited in the number of sets you can use, and you have to do a minimum of eight pages for each scene. You also have to get your characters on and off, as on the stage, with many entrances and exits. On a one-camera film show you don't have these problems—you can do a lot through editing, really control the pace. But one of the disadvantages of film is that you don't know what you have until you get into the editing room. You spend a lot of time talking to your director and camera operator to get some sense of how the shots are lined up, but you're never sure until you see it. On tape you see everything. By the time you shoot the actual show, you've seen every shot beforehand. There are no surprises.

Another disadvantage to a one-camera film approach is that you start at six-thirty in the morning and finish at six-thirty at night. It's very hard for the actors to be funny under those conditions, although *M*A*S*H* succeeded very well. But in my opinion it's difficult to keep the comedy energy up.

What about the look of film versus the look of tape?

GOLDBERG: No question that film looks better. It has depth, and it gives you a very classy-looking product. When you use tape, you can't light it quite as well, although there have been significant improvements, and this is getting to be less of a disadvantage. In the early days they just blew you out with their light. But now, particularly on *Family Ties,* we're taking great care to give it much more of a film look. Maybe we're not as good yet, but for me the difference isn't worth all of the uncertainty of shooting film, not to mention the expense.

When you did Making the Grade, *you directed for the first time. Did you enjoy the experience?*

GOLDBERG: No, I didn't like it very much. It's all about

things that you don't want to be involved in. I prefer to be the producer working with the director. Television is a producer's medium, and the only thing that really matters each week on *Family Ties* is that I like the show. It doesn't count if the director likes it and I don't. Now we have terrific directors most of the time—Will MacKenzie and John Pasquin direct most of our shows—and I find that they come from an area that I'd never come from, so we're getting the best of it, the best of both worlds. Even though they don't have the final say, they have a great deal of latitude. They come up with great stuff on their own, and I'm free to worry about the script. Whereas when I was directing, I got bogged down with all the directing details and didn't have a chance to improve the script.

Making the Grade *wasn't a success. What do you think were some of the problems?*

GOLDBERG: My first mistake was to accept a network order for only six episodes. That's just not enough time to launch a complex series. But I had just come over to Paramount, and they were paying me a lot of money, so I felt, well, at least we've got something going, we're in the game, and maybe lightning will strike. But it was definitely a mistake, because just when I was getting a clearer conception of the show, we were already canceled. There were other mistakes, including the fact that we didn't focus enough on the lead character—we got a whole ensemble thing going right away—but I never should have accepted a short order.

Most people overlook the fact that part of the producer's function is deal making, and it's a factor that can either help or hinder a project right from the start.

GOLDBERG: It's a very tricky area. You may lust for an actor, for example, who is creatively perfect, but the cost may eventually kill you. The decisions sometimes conflict.

Family Ties *is your most successful series. How did it evolve?*

GOLDBERG: It started at CBS as a one-hour drama. I think they were looking for a 1980s version of *Eight Is Enough*. I had a deal with CBS that I would write four pilots and they would make them—which really means that if they *didn't* make them, they had to pay me anyway. It's a method of protecting yourself economically. I met with a man named Scott Seigler, who's no longer with CBS, and we talked over different ideas. We finally came up with the concept of a sixties radical couple whose children are conservative. It was something that was happening to all of our friends who went through the sixties. I remember Scott said, "Hey, let's do your life." I wrote a first draft, and everybody called me and said it was the best thing they'd gotten all year. I was very excited. I started getting casting ideas. Then the next day they told me that it wasn't going forward. Harvey Shepherd, the executive in charge of programming, didn't like it and that was that.

I was very upset, because I felt they had really jerked me off, and I started yelling and screaming. I said, "Well, what's *your* job if Harvey Shepherd makes all of the decisions? Maybe you should turn your check back in." The thing is that at CBS all of the power is centralized in Harvey Shepherd, and they've had a great deal of success. But I felt it was shortsighted of them to cut me off at such an early stage. Whether they loved it or didn't love it, I think they should have said, "Well, we trust Gary, we've made this big deal with him, maybe we don't see it yet, but maybe it's there and we should at least give him a chance to do the pilot." That's the relationship I thought we were getting into when I signed the deal with them.

Luckily my attorney, Skip Brittenham, had arranged for me to take any rejected pilots somewhere else as long as I reimbursed CBS for the cost of developing the script. So I called Brandon Tartikoff at NBC and told him I had a project that CBS had turned down. He was very enthusiastic. He read the hour script, loved it, and he made the suggestion that I think insured the success of *Family Ties*, which was that we should do it as a half-hour show.

What did you do, as a producer, in terms of casting the pilot?

GOLDBERG: That was my most important job, because I've become convinced that the success of a television series is ninety percent casting. The other elements have to be there, but if you don't have this X-factor—whoever it is the audience is going to identify with and want to invite back into their homes every week—if you don't have people they like, you're not going to get the chance to let those other elements work. There has to be somebody special there.

We have a casting director named Judith Weiner, and she is really fabulous. When we began casting the pilot, she started to bring actors in. I had written the part of the mother with Meredith Baxter Birney in mind. We made the deal, we set her, and that was it. She didn't read; I just had an instinct that she could do it. For one of the daughters Judith brought in a young actress named Tina Yothers, who had just finished a movie called *Shoot the Moon*. Judith said, "You must meet this girl, you're not going to want to see anyone else," and Tina came in and read four lines for the part of Jennifer and we decided immediately that she was right. Justine Bateman, who plays the older girl, wasn't even a full-time actress. Professional actresses were too slick for the character that we wanted, so Judith started going to local high schools and interviewing kids in drama classes, and that's how she found Justine.

The two characters that were less easy to cast were the father and the son. Michael Gross, the dad, was cast at the last minute. We had a lot of difficulty finding this image because it's a very hard part to play—a man in his late thirties or early forties who's attractive and who can do comedy. We found Michael in New York. Gretchen Rennell in the Paramount casting office in New York put him on tape and sent it to us. We looked at it, liked his quality, and flew him out here.

How did you find Michael J. Fox for the part of Alex?

GOLDBERG: Michael is one of the hottest actors on television today.* Gets more mail than anyone on the Paramount lot. And when he first came in, I turned him down. He wasn't what I was looking for. At that point we had been negotiating with Matthew Broderick. But his dad was ill and he didn't want to do a series—maybe he had a sense of other things to come—so he backed out. And in comes Michael J. Fox. For whatever reason, I said no. Judith said, "You're making a major mistake; this kid is fabulous." And I'm saying, "Judith, I happen to be the creator of the show. I know what I want and this fellow isn't it." And she's hammering at me every day, driving me nuts about Michael J. Fox and that I've made this terrible mistake.

Then we go to Washington where they're premiering *Making the Grade* for the press. It was very well received, and everyone was particularly complimentary to the cast. So I called Judith and say, "I just want you to know that your work is really being lauded here, congratulations." And she says, "You're in a good mood." I say, "I'm in a great mood." She says, "Would you do me a favor?" I say, "Anything." So she says, "Will you see Michael J. Fox one more time?" I say, "Okay, Judith, just for you, but I know he's not the guy." I come back, see Michael J. Fox again, and he's fabulous. I turn to Judith and say, "Why didn't you tell me about him?" And that was it. Thank God for Judith Weiner. Without her there'd be no *Family Ties*.

Producing an episode of a situation comedy takes a week from start to finish. What's the process, step by step?

GOLDBERG: On Monday morning at ten o'clock we all

*Fox has since achieved motion picture stardom in *Back to the Future*.

sit down at a table and read the script for that week's episode. From that point forward everything leads to the taping of the show on Friday night at seven. After the reading we all talk about our responses. And maybe the actors will say that something didn't work, that they don't know why they'd be doing this or that. Depending on how we feel about the reading, we may ask them to start working on it, that it will eventually become clear. What is a given here is a lack of ego on the writers' part, because if an actor doesn't want to say a line, he's not going to say it. On the other hand, our actors trust us, and if we say, "Look, this is going to work, just find it, it's there," they'll give it a try.

Are you doing any blocking at this point?

GOLDBERG: No, we haven't gotten up from the table yet. After the reading the staff goes back to the office and starts making changes. On *Family Ties* there are five of us, and whatever titles we have, we all function as one writing unit. While we're working, the actors and the director will now start to put the show on its feet, with script in hand, using the script we've just read. We will not see the show again until the next evening.

When we first started, we used to come down on Monday at the end of the day, but the actors and the director felt they hadn't yet had a chance to get a true sense of whether the material worked or not. So we rewrite and send the changes down, and they put them in and make adjustments, and it's all very rough. But now, after so many shows, nobody has to spend time talking about what the characters are like, so it's just dealing with the particular problems of the particular script we'll be shooting that week.

On Tuesday at four we'll usually see a run-through of the whole show that includes the changes we've made. The actors do it, and we make notes. After the run-through we'll sit down at the table again and talk about the script.

Now we're getting more serious. The actors will be saying, "Look, we tried that and we're really having trouble with it." And we'll be making comments about the blocking, telling them, for example, that we think it hurts when somebody walks on a joke. We hold back a little because we don't want to get too specific too early in the week. The one thing you want to avoid is overload, so that the show peaks on Wednesday instead of Friday. A good director can control the pace of what the actors are doing. The actors are working to make us laugh, but they hold back a little too—they're waiting for the audience. And if, for instance, Michael J. Fox comes to me and says, "I can make that work, but I don't want to do it now. Trust me"—well, that's fine, I don't even think twice about it.

Anyway, on Tuesday night we stay in the office from five to midnight and rewrite the entire script. And those rewrite sessions are fabulous for us. We have them catered, and we indulge ourselves in an orgy of laughter and food. The combined energy of everybody is better than any one person. My function, normally, is to make the final decisions, but our rule is that there are no censors. No idea is to be dismissed until it's had a full hearing. There are many writers, you know, who never come up with *the* idea but who do come up with the door that opens onto the idea.

Your job, from Monday to Friday, seems to be more that of a story editor or a writer than a producer.

GOLDBERG: Well, I do produce if an emergency comes up. I mean, I might have to replace a guest actor. But I'm also editing last week's show and casting next week's show, so the producing functions never stop.

What happens on Wednesday morning? Do you go back to the table again with the rewrite?

GOLDBERG: Yes, at ten o'clock. We read the new script. There may be one or two areas that still need help. We'll polish them off Wednesday morning and see the show again on Wednesday night to make sure that it's in place. On Thursday the cameras come in, and after that you can't really do a lot of rewriting because the shots are geared to the dialogue.

Do you personally go into the control booth on Thursday?
GOLDBERG: No. I have a hookup from the studio into my office. The directors we have are very good and don't need me to sit behind them. When they run the scenes on Thursday, I'll punch up my monitor and watch it. If I see a major error or have a major difference of opinion, I'll call and say things like, "You've got the wrong guy there for that joke, or that shot is so wide we can't use it." Because I see the quad split—that is, what all four cameras are shooting at the same time—I might say, "Put camera three on the line instead of camera two." Anyway, John and Will are very good at this, and my input is usually minimal here.

Late on Thursday we see a camera run-through and we just watch the monitor. We give final notes to the actors, who are usually very close, and then we talk with the director, going over the script page by page. Usually our notes are minor, just housekeeping stuff. We make very few changes on Thursday night because it's disturbing for the actors to change things at that point. So even if we see a chance to make things a little better, we try to resist— that is, unless an actor has a real problem with a joke or a bit of business.

Keep in mind that our actors are very inventive and contribute heavily to the show. I don't care where an idea comes from—if it's good, I'll use it. Most of the time we don't even remember whose lines are being used. When we were sitting around celebrating our fiftieth show, nobody could remember whose lines were whose. A good show really reflects the entire group. When the show works, it works for all of us. If it doesn't, then I'm responsible.

What time do things get started on Friday?

GOLDBERG: We come in at twelve forty-five. We shoot the show out of sequence, without the audience. We do it that way for two reasons. For one thing, we have kids on the show, and we lose them at nine-thirty, because of the state labor laws. So we want to use them first. Also, we want to finish all of the shots in one set before moving on. And the reason we shoot without an audience is to relieve the actors of pressure. We want them to go through it a few times in costume, with all of the cameras, and make whatever adjustments are necessary.

By the time the show shoots in the evening, we already have an entire taped version that's okay. So we don't have to stop, even if somebody makes a mistake, when we do it at night. We're covered. We have everything we need, although usually it doesn't have the magic and the luster that the audience will bring to it.

What do you do with the tapes?

GOLDBERG: I'll take them home over the weekend—the tapes from the afternoon and the evening—I'll look at all of the performances, and then I'll intercut them. For example, I could have someone's close-up from the evening show, and he or she would be talking to someone else's close-up from the afternoon show.

How many times do you tape the program?

GOLDBERG: We tape it, literally each scene, four times. Three without an audience, one with the audience. Normally the show we tape with the audience comprises about eighty-five percent of what goes on the air.

Why do you do it so often?

GOLDBERG: Just to get everyone real comfortable. I don't think the evening performance would be as good unless we did the other shows in the afternoon.

You've just described an enormously busy week. Yet this season you have a second *show on the air. It's called*

Sara, *and it's about a young attorney in San Francisco. How do you manage to do two series at once?**

GOLDBERG: I'm not able to do it. At least I'm not able to do it well. *Family Ties* is a smoothly running show. The people on the staff—Michael Weithorn, Lloyd Garver, Alan Uger—can do it without me. So I thought, when *Sara* was launched, that I could turn *Family Ties* over to them, lead the country gentleman life of an executive producer, and spend my time day-to-day on *Sara*. But I realized I couldn't do it, it didn't make me happy.

I love *Family Ties,* I can't live without it, and I'm going back to it in the fall. Someone else will do *Sara*. Ruth Bennett, who cocreated it, will assume the functions on *Sara* that I serve on *Family Ties,* and I'll just read scripts and try to be of some help to her while I collect a salary. But I can't do it full-time. You can't produce two shows that are going simultaneously. I prefer to be down on the *Family Ties* set saying, "No, the curtains should be blue." That's the kind of thing that makes me happy.

What are your relationships with the networks?

GOLDBERG: At the moment NBC is the only place I would work. I don't want to spend a lot of time explaining things to people who are not as quick about comedy as I am. And that would be everyone at CBS and ABC right now. Taste is a matter of opinion, and what I resent about ABC and CBS is that they act like they know they're right. Basically all you can say is that this is how I feel—there is no such thing as being right. If Harvey Shepherd wants to produce a show, then he should go out and produce it. But if *I'm* hired to do it, then I'm foolish enough to think that I should make the decisions. That doesn't mean I don't want to hear from the network. I do. And I respect Brandon Tartikoff at NBC. I think he has a keen mind and he's real funny, and I want to know how he reacts. But in the final analysis my opinion should count more than his.

---

*Sara was canceled by NBC shortly after the interview.

And yet he disagreed with you on which episode should open the season on Sara *and you deferred to his opinion.*

GOLDBERG: He was very passionate about which show we should lead off with, and it wasn't as big a deal to me. He didn't tell me to do it, he asked me to trust him and said it meant a lot to him. I'm not as strong as he is in the areas of programming and research. That's his strength, not mine. So I bowed to his better wisdom. I said, "If you're so comfortable with it, let's do it."

Do you spend a lot of time reading, going to the movies, or watching television?

GOLDBERG: I've been trying to keep reading, because that's vitally important to me, but I've hardly seen any movies this year, and I haven't watched much television because I have two daughters and I don't want anything to distract from the time we have to spend together.

How do you find the people who work with you on your show? Are they friends, are they recommended? How do they come to you?

GOLDBERG: We're very open on *Family Ties*. Until recently I'd read anything that came in. We like to use people who haven't done anything, people who are bright and show the right instincts. Then we throw them right into it.

For example, this year I felt we needed to shake up the staff a little bit. We were all very comfortable with each other, and we were all playing certain roles, maybe getting stale in those roles. I spoke with Diana, who's a Ph.D. in communications, and she said one thing that might be good would be to bring in somebody fresh. That could shake up everyone in the organization. So I read a script from a kid named Marc Lawrence that was very good. It was a spec *Family Ties* script.* Came in from an agent in New York whom I had never heard of. So I called Marc in

*A spec script is one that is written without assignment, purely on speculation.

New York. He was an NYU Law School dropout, and he sounded like a very warm, funny guy. He was young, about twenty-four years old, I think. We decided to fly him out here, spend some time with him, and see what he was like. And he's this terrific kid. He's a wonderful young person with a lot of energy, and very funny. Everyone on the staff liked him, and we decided to make him story editor this year. And he'd never done a thing. Just dropped out of NYU Law School which, as far as I'm concerned, is a very good opening thing to do.

Having him here is exactly what I'd hoped it would be, because he was so fresh that it made us all remember how exciting it really is. From the moment he came on, everything really brightened up again for all of us, even though I don't think he contributed a word to the first few scripts. But the table was real hot, and things were going great. It gave us someone to worry about and to mother. We found Michael Weithorn the same way. Script through an agent. He was a teacher. He's now the supervising producer of the show and, in my opinion, the best comedy writer in TV today. Then there's Ruth Bennett. Again, script from an agent. She wasn't even in the country when we hired her; she was in Israel. We used to sit around and think what she would be like. Her script was so warm and funny that there was no way she wouldn't be just like her work. And she was.

I'd rather have new, untried writers than older writers who have become disenchanted; I just hate that negative energy. We don't think that what we're doing is anything other than terrific. And we don't think it's anything other than a privilege to be doing what we do. It's a very fortunate way to be able to spend your time.

The Writer
SCHILLER AND WEISKOPF

Bob Schiller was born in Los Angeles in 1918 and graduated from UCLA, where he majored in Economics. Bob Weiskopf was born in Chicago in 1914 and spent two years at the University of Chicago. Both separately and in collaboration, the two men have been writing radio and television comedy for over forty years. They were on the staffs of two classic TV series, I Love Lucy *and* All in the Family, *and together created their own shows* (All's Fair *and* The Ann Sothern Show). *They are the recipients of two Emmy Awards for their work.*

Bob Schiller, what was your first professional credit?

SCHILLER: It was in 1946 on a radio show called *Duffy's Tavern.* After that I did a number of other radio shows, including *Abbott and Costello, December Bride,* and *The Ozzie and Harriet Show.*

I began writing for television in 1950, in New York. The first TV show I wrote was one of the segments of the *Four Star Review.* They were live shows, with four stars alternating. I worked on *The Danny Thomas Hour.* Then I did *The Ed Wynn Hour,* and I eventually worked on all of the Ed Wynn and Danny Thomas hours.

Did you work by yourself or in collaboration?

SCHILLER: For the most part I collaborated. Interestingly my first collaborator in television was a young man named

Joseph Stein, who later wrote the book for the Broadway musical *Fiddler on the Roof.*

Bob Weiskopf, what was your major at the University of Chicago?
WEISKOPF: Baseball.

You also started out in radio, didn't you?
WEISKOPF: Yes, with Eddie Cantor in 1940. Then I wrote for the Rudy Vallee, Joan Davis, and John Barrymore shows. After that I spent nine years with Fred Allen in New York. I never worked on a situation comedy in radio. I usually did variety shows. I got into this business by writing jokes. Funny things for funny people to say.

Did television situation comedy evolve from radio?
SCHILLER: Yes. I think that *The Goldbergs* and *Henry Aldrich* were the prototypes. Some of them were on five days a week for fifteen minutes. *Amos and Andy* was another one. And funnier than the other two because of the ethnic humor, which we're not allowed to do anymore. I think the absence of ethnic humor on television has mellowed out everything. There was lovely, funny humor on *The Goldbergs* and *Amos and Andy.*
WEISKOPF: I think ethnic humor in good taste is perfectly acceptable.
SCHILLER: The trouble is, some people feel that any ethnic humor at all is in bad taste.

What kind of show was Duffy's Tavern?
SCHILLER: The show would open with a monologue, which certainly isn't situation comedy. Archie, the bartender, played by Ed Gardner, would be having a one-sided conversation with the never-seen, never-heard Duffy on the telephone. Then characters would walk into the bar. Eddie, the black waiter, would be there and do a few jokes about that week's guest star, then Miss Duffy would come on and talk about her sex-starved existence, then Clifton Finnegan would do a few "dumb" jokes, and finally the

guest star would show up. It was all very loosely structured, but funny and with some good satire.

WEISKOPF: Most of these shows centered around the
guest star. You'd write for the star of the week. If you had
Charles Boyer as a guest, you might do a sketch about
Boyer in a French restaurant or about a woman who swooned
when she saw him.

What would you call a radio show like The Life of
Riley?

SCHILLER: That was a situation comedy. But the best
example was *Ozzie and Harriet.* Like *Riley,* it moved from
radio to television. It was well structured, well plotted,
and it dealt with the kind of characters you knew. They
rarely did anything out of the ordinary.

WEISKOPF: Also, it was one of the first times that comedy
was performed by people who weren't comedic. Ozzie and
Harriet weren't comedians or actors. Ozzie Nelson was a
bandleader and Harriet started out as a vocalist, a singer
in his band. They eventually brought their own two kids
onto the show and created a successful, long-running family relationship. The country watched those kids grow up.

*You seem to differentiate between comedians and comic
actors.*

SCHILLER: Well, nobody ever died laughing at Ozzie or
Harriet Nelson. But the situations were funny and interesting, little vignettes about family life.

WEISKOPF: True comedians began to phase out with the
demise of vaudeville. The only comedians you have today
are stand-up comics who play nightclubs like the Comedy
Store, or else a few resorts left in the mountains. There are
certainly no theaters in America where you can do a funny
act.

SCHILLER: There are still a few funny people left. Bill
Cosby's funny. In fact, the three funniest men in America
today are all black. Cosby, Richard Pryor, and Eddie

Murphy. And only Cosby is on television doing situation comedy. He's doing a black version of *Ozzie and Harriet*.

WEISKOPF: You can't blame comics for not doing television. They make a lot of money doing films and concerts, and it's much easier than doing a weekly TV show.

Cosby, Pryor, and Murphy are essentially comedians; their roots were in clubs and they all did stand-up work. Isn't there a place for an actor who can play comedy if the role requires it?

WEISKOPF: Sure. There's a place for, say, a Cary Grant or an Irene Dunne. They played what was called "light comedy." It was sophisticated, a category by itself. But when you went to the movies to see Red Skelton or Charlie Chaplin, you laughed out loud. Maybe a chuckle for Cary Grant, but I remember when I saw a Chaplin film, someone in the audience laughed so hard, he started coughing and had to leave.

When did you two meet?

SCHILLER: In 1953. In the den of my former house. The meeting is now commemorated by a plaque. Weiskopf was looking for a nursery school for his oldest child, who's now a television writer-producer, by the way. He was told that my wife was *au courant* on nursery schools, so he dropped by and we met.

Is that when you decided to become writing partners?

SCHILLER: No. Weiskopf had a deal to do some *Make Room for Daddy* shows, and I was on my way east to do *The Red Buttons Show* with his head writer, Larry Gelbart. I had introduced Larry to his wife, and to get even he put me on the show. When I came back, Weiskopf was looking for a partner. He saw a telex at the William Morris Agency saying that I was returning, and figured that I'd be as good a partner as any.

Why is it a tradition in the comedy field for writers to work in collaboration?

SCHILLER: I think one of the reasons is that it's terribly lonely. Another reason is that in comedy most of us don't trust our own sense of humor. You have to be awfully secure to do that. I guess Neil Simon is an exception. So you collaborate because it's easier, you have a sounding board, and if it doesn't work, you can blame your partner. They're handy for that.

How do two writers work in collaboration? Are you both in a room from first to last page?

SCHILLER: Usually. On very rare occasions, when we're under tremendous deadline pressure, we'll split up pages and scenes and do them separately. But that isn't often. You have to remember that nowadays there are other writers on most shows that we do. The way things are now, unless you're a free-lance writer working at home, you're writing in an office with other people around. Script supervisors, story editors—all of which are fancy names for rewriters.

Television situation comedies are usually staff-written. Do free-lance comedy writers exist anymore?

WEISKOPF: Oh, yes. They exist—but just barely.

If one of them comes in with an idea, who does he present it to?

SCHILLER: The story editor or producer, or both, or a script supervisor. I've never really been able to understand the differences between all of those titles, because we've functioned in each of those capacities and we wind up writing just as much when we're producers or story editors as we do when we're outside writers.

WEISKOPF: I think the chief function of a free-lance writer on a comedy series is to come in with an idea, because in most cases, at least until the show is fully staffed, it's difficult to come up with twenty-two or twenty-four good story ideas. If you're lucky, you'll get half a dozen from the outside. Then the attitude is: "They don't know the show. Let's buy the idea and let the guys on staff write it.'' And that's what eventually happens.

How many staff writers would there be on a situation comedy today?

WEISKOPF: Between four and six.

SCHILLER: That includes the producers. Most producers in the comedy field are writers. When you make a writer a producer, you get more from him; you get two functions from him rather than one.

WEISKOPF: If you do use a free-lance writer, the staff will usually get together when he's not there and make notes on his material. Then the producer and/or story editor will present the notes to him.

SCHILLER: But there's no particular pattern. In my nearly forty years of personal experience, I don't think any two shows have been the same. The broad, overall picture is that every show is a problem, each episode has its difficulties, and the mix of people working on it, and what they do, constantly changes. You can't lay down any firm rules. For example, we didn't have any input whatsoever from a staff when we wrote our first script for *Maude*. We finished it, brought it over to Norman Lear's house, and then we did a very minor rewrite. We said to ourselves, "Everybody complains about Norman Lear being a big rewriter, but this is a cinch." Of course, the reason the rewrite was so insignificant was because there was a deadline—the thing had to be done the next week. Believe me, after that it was never a cinch again.

What you're saying is that the situation comedy script exists to be rewritten.

WEISKOPF: Yes. And that's not always the best thing. I have a chip on my shoulder about this, and I think it's legitimate. Bob and I did that first script for Norman with one normal rewrite, which took us perhaps a day. And the script came out fine. Now I hesitate to believe that was the only script we wrote that was that good. Yet all of the others we did went through all kinds of hassles—rewriting, and fixing, and futzing around day and night. Do you have any idea what goes on the air when you keep throwing things out? What goes on the air is the last thing you write, at three in the morning, when you're exhausted. I have grave doubts about the last version of a script being the best version.

Are these shows generally better because of the rewrites or just different?

SCHILLER: Many times, just different. We used to complain to Norman about all of the rewriting. We didn't feel it was necessary. But he felt the shows improved. Frankly, I think we actually hurt some of the shows by rewriting. We lost an awful lot of good stuff. Every time we did a run-through we'd rewrite. Sometimes we'd even rewrite after the audience went home. We'd put in new lines. Now that's idiocy. How do you know the audience is going to laugh if they're not there? And Norman would answer, "Easy. We'll punch a button."

WEISKOPF: I used to scream, "Why are we sitting here at eleven-thirty at night writing a new line when we'll never know if it's funny because the audience isn't here? If you're going to put in a laugh, you might as well stick it in for the old line."

SCHILLER: When you think about it, it's amazing. What we were doing was performing miracles every week. We were putting on a full two-act play that, according to Norman and a lot of other people, was just as good as anything on Broadway. We were, in effect, breaking it in in Detroit, taking it to Boston, and then to Philadelphia, and then on to Broadway, and we were doing it every week.

Before you went with Norman Lear's company, you were involved with one of television's classics, I Love Lucy.

SCHILLER: That's right. We came on in the fifth year and

did the last two seasons. After that we did all three years of the *Lucy/Desi Comedy Hour*, and the first two years of the *New Lucy Show*. A lot of *Lucy* shows.

Would you say the Lucy *shows were blends of sketch comedy, farce, and situation comedy?*

SCHILLER: In a way. A sketch is usually a blackout or an extended blackout that describes a very minor incident, and it doesn't necessarily depend on continuing weekly characters or a strong story line. You'd usually find sketches on variety shows that had guest stars.

WEISKOPF: If Humphrey Bogart was the guest, you'd do a gangster sketch.

SCHILLER: On *Lucy* you had a mix at times. For example, Bob Weiskopf mentioned Charles Boyer. Okay, so we had Charles Boyer on a *Lucy* show. Now, Desi/Ricky warns Boyer to stay away from his wife or else she'll get him in trouble. When she meets Boyer, he denies that he's Boyer, and now Lucy's in a sketch to try to make Ricky jealous by taking this imposter, who really *is* Charles Boyer, and teaching him how to be Charles Boyer.

WEISKOPF: She says, "You may look like Charles Boyer, but you don't talk like him or act like him, so I'll have to teach you."

Was there any improvisation on the Lucy *shows?*

WEISKOPF: Never.

SCHILLER: Oh, there were normal rewrites, but the actors trusted the writers—a rarity in this business—because Desi Arnaz had complete confidence in them. Desi, by the way, is the most underrated producer and director in television. He, like Ozzie Nelson, took the trouble to learn every single facet of what goes into a show. In addition, he was a charmer, and his writers would do anything for him.

The show was famous for Lucy's physical comedy. Was that laid out in the script?

SCHILLER: Yes. You can watch a show and follow the script line for line and gesture for gesture—they'll match.

WEISKOPF: The director would stage the moves, but they were almost always in the script. And incidentally, if Lucy didn't feel comfortable with something, she wouldn't alter it on her own. She'd call the writers and confer with them.

As you mentioned, Lucille Ball did a series of shows that were an hour in length, but there have been very few hour-long comedies. Why? Can't comedy sustain on television for sixty minutes?

WEISKOPF: It's very difficult to write an hour's worth of situation-comedy material on a weekly basis. We did it on the *Lucy/Desi Comedy Hour*, but we only did four or five a year, and we had guest stars interacting with our characters. Each show took us six weeks to write. You don't have that kind of time on a weekly situation comedy.

SCHILLER: You can do an hour-long variety show, but that's different. An example would be the old *Gleason* show. It was a variety show, and in the middle of it he'd do a segment of *The Honeymooners*.

WEISKOPF: Last Thanksgiving we had our family together. It's normally a tense situation when families get together for an entire day. But this year the time passed beautifully. You know why? Because the old *Honeymooners* was on television all day long, from six A.M. until two the following morning. We didn't even have to talk to each other.

You don't see much, if any, slapstick comedy on television today. Is slapstick dead?

SCHILLER: Slapstick comedy is alive. Slapstick comedians aren't.

WEISKOPF: You're not going to see something that performers can't do.

SCHILLER: What's interesting is that the greatest comedian who ever lived was Charlie Chaplin. And Chaplin did slapstick. He added heart, but it was still slapstick. A major exception to the trend away from slapstick is John Cleese, the English comedian from *Monty Python*. He's one of the funniest men alive, barring none. The series he cocreated and starred in, *Fawlty Towers*, is brilliant. Wonderful knockabout comedy. Slapstick comedy. And he gets away with it because he's funny. He even walks funny. All great comedians walk funny and eat funny.

You spent a lot of time working for Norman Lear, first on Maude *and* All's Fair, *and then on* All in the Family *and* Archie Bunker's Place. *It's been said that his shows were very much like radio comedy—all dialogue, usually of a confrontational nature, and with little visual humor.*

SCHILLER: That's a good description of it. But Norman did something else as well—he added social issues to comedy. Not that social commentary is necessarily good, in and of itself, but he did it well and it was funny. That's the most important thing: The shows that he was putting out were funny. The fact that they were also carrying a message was an added plus. They had content, they had balls. Rather than a guy living with two girls who says he's a homosexual which was used only for titillation.

What's your feeling about The Mary Tyler Moore Show?

SCHILLER: I never felt, as others did, that her show had a great deal to say. When we were doing *Maude*, I always said we were flying like the Wright brothers but nobody knew we were up there. People would rave about how meaningful the Moore show was, and my partner said we did a two-parter on alcoholism and *The Mary Tyler Moore Show* retaliated—they did a three-parter on mayonnaise. But it was a funny and warm show, well written and performed, and in the long run that's what it's all about.

In addition to alcoholism, you also did shows about death, abortion, and impotence on Maude, *and rape on* All in the Family. *Was this because of Norman Lear?*

WEISKOPF: Yes. He wanted to deal with those subjects. He'd say, "Let's do alcoholism." Then we'd go home to try and come up with a story and I'd say, "That son of a bitch, I wish he were here."

SCHILLER: Once again, you have to be funny. To get your point across—that alcoholism is dangerous and that rape is not particularly good for the country—you have to get laughs along the way. Because if you're not amusing, nobody is going to watch. It was quite a challenge.

Any problems with network censorship?

SCHILLER: Not particularly. We've been fortunate in working on successful shows, and when you're a hit, the censors generally leave you alone. But I do remember that when we were doing *Maude* and Gene Reynolds was producing *M*A*S*H*, he was always complaining that we were getting away with murder and he wasn't. When *M*A*S*H* first started, it wasn't too successful, so consequently he came in for a lot of network harassment.

When you did have problems with standards and practices, did Norman run interference for you?

SCHILLER: He'd leave it to his producers until it got to the point where it was a standoff. Then he'd come in. Sometimes he'd win, sometimes he'd lose.

How do you feel about some of the more recent situation comedies? Shows like Cheers *and* The Cosby Show?

SCHILLER: You happened to pick the two best shows in comedy today, to my taste. I think *The Cosby Show* is funny because Bill Cosby is funny. I also think the writing's good, the acting's good, it's well directed and well produced. And I think it's making a subliminal statement for tolerance, which I think is wonderful.

What is your attitude toward the so-called new forms of television comedy, as personified by Saturday Night Live?

SCHILLER: I think that most of the comedy of that genre is written for teenagers, and teenagers and I don't have the same kind of sense of humor. They're out to shock their elders.

WEISKOPF: A lot of it does seem to revolve around shock. It all started with the Smothers Brothers. They would shock you, shock the audience, by doing comedics about certain taboo subjects.

But that's exactly what you did on the Lear shows.

SCHILLER: The *Saturday Night Live* people were doing a different kind of shock. Schlock shock. They just wanted to be outrageous. They dealt with drugs, for example, but not in a negative sense. I used to tell Michael O'Donaghue, one of the writers, that he was obsessed with death. He was the Brian DePalma of comedy.

Perhaps the impact of the show had something to do with the feeling that anything could happen because it was live.

SCHILLER: *Everything* was live in the early days of television. That's what I used to tell my son, who later became a writer for *Saturday Night Live*. He hadn't realized that. We dragged him to New York when he was a year old so that I could work on some of the shows I mentioned. All of them were live. No, I think the reason *Saturday Night Live* did so well was the fact that every generation has to give a kick in the pants to the generation ahead of it. And that was their way of punishing us for bringing them into the world. They did it with rock and roll, they did it with *Saturday Night Live,* and they've done it with drugs.

With an attitude like that, aren't you open to accusations of becoming fossilized? Can't comedy move in new directions?

WEISKOPF: Well, I was beginning to think I was a dinosaur, but what's the biggest hit in television comedy today? *The Cosby Show.* Apparently a lot of people think it's funny, and it is. As we said, it's back to *Ozzie and Harriet.*

SCHILLER: By the way, in their infinite wisdom, ABC turned down *The Cosby Show.* Now they've ordered up a bunch of black shows. They obviously must think the reason it's doing well is that Cosby's black. What they don't realize is that he could be orange and it would be the same show because he's funny.

How astute were the stars of your various comedy shows in terms of judging material?

SCHILLER: The successful ones were astute. Take Cosby again. He obviously knows what he's doing. He has a hand in all of the scripts, he sprinkles them with routines of his own from his concerts. Most comedians will know what they can do best and can be very helpful.

What about actors who play comedy as opposed to comedians?

SCHILLER: To give the devil his due, Carroll O'Connor knew Archie Bunker better than anybody in the world.

WEISKOPF: He did a lot of rewriting—sometimes improving and sometimes destroying material. He wanted to be the big creative cheese.

SCHILLER: There's an unconscious—and sometimes not so unconscious—conflict between writers and performers in comedy. By and large the performers will think they know the persona they're projecting, and they think they should be the final judge of what's right for that persona. You can't blame them—

WEISKOPF: I'm sorry, I do blame them.

SCHILLER: They're the ones who have to go out and face the audience.

WEISKOPF: No one twisted their arms. They could be floorwalkers at the May Company.

SCHILLER: Well, nobody twisted your arm to be a writer, so you have to take these indignities as they come. Comedians, particularly in the old days, didn't like to admit they employed writers to come up with all the funny things they said. They knew they were dependent on writers, so they'd rewrite the material to prove to themselves that they were contributing.

There seems to be a trend toward character comedy, with humor arising through a given situation, instead of so-called "joke" comedy. In the theater, Neil Simon is often accused of being preoccupied with jokes and one-liners.

WEISKOPF: I don't know why there's such a big onus on jokes. The first thing you hear, when you become connected with a new show, is, "Oh, we don't do jokes on this show, just character." Then, of course, when the show isn't funny, they start to scream, "Where are the jokes?"

SCHILLER: Usually the person who says they don't do jokes can't write them.

WEISKOPF: In radio Eddie Cantor once said, "Boys, Milton Berle tells the best damn jokes in the world, and he's not on the air." So we did a show with a minimum of jokes. After the show the first thing out of Cantor's mouth was, "Boys, where are the jokes?"

SCHILLER: There's nothing wrong with comedy arising from character and situation, but there's also nothing wrong with a good joke. I mean, God knows our social contacts are greased by jokes. One of the first things that happens whenever you get in a room is that you tell jokes to break the tension.

What were some of your early influences?

SCHILLER: I was weaned on Robert Benchley, Thurber, and S. J. Perelman.

WEISKOPF: I have one favorite author—Ring Lardner. And he wrote jokes in his stories.

Are there any questions you'd like to answer that haven't been asked?

SCHILLER: There is a question that most interviewers get around to asking.

What's that?

SCHILLER: "Are there any questions you'd like to answer that haven't been asked?"

Well, are there?

SCHILLER: We're often asked how to break into TV comedy.

WEISKOPF: And we tell people to write a sample script. Pick a show you like and think you could write, and then sit down and give it a go.

SCHILLER: Usually we never hear from that person again.

WEISKOPF: And if we do, we change our telephone numbers.

SCHILLER: Seriously, every now and then a good first effort comes across our desks and we'll try to get it to the proper producer. We've discovered some good talent down through the years.

WEISKOPF: Plautus, Demosthenes, George S. Kaufman—they all sent us first drafts.

Can comedy writing be taught?

SCHILLER: There's no way you can teach somebody to write funny. You have to be born with it. My first employer, Ed Gardner, said, "I look for people who think crooked." A comedy writer will never give you a straight answer. You have to play with words, play with thoughts, play with ideas. I think you have to have a warped view. And, of course, a sense of humor. Which an awful lot of people don't have—as witnessed by the poor comedy on television that gets high ratings.

THE TV SERIES: COMEDY

The Director

JAY SANDRICH

Jay Sandrich was born in Los Angeles, California, in 1932. He graduated from UCLA with a Bachelor of Arts in Theater, and after a lengthy apprenticeship as an assistant director, he has become one of the most successful directors in television comedy, having directed the pilots for such series as The Mary Tyler Moore Show, The Bob Newhart Show, Soap, Benson, W.K.R.P. in Cincinnati, Golden Girls, *and* Off the Rack. *He directed the pilot presentation and, as of this writing, all of the episodes of* The Cosby Show. *He has also directed several TV movies and a feature film,* Seems Like Old Times, *with Goldie Hawn and Chevy Chase. Sandrich has won three Emmys and two Directors Guild awards.*

Did you have any ambition to be a director when you were growing up?

SANDRICH: None at all. My major interest was sports. I wanted to be a shortstop for the Brooklyn Dodgers. I became a director by being in the right place at the right time, plus that wonderful thing that helps so many people in this business, nepotism. My father was a feature film director. He did most of the Astaire and Rogers pictures, and comedies like *Skylark* with Brian Aherne and Claudette Colbert. But I really had no interest in the business.

I've always felt that if my father had worked in the automobile business, I'd be in the automobile business.

I had no burning desire to direct. I didn't grow up studying motion pictures. I didn't think of movie stars as gods and goddesses. It was really just a profession that I gravitated to because of my father's involvement and my geographical closeness to it. He died when I was thirteen, and I suppose I took my first step toward becoming a director when I was in college and I got a call from a friend telling me I had better join the Directors' Guild. They were changing the eligibility rules, but as the son of a member I could join as long as I signed up within six months. So I did.

Then, in my senior year, I worked as a second assistant director on *The Lone Ranger*. The man who was directing it had worked for my father, and he helped me get some experience by allowing me to be on the set. At the time I knew nothing. I just followed a second assistant director around. Then I went into the army right after the Korean War. I was with the Signal Corps for two years making training films. Frankly, I didn't really know what I was doing.

Where was your next professional experience?
SANDRICH: At Desilu. When I was in the army, I noticed that all of the shows I liked—*I Love Lucy, Danny Thomas,* and two or three others—were done by Desilu. So when I was discharged, I called up Argyle Nelson, who was the production manager for Desilu and who had also worked for my father. They hired me as a second assistant director.

At that time we worked a six-day week. I spent two days on *Lucy,* two on *December Bride,* and two on *Our Miss Brooks*. A second, by the way, didn't have much to do. It was mostly paperwork and knocking on actors' doors and saying, "Sir or ma'am, would you please come out on the set?" Somewhere along the line there were layoffs because production shut down, so I left and got a job at another studio.

Then I got a call from Jack Aldworth, who was the first assistant director on the *Lucy* show, asking me if I wanted to come back and work as a first on *Lucy*. I said yes, absolutely. I thought he meant the second assistant. But it turned out that he did mean the first assistant director because he had moved up to become the associate producer. It was the last year that *Lucy* did half hours. I was twenty-four years old.

You seem to ascribe most of these job opportunities to the fact that you were your father's son.

SANDRICH: He left me a legacy with a lot of people who cared for him. Obviously I had to be able to learn and handle what I was given, but without the name I probably wouldn't have gotten the jobs in the first place. I was really very fortunate. Jack Aldworth took me by the hand and wet-nursed me through for the first six months.

Essentially, when you're an assistant director on an audience show, it's like being a stage manager. There are none of the complicated problems that a first on a one-camera location shoot has to deal with. So I had the opportunity to watch and learn. I watched the directors, I watched the actors, and I was constantly asking questions. I learned a lot about the technical end.

In those days college didn't really prepare you to be a director. You went to lectures and you saw films, but it wasn't much in the way of preparation. I didn't know what I wanted to be—I never really assumed I'd be a director—but as long as I was watching, I wanted to know why a director would do this, or that, or why the camera was here instead of there.

I stayed with *Lucy* for about one year after it became an hour show, then I switched over to *The Danny Thomas Show* and worked with Sheldon Leonard, who had a great influence on my career. I was his assistant director for about five years. He gave me the opportunity to read scripts, and eventually he let me become an associate producer, which meant that I was going to dubbing sessions and supervising laugh tracks. I also began to learn about editing, which I think is an important prerequisite for any comedy director.

How did you get the chance to direct your first show?

SANDRICH: *The Dick Van Dyke Show* wasn't getting good ratings, so at the end of its first year the network canceled it. Sheldon was directing a *Danny Thomas* at the time, and in the middle of the show he left and flew to wherever the company was located that sponsored *Van Dyke* in order to make a pitch to keep the show on for a second year. But he hadn't completed the *Thomas* episode, so he turned to Danny and said, "You direct it." And Danny turned to me and said, "You do the cameras." So Danny directed the actors and I told the cameras where they should go.

It was a three-camera film show. Each camera has an assigned spot that is marked with a piece of tape on the floor. It's like watching a ballet. You have to move cameras at certain times, although you don't want all of them moving at once, and since it isn't tape and you can't see what you're doing, you have to somehow edit it in your mind. But I had been watching for a long time, and I did it.

A few years later Sheldon stopped directing entirely because he was busy with other things. They started bringing in directors from the stage and from live TV. Most of them hadn't done that kind of show, and they were smart enough to recognize that they didn't know the technique, so they allowed me to help out. Then Danny started directing all of the shows and I did the cameras for him. Finally they decided that during the last season Danny wouldn't be in every episode—they'd just have the family and he wouldn't appear. So I directed two of the shows he wasn't in.

You worked with the actors as well as setting up camera positions?

SANDRICH: Yes, and it was a wonderful, frightening experience. One week I'm the assistant director, the next week I direct, and the following week I'm back to being the assistant again. I remember that just before I directed my first show, I literally hoped I'd get a phone call saying the studio had burned down. I didn't want to go to work. I was afraid that if I said to an actor, "Why don't you go here?" he'd say, "No, I don't want to do that," and I wouldn't know what to do. Or I'd come up with a joke and everybody would think it was terrible. Which happened. But somehow I struggled through. I guess I didn't allow them to see how nervous I was.

Since those days, aside from directing individual episodes, you've come to specialize in pilots for new series. Are you closely involved with the casting?

SANDRICH: Yes. But the first thing I consider, before I commit to do a pilot, is how much I like the script. Am I amused, am I entertained, am I moved, is it something that I'd want to watch? If I don't want to watch it, I don't want to direct it.

Then, assuming I get a script that appeals to me, the next step is to find the actors who can make it come to life. If I'm not involved in the casting, I won't do the pilot. Obviously I work in concert with the producers. And normally the writer.

There's an adversary position in Hollywood between a lot of directors and writers, and I don't know why. If you like the script, you've got to like the writer's mind. And if you like his or her mind, then you want to have that mind around—unless the writer really wants to direct the script. I want the process to be collaborative.

During casting, what I personally look for in the actors is what I call "long-staying depth." Sometimes people can come into the office and give a wonderful reading that's glib and funny, but the question is whether or not an audience will keep liking these people week after week after week. You want to feel that you're setting up a show that's going to be around for a while. After all, a pilot is just a selling tool. It's really for no more than five or six people at the network, and for testing purposes. So I feel it's a director's responsibility, aside from setting a style, to cast it so that as the weeks go by, and some of the scripts may not be particularly good, there is still a depth and durability to the actors who are regulars on the show. I think casting is forty-five percent of comedy directing. The writing is forty-five percent and ten percent is technical.

You've been with The Cosby Show *from its inception. Was it a typical experience for you?*

SANDRICH: No, it was atypical. I got a phone call from Marcy Carsey and Tom Werner, the producers of the show, saying that NBC had bought the idea of a series to star Bill Cosby, and that they had committed for six episodes. There was no premise, no story, and no script. The network wanted a ten-minute presentation so they could show it to their affiliates. Now, I adore Cosby, I love his work. I had directed some of his old half-hour shows and I had enjoyed the experience. But when they called me, I said I had to see a script. Because if I'm not happy with the script, or if I disagree with the premise, then I make life miserable for everybody, myself included. I told them that I couldn't commit to something when there wasn't anything to read. So they said it wasn't going to be shown on the air, it was just a presentation film with Bill and whatever casting could be put together within the time limitations, that they realized I needed a script but they just didn't have one at the moment, and would I do it?

Well, I broke a cardinal rule. I accepted. I said okay because of Bill Cosby and because of Marcy and Tom. But I really worried about it. I was doing another pilot, and I kept calling in to find out how things were going. The writers involved didn't work out, and there really wasn't a concept yet. When I finished the other pilot and we had our first meeting, I suggested they try to get Ed. Weinberger to write the presentation. After a series of negotiations they set Ed. and Michael Leeson. Then, finally, the basic premise of the show emerged. It was going to be about a father, a mother, and a family, based upon Bill's comedy material. Surprisingly enough, it took a lot of meetings to come up with that because it was not Bill's original concept of the series he wanted to do.

How did you assemble the cast?

SANDRICH: There was time pressure because the network had to announce their schedule, so we had to tape by a certain date. Tom Werner and I went to New York to look for actors, but we didn't have a script and we had no idea of what we were going to do. All we knew was that Bill Cosby's real son, who was fourteen, was six-foot-two, and Bill wanted a young actor who was the same age and height. So we had to find somebody who was six-two, and Bill wanted us to find a wife who could speak Spanish. That was very important to him. To this day I don't know why. Also, the actress who played the wife would have to be attractive and a wonderful reactor.

We talked to casting directors, we told them our needs, and we saw a lot of actors for all of the parts. One day a little child came in—we were led to believe she was five and we later found out she was four—and she just knocked us all out. At the time the part of the youngest child was supposed to be a boy, but I said we had to take this little girl back with us.

We took five children to Los Angeles, plus two wives. Malcolm Warner, who now plays the son, came in on our last day of casting after we had reassembled in L.A. Tempestt Bledsoe was found by NBC casting in Chicago at the very last minute. We did all of our casting without a script. We took scenes from other shows. The little children were reading scenes from *Punky Brewster,* the wives were reading from a Carsey-Werner series that starred Madelene Kahn, and the older kids would read from *Diff'rent Strokes.* None of the scenes had anything to do with *The Cosby Show.*

How long did it take to tape the presentation?

SANDRICH: We had two days. We rehearsed one day and taped it the next. It was an amazing experience for me, because when we went on camera, my wife, who had just come into the studio, asked me how things were going, and I said I didn't know. I had no idea what I was going to do, I didn't know where I would make the cuts; I mean, it was just too hectic. It was so under-rehearsed. And then, the minute we started to tape, it became magical. Because Bill comes to life when the audience is there. He became Bill Cosby as we know him. The kids were great, everything worked, and the audience loved it.

We did the show twice, once in the afternoon and once in the evening. We were never able to cut it down to the planned ten minutes—I think it ran for fifteen or sixteen minutes. We sent it to the network and they said they wanted to schedule the series beginning in September. We still had to shoot about twelve additional minutes to make the presentation into a full half hour, which we picked up, a scene at a time, as we taped other episodes of the series.

Now that you're settled into the routine of the show, how many times do you tape each episode?

SANDRICH: Twice. We do a four-thirty show and a seven-thirty show. *Cosby* is different from most other series. It's certainly different from *The Mary Tyler Moore Show,* where even after seven years, we still rehearsed five days a week. Because of Bill's way of working, we really don't rehearse a lot. *Cosby* rehearsals are more or less just finding out what works and what doesn't. He likes a certain sense of freedom, and the other actors are wonderful because they can deal with it. Phylicia Ayers-Allen, for example, who plays his wife, has learned to go with him wherever he's going until she gets the feeling she's got to bring him back to the script. He improvises a lot. Brilliant stuff. He's a performer who loves the audience and feels he has to entertain them. And if he's not quite sure what he's going to be doing, he can constantly challenge himself, which can also be a challenge for the director.

What we do is have all four cameras recording at all times, and I will cut from one camera to another for the sake of the audience, because many of them are watching the monitors in the studio. But the camera cuts I make while we're doing the show are not necessarily the ones that will go on the air. The final version is reedited, using material from all of the cameras. We tape on Thursday, and on Friday I sit with the editor and select moments from the two shows we've done to combine into the final cut.

What goes on in the control room during The Cosby Show?

SANDRICH: Let me give you a contrast. I recently did a pilot for a series called *Golden Girls*. The actors were very disciplined, and we had two weeks to rehearse. I knew exactly where every camera was going to be. It was very calm in the control room.

On *Cosby,* however, it's pandemonium. Sometimes I have no idea where I'm going to go. Sometimes Bill will do something so brilliant that my whole thought process is stopped because I'm laughing so hard, and there are other times when nothing seems to go right. Very rarely have I ever walked out of the control room after a *Cosby* show and said, "This is a wonderful show." I've always hoped that we could use the bits and pieces to *make* it a wonderful show.

Normally I'll have given the associate director a blueprint of all the shots I want: close-ups here, two-shots, masters, all of that. And it will be marked down in a script. Then we spend a camera day getting those shots with the camera crew. So they'll know that camera one has shot twenty-seven, and it's a close-up of Bill, and shot twenty-eight is on camera four, and it's a close-up of Phylicia. And then, as the show goes on, the AD is always calling off numbers so they'll know what number they're on. But on *The Cosby Show* it doesn't always work out that way, because different things will happen, new lines will come in, and I won't always know where to cut. So it's craziness during the show. The cameras are constantly moving, and in the back of my mind I'm thinking, "If that shot doesn't work, how am I going to get to the next shot, and did we do that line correctly in the first show, and was the camera moving or focusing or just not there at a particular moment I'd like to use?"

If many in the audience are watching monitors, is it true that you control their laughter, or at least the duration of their laughter, by your cutting decisions?

SANDRICH: Yes. I sit next to the technical director, and I snap my fingers when I want him to push the buttons that cut from one camera to another. The audience will laugh at a shot, and if we cut too soon, they'll stop laughing. If we stay on a close-up too long, they'll just keep laughing and laughing, which can be too *much* of a reaction. I feel that's part of directing, the timing. Even though we can repair things in the editing room, I want to try to make it as good as it can be for the audience in the studio.

The Cosby Show *is done in New York. Is there much of a difference between taping a series in New York and doing it in Los Angeles?*

SANDRICH: Not anymore, but there was when we first started. Since there were so few properly equipped television stages in Manhattan, we ended up on a stage in Brooklyn that hadn't been used for several years. The tape cameras were about sixteen years old, so we were having terrible technical problems for the first half dozen shows.

We gradually worked these problems out with the help of Grant Tinker. Some of the business people at NBC didn't want to invest too much money in the show's production because it wasn't on the air yet, and it might not be successful. It finally came down to going to the head of the network, Grant, because he's a man who really cares about quality product.

How are the New York crews?

SANDRICH: Now they're terrific. But it was a struggle at first, because they weren't used to working the way I was. They were comfortable with a much more "wing-it" type of operation. But in order for me to edit, I have to count on certain shots being there at certain times. It took awhile to find camera operators who were willing—and I don't mean that they were against it—but who were willing to change their methods. Now we have a really wonderful crew. There are still some technical problems with the studio, but they're supposedly fixing things up.

Do you have a bias against certain kinds of material?

SANDRICH: Yes. Television goes into the home, and I think all of us should have a sense of responsibility to our audiences. I don't want to do any comedy that deals with destruction. I don't want to do any comedy that makes drugs acceptable or objects of humor, and I don't want to say something that I don't really believe in. Now, this comes from the man who directed *Soap*. But I felt that *Soap* had a moral sense. It made fun of certain attitudes, but its basis was family and love.

As for *The Cosby Show*, Bill has a definite concept of teaching, of what he wants to say. For me it's a pleasure because he and I are usually in agreement about the show's point of view. Another thing I don't want to do is a show that's just for children. If I, as an adult, don't want to watch it, then I don't want to direct it. Although *The Cosby Show* reaches children, it is not a show *for* children.

It's written for grown-ups and tries to treat children as thinking human beings.

Do you have any particular approach to directing comedy?

SANDRICH: Well, I like pace. When people are sitting at home watching television, there are a lot of distractions. So a director has to keep things moving. By pace I don't mean that the words have to be rushed, but a lot of actors tend to draw out their sentences. So my style—and it's not just my style since George Abbott has used it for years—is pace.

But I also think there are times when it's important to slow "moments" down. That doesn't mean everything should be overly dramatic. That's a mistake, and it causes you to lose impact. I'm interested in relationships, so I don't like to play everything in close-up. I like to see two people relating. On most of the shows I've done I tend to use a lot of medium shots of two people talking. If the actor is good, I don't want to interrupt it by cutting back and forth.

Is there such a thing as comedy acting? Frequently on sitcoms, the actors seem to be pushing too hard.

SANDRICH: The good comic actors are good actors. They find the reality of a situation, the truth of a moment, and then they exaggerate it slightly. The less it has to be exaggerated, the more honest it is and the better it is. But sometimes exaggeration is valid. Bill Cosby has a wonderfully expressive face, and that's the face he uses in real life.

There are different kinds of comedy actors. Mary Tyler Moore is not a comedienne like Carol Burnett, but she's a great reactor. She can also make you care about her character's problems, and that's a very important thing. You look at some of the comedy shows, and they're so lacking in reality that the audience isn't interested in whether the characters solve their problems or not.

Then there are great physical actors like Dick Van Dyke.

I remember once, when I was doing the *Dick Van Dyke Show,* we had a scene that wasn't working. His wife, just for something to do as the scene opened, was sweeping the floor as he entered. I suggested that instead of sweeping the floor, what if it had just been waxed? Well, Dick came in the door and improvised three of the funniest physical bits I've ever seen, all without falling.

What you hope to do as a director is set up a situation for these brilliant comic minds. I'll never tell Bill Cosby how to read a line. I will say that something was over- or underacted, or that instead of reacting in a certain way, he should try something else. If he agrees, he'll do it. But you can never tell somebody like Cosby or Van Dyke or Mary Tyler Moore how to do something because they're so innately good at what they do. The really top comedy actors are extremely bright people, and the way to help them is just to give them another point of view.

How does "funny" enter into the equation of situation comedy?

SANDRICH: "Funny" comes from the script. If you have a script that works, then the actors and the director can find the humor. I've done many shows where the scripts weren't funny. We'd spend a lot of time on them—they would pass and be okay—but they weren't funny. Basically it all comes from the writing.

Have you ever done any writing yourself?

SANDRICH: No. I've collaborated with writers and I've worked on scenes in scripts, but I've never had the courage to sit down and do it myself. Also, I've worked with such wonderful writers that it isn't necessary.

You produced the first season of Get Smart. *Since then you haven't produced. Why not?*

SANDRICH: To me, producing comedy is a writer's function. It's fixing scripts that don't work, rewriting seven days a week, and never being able to relax. Because even if this week's show is wonderful, next week's script is a disaster, and there might not even *be* a script for the week after that.

I've learned that I'm happier with what's happening on the stage right now. When I'm not at the studio, there's not much I can do. I mean, I'll give my opinions to the writers and definitely to the producers, but they're the ones who will have to sit up all night and try to fix it. When I was a producer, I used to wake up at four in the morning and say, "My God, I haven't done this or that." But now, as a director, I only deal with things when I'm there. I like to wrestle with immediate problems, not the problems of the future. I think producing television comedy is the hardest job in the business.

You directed a feature film, Neil Simon's Seems Like Old Times. *What were some of the differences, aside from having more time and more money, between that and your television work?*

SANDRICH: One of the problems for a director in features is that other people can change his material. In television, there isn't time for that. In TV the director cuts it, and more often than not, his cut is the one that airs. When I did *Seems Like Old Times,* there was a difference of opinion between me and some other people because they thought I paced it too quickly. Fortunately, when we ran it in front of an audience, they loved it. If they hadn't, the picture probably would have been recut.

There's also another problem in features—you're not always allowed to cast the best actor. Instead you cast for box office. In television we cast whoever we want. When we did *Soap,* we didn't have one name actor. On *The Cosby Show,* aside from Bill, we had complete casting freedom. Television makes its own stars. If an actor is wrong for a part, it's not going to work, no matter who the director is and how many rewrites you do. Still, making the picture was a wonderful experience for me because doing a Neil Simon script is a director's dream. I had heard that he wouldn't let a word be changed, but it's not true. If I made a suggestion and he liked it, he'd go with it. At one point we came up with a physical bit that knocked out four pages of dialogue. When we told him, he said, "Lose the dialogue."

Another pleasure was having two full weeks to rehearse. And Goldie Hawn and Chevy Chase were really wonderful to work with and to know as people.

In addition to directing a theatrical feature and situation comedies, you also did a "special."

SANDRICH: Yes, For Lily Tomlin. I did it because if someone says to you, "Would you like to work with Lily Tomlin?" you say yes. It was a rewarding experience. It was essentially a series of sketches. We kept some, we threw some of them out, and Lily did a lot of the writing herself. My tendency is to look at a sketch as a modified half hour, and I feel it has to have a certain sense of intelligence and reality. The show was a mixture; we did some of it in front of an audience and some of it on film. There was also a dance number where we used four tape cameras.

Why are so few women directing situation comedy?

SANDRICH: That's changing. I was fortunate to be able to work with two female ADs who are now both directing. But the business is very chauvinistic. When something's on paper, it doesn't matter who writes it, man or woman. But many executives, producers, and actors don't want to deal with a woman telling them what to do. Actors are often in conflict with a director. That shouldn't be true, but it is. When you tell somebody you want them to do it again, in effect you're saying that it could be better, that it didn't please you. And a lot of men don't want to hear that from a woman.

Also, women weren't given the opportunity to learn the technical end. A director has to deal with actors and writers, but he or she also has to know the mechanics. If the camera is put in the wrong place, the jokes just won't work. Now women are getting the chance to spend time in these areas, and there are some fine women directors coming up. It's really a matter of training and opportunity.

Do you let people audit your shows?

SANDRICH: Yes. Somebody will introduce me to someone who will want to come in and watch. Usually I accept people who are equipped to understand what's going on. I mean, they have to have some experience directing.

Any advice for would-be directors?

SANDRICH: Yes. Write. If you're a good comedy writer, than at some point you can say you want to direct a script. Another thing, particularly if you're in college, is to accumulate a broad knowledge about everything you can. In school I honestly feel that one should learn more about life than directing. Obviously there are certain technical aspects one can pick up: You can learn about editing, or if you want to become a cameraperson, you can learn about lighting. But I really do feel that to prepare yourself for this work you've got to know literature, you've got to know language, you've got to know history. A good director has to bring a certain sense of the world, and an intelligence, to the material. If you concentrated exclusively on television and motion pictures when you're young, then you may not have the broad knowledge you need when you're in your forties. When I went to college, I took a lot of courses that had nothing to do with film. A widely based background is essential, because when you're a director, people ask you so many questions about so many things.

A final point is that you shouldn't expect a career to happen quickly. Most young people want to be directors by the time they're twenty-five; they want to be making a lot of money when they're thirty. It takes a long time and a lot of breaks to get ahead in television. And sometimes tremendously talented people don't make it because they give up. I never felt I had a lot of talent, and I never felt I had a great sense of humor. But I spent a lot of time at my job. I was an assistant director for eight or nine years, so when I got the chance, I was well prepared. I was very frustrated that I wasn't directing earlier. But now that I look back, I realize how much I was learning. So have patience. That's the best advice I can give.

PART TWO
THE LONG FORM

PREFACE

Aside from the criminal underworld, the military, and the local high school, the television industry may be one of the last remaining bastions of jargon. TV folk have to deal with "preemptions," "sweeps," "overnights and nationals," "soft and hard" ideas, "gang" comedies, "open and closed" mysteries, "backstory," "franchise" (a word having nothing to do with Kentucky Fried Chicken), "step outline," "development deal," "TVQ," "pickup subject to casting," "lead-ins," and, finally, that most terminal of words, "cancelation."

Still another phrase—"the long form"—has been much in vogue for the past twenty years. Originally coined to describe TV series that were more than an hour in length (i.e. *The Virginian* and *Arrest and Trial,* both ninety-minute programs), it eventually came to include ninety-minute and two-hour television movies, miniseries, and so-called "two-parters" such as *Fatal Vision* and *The Atlanta Child Murders,* which were aired in two-hour segments on separate evenings.

The first extra-long (one is tempted to say "king-size") television movie was *Vanished*. Based on a novel by Fletcher Knebel, it was produced by Universal and aired in two parts in 1971 by NBC. The actual running time of the film, minus commercials, was three hours and ten minutes, putting it in a league, at least in terms of length, with *Gone With the Wind*.

Rich Man, Poor Man, shown on ABC in 1976, is given credit for being the first miniseries, although ABC showcased a six-and-a-half-hour version of *QB VII,* the Leon Uris best-seller, two years earlier. *Rich Man* was twelve hours long and aired as six two-hour motion pictures over a period of seven weeks. It paved the way for *Roots, Shogun, The Thorn Birds, Space,* and dozens of other miniseries, including such superb British imports as *Brideshead Revisited, The Glittering Prizes,* and *The Jewel in the Crown.*

The TV movie, or Movie of the Week (MOW) had its birth in 1964. Prompted by the need for product to replace the diminishing reserves of theatrical feature films, NBC and Universal Studios came up with a new way to package the anthology concept. They began by dispensing with the dirty word "anthology" altogether. Instead these films would be shrewdly promoted as a first look at newly minted motion pictures made especially for television. Viewers would be unaware that they were meeting their old friend, the anthology, in a new guise.

Ironically the first television movie was never put on the air. It was an adaptation of Hemingway's short story *The Killers,* and one of its stars was an actor in the twilight of his acting career named Ronald Reagan. Deemed too violent for home consumption, *The Killers* was given a theatrical release.

In its various forms the TV movie has survived in a fickle medium for over two decades. Even pay-cable companies such as HBO and Showtime have invaded the field with films and miniseries of their own.

On balance, this has been a fortunate circumstance for viewers, since the occasional MOW can rise above the banality of most prime-time fare—and even above most motion pictures. Over the years TV has been graced by such impressive works as *The Autobiography of Miss Jane Pittman, Tribes, Brian's Song, The Glass House, Catholics, I Heard the Owl Call My Name, The Law, Love*

Among the Ruins, Bill, Bitter Harvest, Gideon's Trumpet, Adam, Something About Amelia, On the Minnesota Strip, and *Friendly Fire,* to name only a few.

Miniseries have seldom been the equal of TV movies in quality or creative flair, chiefly because they are often based on books of no particular literary merit. What the networks offer, sagas such as *Evergreen* and *Ellis Island, Hollywood Wives* and *Rage of Angels, Scruples* and *Mistral's Daughter,* are invariably simpleminded adaptations of best-sellers that have lavish production values and large casts of well-known actors but lack subtlety, daring, or anything resembling depth of characterization. With few exceptions miniseries are popcorn fare, the equivalent of what the publishing world calls a "trashy read."

Television movies, on the other hand, can afford to take chances; the investment in money and airtime is not as substantial. If a miniseries fails to attract an audience, it can demolish a network's standing for weeks at a time, but a MOW is only a one-shot; if its ratings are low, they can be absorbed without much damage.

This is not to say that television films are free from problems of their own. They have suffered greatly in recent years from what has become the institutionalization of network controls. In the past, when the early "World Premieres" were made, NBC had only vague-sounding "rights of consultation over star casting." Producers were more or less free to put their films together as they saw fit.

Today, however, license fee contracts for every television movie grant the networks "rights of approval" over the writer, the director, the producer, as well as all actors, the casting director, and the composer. It is now standard operating procedure for a producer to call the network executive who oversees his particular film with a list of actors, in order of preference, to see which one he will be permitted to hire.

Some producers resist these encroachments, and if they are articulate enough, or stubborn enough, or have sufficient "clout," they will win a victory here and there. But others, who are dependent on the sufferance of the network for their jobs, tend to be a bit more pliable.

The inevitable result of this acquiescence is a homogenization of the elements of picture-making, a quality of sameness. Innovation is superceded by a reliance on the tried and the true. Theatrical instincts take second place to the network's perception of which actor is "hot" at any given moment in time, in terms of a potential to deliver ratings. Since an actor's "name value" is often unrelated to his suitability for a part, miscasting abounds.

New writers and new directors also have problems getting on the "approved" list. It is easier for them to break into series television than into TV films and miniseries. The situation is exacerbated by the fact that many second-level network executives are young, with only a short-term knowledge of the medium. Their powers of recall do not extend beyond the previous season's television series or hit motion pictures; they will react with blank stares to the mention of time-honored names that are not of recent currency.

In addition to the loss of creative controls the makers of television films must also deal with the networks' ever-changing insights into what the public wants. For most of their incubation period TV movies were essentially melodramatic programmers and pilots for potential series. Viewers were not expected to respond favorably to "soft" stories or character studies.

Then, unexpectedly, *My Sweet Charlie,* which was both soft and a character study, made its mark in the ratings. The door opened a crack and for a number of years there was a rash of interesting, provocative, and unusual MOWs.

At the same time several trends began to emerge that were less than promising. An early TV film called *Brian's Song* has the unhappy distinction of spawning a genre that came to haunt the airwaves: the so-called "disease of the week," in which the protagonist, always the victim of some incurable malady, is able to triumph over adversity until he or she expires, usually in a well-lighted close-up.

Another trend, even more pernicious, is the networks' love affair with something called "high concept," meaning a story line that can be boiled down into a phrase or two that will, in theory, jump off the page in *TV Guide* and all but coerce the viewer into watching. For example: *Hamlet. Father murdered. Son pretends to be demented as part of diabolical revenge scheme.*

Failing a "high concept" premise or a new twist on a fatal disease, the networks respond avidly to stories about prostitutes, mistresses, and rape. What they are *not* interested in are so-called "people" or "relationship" stories, unless the plots lend themselves to exploitable gimmicks or promotional hooks.

TV movies, far more than miniseries, are affected by the cyclical nature of the medium. When the economy is in a slump, the networks will send out a call for "light, escapist entertainment." The assumption is that viewers, innundated with problems of their own, will not respond to even a whiff of grim reality on their television screens.

Then a long-form production, such as *The Day After,* will come along, dealing in graphic fashion with the horrors of nuclear annihilation and violate the expectations of the trade by piling up almost unprecedented ratings. Suddenly "light, escapist entertainment" will be relegated to the back burner and "issue-oriented" drama will be back in vogue. At that point viewers will be subjected to a flood of films about wife-beating, teenage suicide, incest, and whatever other social problems have yet to be explored by the pioneer of "problem dramas," *The Defenders,* or by Norman Lear and other practitioners of the "issue-of-the-week" gambit.

After two decades television movies seem to have settled into a predictable rut. Now more than ever, the discriminating viewer must settle for a diminishing number of exceptions to the general run of formula films. Similarly the miniseries has found its niche and seems bent on continuing its tendency to mine the inexhaustible lode of second-rate popular fiction. This is unfortunate, since in the past both of these programming forms (in particular the MOW) have provided the means for experimentation, as well as a forum for some of the medium's major talents.

Unhappily for both the networks and the members of the creative community, there appears scant hope of a satisfying resolution of differences; their conflicting needs all too often place them in opposition. Networks are in business to deliver ratings. For them, numbers are almost a moral imperative. Network executives have no objection to quality—they prefer it—but it is far from their main priority. Writers, producers, and directors, on the other hand, often have a different goal—the desire to do good work. They have no objection to popularity, but ratings are not necessarily their primary concern.

Since these points of view are virtually antithetical, the two camps try to reconcile their differences by a never-ending process of horse trading, compromise, and jockeying for control. The result of this perpetual in-fighting (which is usually conducted in an amiable fashion) are films that are hybrids, pulling in several directions at once and unsatisfying as either art or commerce.

Still, many of those who make their living in episodic television aspire to the Movie of the Week and the miniseries. At their best, these productions are showcases. They can add luster to established reputations and have frequently launched careers. Directors such as Speilberg, John Badham, Michael Ritchie, and Dick Donner attracted attention with their television films and moved on to theatrical motion pictures. Sally Field established herself as a serious actress when she appeared in the TV version of *Sybil*. Writers, rendered all but anonymous by the restrictive formats of episodic series, have a chance for individual expression and therefore the possibility of being noticed.

More important, at a time when the costs of theater and motion pictures make risk taking all but obsolete, the long form offers the opportunity—however rare—to handcraft a single piece of work that will be worth watching.

The Producer

ROBERT PAPAZIAN

Robert Papazian was born in Boston, Massachusetts, in 1941. At an early age he moved to Los Angeles where he attended California State College and received a Bachelor of Arts degree in Speech-Drama. For most of his career Papazian has functioned as a producer, first at a network and then with various independent suppliers. He now runs his own company, Robert Papazian Productions. Among the television movies he has produced are Crisis at Central High, *for which he won the Christopher Award,* Murder by Natural Causes, Stand By Your Man, Why Me? *and* The Day After, *which was nominated for twelve Emmy Awards.*

How many movies for television have you personally produced?

PAPAZIAN: Almost thirty. Some were two hours, some were ninety minutes; one of them, *Crisis at Central High,* was two and a half hours long; and *The Day After* ran for three hours.

What are the producer's responsibilities on a TV movie?

PAPAZIAN: There are usually two categories under the producer heading. One is the executive producer. He's generally the man—or woman—who takes an idea to a network, be it a book, an article, or an original concept. It might even be a completed script that he's either written or acquired. Let's say he sells it, whatever it is, to the network. At some point, after developing it with a writer, he may get a go-ahead to picture. Then, if he's not going to oversee it himself, he might hire a producer. That's where I come in.

My function is to make the film for the money provided while maintaining the integrity of the script. A good producer should be a jack-of-all-trades. He has to be able to read a script and see what, if anything, is wrong with it. He has to know how to make story suggestions to the writer, both from a creative and a production standpoint, and, if necessary, he may even have to rewrite a scene or two. He should be able to budget and schedule the picture, work with the director on location choices, script revisions, and the selection of the crew. He gets involved with the look of the movie, including makeup, wardrobe, hairstyle, and art direction. He should also be familiar with all of the business affairs areas, especially with negotiation of a license fee with the network. He should work with the executive producer and the director during casting, and he may negotiate the actor deals through the casting director. He should know how to supervise administrative functions such as cash flow, accounting, and cost reports.

In terms of post-production he should be able to look at the director's cut and, if things aren't right, sit down with the editor and correct them. He should be knowledgeable enough about music. to speak with the composer concerning the requirements of various scenes. His responsibilities extend to the supervision of the scoring and the dubbing process. When the picture is mixed, he should know how to correct an answer print, making sure that the color is right and that the soundtrack is clean and has been transferred properly.

Finally he should follow through with whatever distribution deal has been made. It all comes down to planning the financial elements of the movie and weaving them together with the creative elements—without doing damage to either side.

What does the production manager do?

PAPAZIAN: When we arrive at the overall plan, he's the one who follows through with the coordination of the production elements. He's responsible for hiring the crew based on the approved budget. He makes sure that the department heads are informed about any changes in the script. He works with the location manager and negotiates those deals, and he coordinates with the first assistant director in terms of each day's work. Basically he's the right arm for the producer during the stages of preproduction and production.

Do you do the schedules for your pictures?

PAPAZIAN: Yes. I've had some experience directing, so the first time I read a script, I read it as a director, asking myself how I'd approach various scenes if I were directing it. Then I analyze the material in terms of locations and production needs. When there's a scene that takes place in a factory and the setting is essential, then obviously you have to film at a factory or something that looks like a factory. But there may be other scenes that can be filmed anywhere. I call these my "swing" scenes. I pile them off to the side, so that on a particular day, if we don't have a full schedule, I can use one of these scenes to fill out the day's work without a production move, that is, a company move from location A to location B, which can cause unnecessary expense.

So you lay out a scene-by-scene, day-by-day projection of the film.

PAPAZIAN: Correct. Every scene in the script is represented by what is called a strip. Strips are flexible pieces of cardboard about fourteen inches long and half an inch wide, and they fit, side by side, into a holder called a board. All of the elements of a given scene are written on a corresponding strip: the actors, the extras, some of the requirements like cars or animals or welfare workers for child actors, whether it's day or night, the page count of the scene, and a description of the scene in a few words. You wind up with a multitude of these strips, and you put them on the board in script continuity. That's when you begin to see the dynamics of the problems. Since it costs a great deal to carry actors, I start by boarding strictly for cast, trying to keep the actors down to the lowest number of days. This doesn't apply to the stars because they're usually contracted for the run of the picture.

Naturally, when you lay out a schedule in this fashion, you may keep the cost of the actors down, but you can increase the cost of production. You may have created a lot of unnecessary moves. So you try to find a balance. I keep juggling the scripts around until that balance is found. Also, by involving yourself with the casting director when the actors' deals are negotiated, you're sometimes able to make arrangements that give you more flexibility.

Does your schedule dictate changes in the script? Or is that the tail wagging the dog?

PAPAZIAN: There are usually certain scenes that don't necessarily have to be filmed the way they're written. I don't go to the writer and say, "Look, this scene is going to cost too much money." What I try to do is give him creative options, alternatives that won't damage the script but that might be less expensive. Sometimes these options work, and as a result the writer may create a stronger scene. From his point of view he's not doing it for my scheduling convenience, but it has that effect. Finally the board is frozen, although during shooting it's sometimes necessary to change things around. But once it's set, the information is disseminated to the production manager, the first assistant director, the location manager, the wardrobe people, the property people, and the director. From that point on everything starts to flow according to that schedule.

You now have your own company. How did that come about?

PAPAZIAN: When I was in college, my ambition was to be a director. In 1959, while I was still going to school, I got a job as a page at the CBS network in Los Angeles. I had the unique experience of sitting in a classroom listening to theory by day and then going to work at night and seeing how that theory was applied. I paged for *The Red Skelton Show, The Judy Garland Show, The Twilight Zone,* game shows, variety shows, and some of the big dramatic shows. I saw a lot of professionals working on a lot of different projects, and it didn't always jibe with what I was being taught.

After I graduated I worked at Channel 2, a station in Los Angeles owned by CBS, in their broadcast operations department. Then I was drafted for two years. While I was in the service I produced, directed, and wrote Army training films, and at night I got a job at a television station directing sports, news, and round-table discussions. I still intended to be a director, but I began to change my mind, after the Army, because of my experience working on *The Doris Day Show.* I was offered a job as a production assistant—which means flunky—and I took it because I didn't know anything about film and it was a one-camera film show. I was a pretty good flunky, so I was asked to get involved in post-production, particularly editing. I found myself in the editing room, cleaning out wastepaper baskets but also sitting behind an editor's shoulder.

A few weeks later I was on the scoring stage and the dubbing stage. Then the production manager started teaching me how to schedule a picture, and then I got involved with the accountants and started a crash course on budgets. I was beginning to see and experience all of the elements on a very professional level, and I began to take an interest in what it means to produce a picture. Gradually I found that producing was more stimulating than my original intention of becoming a director.

At one time you worked for a network, didn't you?

PAPAZIAN: Yes, ABC. I was hired to be a production supervisor. When I first started, I was given a budget on a series called *Mod Squad,* which was the first in-house series for ABC, and told to do the series budget for the first year. All I knew about budgets was what I had learned on *The Doris Day Show*. So I worked on the *Mod Squad* budget, and it was really boring. I said to myself, "Why the hell are you doing this when you want to be a producer?" But then I began to realize that most producers don't really know anything about budgets. They're handed thirty pages of numbers and they don't know how it relates to the script. With that in mind I started to analyze the components, and I began to understand how a script translates into numbers and what those numbers mean. And the budget I did—after two weeks of agonizing over taxes and fringes and what a guy gets and how do you estimate set construction—that budget became the series budget for the first year of *Mod Squad*. When they finished the season, the show came in on budget—and I discovered I had a talent in that area.

You were involved with some of ABC's first Movies of the Week.

PAPAZIAN: Yes. Barry Diller was in charge, and I was fortunate enough to join his group. My responsibility was production. In a year and a half I think we did a dozen or so in-house movies for television. At that time they were ninety-minute films. We also accepted projects from independent suppliers. Once a picture got a green light and any problems arose, I had the authority to fix them. I was very young—I was only twenty-eight—so rather than throw my weight around because of my insecurities, I sat and listened to the people who were much more experienced than myself. I studied the decision-making process of producers and directors, and even though I had the final say, I'd pretty much approve what they wanted to do. After a while

I started to make my own decisions, formulate my own opinions, and I discovered I was often correct.

How many more steps before you started your own company?

PAPAZIAN: Quite a few. I worked for American International Pictures where I produced two feature films, I became the location producer of a TV series called *Kodiak,* and I was the vice-president of production and business affairs at an independent company called Jozak, where I produced a number of TV movies. Finally I was hired by Taft Broadcasting and ran one of their subsidiaries.

While I was at Taft I met some executive producers who wanted to do their movies for television on an independent basis. I struck deals with them and we went off and made the pictures. After about two years I had turned the subsidiary into a profit-making organization and I decided that the time had come for me to go into business for myself. That's when I set up my own shop. The networks were beginning to deal with independent executive producers instead of the major studios—the business was changing— and my name kept coming up. So I was hired to produce various films for various independents. At this stage of my career I'm also in development on my own projects, but I still enjoy working with other people on their TV movies.

Perhaps the best-known film you've produced is The Day After, *a story about the aftermath of a nuclear exchange between the United States and the Soviet Union. At this writing it's the highest-rated television movie in the history of the medium. How did you become involved?*

PAPAZIAN: In September of 1981, I got a call from Stu Samuels at ABC films, asking me to read a script that was a bit overwritten for a two-hour movie. It was called *Silence in Heaven,* by Edward Hume. The script was so powerful that the network wanted to make it even longer; they wanted it to be a two-night special event, two hours on each night. They intended to end the first two hours just prior to atomic missiles being dropped over the United States. The second half would deal with the aftermath.

Who conceived this idea?

PAPAZIAN: Brandon Stoddard, ABC's senior vice-president of movies for television and the president of their motion picture division.* Brandon and Stu were the ones who hired Ed Hume. They had only a semicompleted script before I came in, and part of my job was to work with Ed and add sixty-odd more pages so that it could be a four-hour presentation.

At what point did a director become involved?

PAPAZIAN: About six weeks after I did. I made up a list of possibilities and we all decided on Bob Butler. The style he created on *Hill Street Blues* was exactly what we felt was needed for *The Day After*.

As soon as he joined the project, he and I began breaking down the script and working on it on five different levels. In fact, to keep us from getting confused because the project was so enormous, we had five different scripts. We had a script that was strictly for story notes. We had a script for special effects notes. We had another script that was just for production. We had a script that we called our "clean" script. And then we had one other script that combined all of the notes. If, on a particular day, we just wanted to talk about special effects, we wouldn't pick up the script that had story notes in it, we'd use the one with our special effects notes.

There were a lot of decisions to make during those early weeks. Bob and I discussed where we were going to shoot it, *how* we were going to shoot it, the number of days needed, the kind of money involved, how to make the story stronger, and how we were going to do things in post-production, especially the blast effects. It was the first

*After a corporate reorganization, Stoddard is now in charge of ABC's television series.

time in my career that a director and I had worked so closely together on a project.

Where was the writer while this was going on?

PAPAZIAN: By then Ed had turned in the additional sixty pages, but we weren't quite ready for him to do a complete polish. We wanted to have all of the information at our disposal before we sat down with him. We wanted to give him our polish notes little by little, without overwhelming him.

What kind of research did you do?

PAPAZIAN: We saw tons of films. I must have read thirty or forty books. We researched paper after paper written by scientists, physicists. We had discussions with doctors, psychologists, chemists—any scientist that we could get our hands on. We talked to people in the military. When Ed Hume was doing his own research, the Department of Defense sent him a manual, which I read from cover to cover. It described various scenarios—limited warfare, a major exchange, the strategies of targets. It was compiled and written by a Senate committee. Informing ourselves took about four months, although it was an ongoing process.

During that time Bob Butler and I went to Kansas, because the story was set around Kansas City and an outlying community. We scouted, we combed the state, and we finally decided to shoot the picture in Lawrence, a small college town—it's where the University of Kansas is located—about fifty miles from Kansas City.

Then, in the latter part of January, we interviewed special effects people, hired one, and started storyboarding the special effects. We had to visualize what the earth would look like after a nuclear explosion. The art director, property master, and all of the other departments would key off these pictures. We had maps of Kansas, maps of the United States. My office looked like a war room. Every time we'd get a new piece of information we'd circle it and say, well, this would happen five miles beyond the center of the explosion, and this would happen ten miles away. While we were doing the storyboards Ed Hume came back—he lives in Boston—and we polished out the final draft.

For a four-hour, two-part movie.

PAPAZIAN: That's correct. Then a budget was formulated by ABC and myself. It was an in-house project, meaning that the network was responsible for it financially. Once we had the script, the budget, and the storyboards, Brandon Stoddard had to make the decision whether to go forward or not. He was very high on the project, but he had to meet with his management and get final approval. This took about four to five weeks. Meanwhile Bob Butler, who had cocreated a series idea for NBC called *Remington Steele,* left us to direct the pilot. Brandon returned with a go-ahead from his management in New York. The budget was approved and we started to prepare. Butler finished directing the *Steele* pilot, re-joined us during his post-production period, and we started refining. We began to handpick the crew.

Then suddenly we were thrown a major curve. NBC decided they liked the *Remington Steele* pilot. It got a go to series—and Butler was committed to direct the first four episodes. That was the problem. At first we thought we could prepare while he did the *Steele* segments, and then he could come back. It turned out to be too illogical and confusing, and we just couldn't work out the time schedule. So Butler had to withdraw. It was an enormous setback, particularly for me. He and I had prepared the movie so well and put so much of ourselves into it, that I felt that fifty percent of it had gone down the drain.

Still, there wasn't time to wallow; we needed a new director. I prepared a short list and Brandon, Stu Samuels, and I selected Nicholas Meyer. He had just finished a special effects movie called *Star Trek II: The Wrath of Khan.* I called the producer of the film, a former TV producer named Harve Bennett, and he gave me a good reading on Nick. Also, Nick is a screenwriter and a novelist, and I felt it would be an advantage to have a writer present while we were in production. If I wanted to change things without bringing Ed Hume from Boston, or doing it over the telephone, I'd have a legitimate writer, who was also the director, on hand.

How long was Nick with the project before you started to film?
PAPAZIAN: He had about a ten-week prep.

Did he do any rewrites on the script?
PAPAZIAN: Not really. He had notes, of course, as every director will. So we did bring Ed to California and Nick gave him his thoughts. Not many, mind you. I went to ABC and discussed the changes we wanted, then Ed sat with Nick and myself for a day, and Ed made the changes accordingly. We were still dealing with a four-hour script.

It must have been difficult for Nick, coming in so late.
PAPAZIAN: It was. Particularly in terms of all the preparation we had already done. I mean, all the books, and all the papers, and all the films, not to mention all of the discussions I had had with Bob Butler. I had stacks of files and my office was like a library. I took Nick to Kansas and showed him all of the locations that had been chosen, and I tried to fill him in on what had taken place for the past six months. The local townspeople, by the way, had read the script, and they gave us their full support. They believed in the project from the start, knew what we were doing, and supported us.

Were you feeling any outside pressure at this point?
PAPAZIAN: Oh, yes. Tremendous pressure. We had kept the project undercover for a long time. We didn't want any publicity, mainly because the movie didn't take a political position. That was a creative choice. The story was not about politics, it was about the effects of a nuclear war.

The problem was that because of the nature of the piece, it was possible for people to read things into it that weren't there. The Right or the Left could use it to justify whatever position they wanted to take. That's why we tried to put a lid on the publicity. But as word began to leak out the media got very interested. They began speculating, and that created pressure on us. People began saying that ABC was taking a serious subject and sensationalizing it.

Did you find that your politics, or Nick's, or Ed Hume's, found their way into the picture?

PAPAZIAN: No. We discussed that thoroughly. Nick has a very definite political position, so does Ed, and so do I. But we agreed that we should never try to influence the project with our personal points of view. It would have destroyed the integrity of the piece.

Was Nick involved in the casting?

PAPAZIAN: Yes. Before he came in, I had some meetings with ABC's casting department, and with Stu and Brandon. We agreed that we didn't need many big names in the picture because the subject matter was the star. But Nick was with us when we decided on specific actors. Jason Robards was always our first choice for the lead. As soon as ABC approved him, I started to open discussions with his agent. By coincidence on that same day, a Friday, Nick happened to get on a plane to New York to visit his parents—and sitting right next to him was Jason Robards. They started talking, Nick told him about *The Day After*, and Jason said he wanted to do it. Nick called me, I sent Jason a script, and by Monday or Tuesday, Jason was set. It's interesting—there were one hundred ten speaking parts, and while we were casting we got calls from a lot of people, many of them important actors, who supported the subject matter and wanted to be a part of the project. The crew got totally involved in it. So did the people of Lawrence.

How many days did you shoot?

PAPAZIAN: Forty days, in Lawrence and Los Angeles. It went relatively smoothly. There were the normal production problems, but there weren't any traumas. The network and I had a disagreement—they didn't want anyone from the media on the set, including the local media—but I felt that in order to gain the cooperation and trust of the people of Lawrence and Kansas, it was essential to involve the local press. We finally worked it out. The only condition was that an ABC unit publicist was present. And that was helpful to me, because I just didn't have time to deal with the press.

Makeup obviously played a substantial part in the picture.

PAPAZIAN: Yes, it did. Michael Westmore was our makeup supervisor, and during our prep he spent a lot of time drawing sketches. We had to show people with cuts, bruises, and radiation burns, and Mike had to find a balance between the reality of the situation and what Standards and Practices would allow. Total reality would have been too much for an audience to bear. I mean, Mike had studied photographs of the Hiroshima victims, but if he went too far in that direction, no one would have been able to watch.

Mike would bring an actor over to us on the set, with partial makeup applied, and Nick and I would have to decide whether it was too much or too little. In one scene—it took place in the university gymnasium—we had fifteen hundred people, all in makeup. It was an immense job. There were three makeup trailers and three lines of extras waiting. We started at four in the morning, and the makeup and hair was completed by eight. Naturally, everyone wasn't made up in full detail, just the foreground people. The background people were just powdered down. But it was still quite a complex makeup operation.

What happened when you completed the film?

PAPAZIAN: ABC's programming people embraced it. They were very positive. Brandon took it back to New York, as a four-hour picture, and showed it to his management. And at that point it was decided, at the highest network level, that it was simply too depressing to run over two nights. Nick later said, "Who wants to watch Armageddon two nights in a row?" So he and I were asked to make cuts in the picture so that it could be a one-night presentation. We weren't given any length restrictions, and they hadn't yet figured out whether it should go on at eight, eight-thirty, or nine. That was still up in the air. Nor did they give us any notes. We went back into the editing room and cut it down to what we felt would be a picture that could run, in its entirety, in one night. Then we screened it for ABC and they gave us their notes.

Didn't Nick Meyer walk off the project?

PAPAZIAN: Yes. At that time everybody was particularly sensitive. The media was pressuring us, and ABC was wondering not only how they were going to present the film to the public, but also how they were going to sell it to sponsors. Brandon was sensitive to certain aspects of the story, and he passed along his notes to Stu for implementation.

Somewhere along the line personalities didn't mesh, and Nick decided to leave for a while. I stayed because I had been with the damn thing long before Nick was involved, and also because it was my responsibility as the producer to see it through. So Stu and I sat in the editing room and made adjustments, some based on his notes, some based on mine. It took us four or five weeks, and then we screened it for Brandon. Other than one small story point, which twisted the movie and gave it a different point of view, everything was fine. But we were all so close to it that we missed the story point, especially me. So thank goodness Nick wasn't involved. Because when he saw the film the next day, he picked up on the problem immediately— Brandon picked up on it too—and explained what was wrong. We made changes, and that was the version that went on the air. Nick participated in the scoring and the dubbing, so the differences were resolved.

Did you originally intend that the picture not have any music?

PAPAZIAN: Yes. While we were in the preparatory stages Nick and I decided that the story had such emotional impact that music might dilute that emotion. But during the final editing we agreed that we wanted to enhance a concept we came to call "America the Beautiful" as it related to the pre-blast scenes. Since the film dealt with the disruption of an entire society, we felt that music should act as a counterpoint, and we began to consider music of a pastoral nature. Nick found Virgil Thompson's *The River*. Thompson, by happy circumstance, was from Kansas City, and *The River* was written expressly for that area. We got the rights and hired David Raksin to compose and re-arrange the theme.

Once David was involved, he pointed out some other places, especially in the post-blast scenes, where music could enhance the mood of the aftermath. We all agreed that music would add a certain elegance to the first half, and because the film was so relentlessly depressing, it would give the audience an emotional release in the second half.

When the picture was finished and you showed it to the people of Lawrence, what was their reaction?

PAPAZIAN: We had four screenings in one day, and over a thousand people saw it. They were dumbfounded. They couldn't believe how powerful the film was, how powerful the subject matter was.

No television movie, and probably no feature film, has ever had so much advance publicity.

PAPAZIAN: It was amazing. The publicity kept growing and growing and growing. At one point we had to send a tape to President Reagan. The Right got involved, the Left got involved. Everyone started taking positions. The media wouldn't let us alone. Every major newspaper was publishing articles. So was *Time, Newsweek, Life,* and all of the magazines. It was a worldwide event, with extensive coverage in the foreign press.

In this country, church groups discussed it, and schools. There was even a campaign to keep children under twelve from watching it. Psychiatrists went on the radio and gave interviews debating its possible effects. Some people said that parents should take classes before the film aired so they could understand what it was about and discuss it with their children. And, of course, the night it aired, ABC gave time to George Schultz, the Secretary of State, so he could make a statement. That was followed by a round-table discussion with Henry Kissinger, Robert McNamara, Carl Sagan, and others. To this day there are still articles being written about the film.

In producing a project of this particular nature you took on something with implications well beyond those of the ordinary TV movie. Did you feel you had any moral responsibilities?

PAPAZIAN: Definitely. There was one particular day, while I was doing research, when I came into my office, looked out the window, and then turned to one of my associates and said, "Why am I doing this? It's the most depressing, the most horrible subject I've ever been involved with." It was unbelievable, the facts I had turned up and the science I was beginning to understand. I was totally depressed for weeks. Because at the touch of a button all life could be eliminated. And somebody else is in control of that. But the point is that I had a very strong feeling that the picture should be made so the American people could know— should know—what the effects of a nuclear attack are like.

Looking back, would you have done anything differently on The Day After?

PAPAZIAN: Speaking strictly as a filmmaker, I wish I could have made it better. There are moments in it that still make me wince. But I think that's a typical attitude when people get some perspective on their work.

How do you feel about the network's involvement with the film?

PAPAZIAN: They conceived it and broadcast it, and I hold them in the highest regard. They were very responsible, from the programming department to the standards department to the publicity department. They were just totally responsible. And I was very proud that they chose me to be the producer.

The Writer

JOHN GAY

John Gay was born in Whittier, California, in 1924, and attended junior college in Los Angeles and Santa Monica. After graduating from the American Academy of Dramatic Arts in New York, he became an actor, then a writer for live television and theatrical motion pictures. In this latter capacity he was nominated for an Academy Award as the coauthor of the screenplay for Separate Tables. *For most of his professional career Gay has concentrated on long-form television movies, having written more of them than perhaps any other writer. Among his credits are* The Amazing Howard Hughes, Captains Courageous, Les Misérables, Transplant, The Bunker, A Tale of Two Cities, *and* Fatal Vision. *He has been nominated for the Emmy, the Writers Guild Award, and the Edgar Allan Poe Award, and has been honored by two Christopher Medals.*

Did you always want to be a writer:

GAY: No, not really. In high school I wrote short stories, but that's all. What I wanted to be was an actor. After I came out of the Coast Guard I went to the American Academy of Dramatic Arts. After that I did one play on Broadway, starring Ruth Chatterton, and then seven seasons of stock—two seasons of winter stock and five seasons of summer stock. I didn't know it at the time, but I was getting an education in the way a play is constructed. Because if you work in stock, and you do as many plays as I did—big parts and small parts—you begin to get a feeling, just by osmosis, of act structure and a sense of beginnings, middles, and endings. It all sinks in. At least it did for me. Being an actor gave me a far greater understanding of playwriting than any other kind of education I could have had.

How did you make the transition from acting to television writing?

GAY: My wife, who is an actress, was doing a live TV show for Kraft. I thought it was terrible. She asked me if I could do anything better, so I wrote a show for the two of us and we sold it. We got it on Channel 9, WOR, in New York. The year was 1949. We were on every night, five nights a week, for fifteen minutes. We had various sponsors when we could get them.

This continued for six months, and then we went to a half hour once a week. I wrote the shows, and my wife and I acted in them. We started with a sitcom and then we went into a mystery-show format where we played detectives. Believe me, it was a very inexpensive operation. We were on the air like that for about another year. I wrote the shows, created parts for my wife and myself, as well as others, and acted in them.

Did there come a point where you had to choose between acting and writing?

GAY: Yes. As a matter of fact, the turning point came when our little WOR show concluded. Which way was I going to go? Should I continue acting or continue writing? I finally decided that I'd write a show in which my wife and I weren't involved and see what happened.

There were a lot of live, half-hour TV shows in those days—*Armstrong Theater, Lux Video Theater*—so I wrote a script and gave it to my agent. Three days later she called me back and said that *Lux* had purchased it. The next day she called and told me that Frederic March and his wife were going to do it. I said to myself, "Well, John, it seems there may be a bit more of a future for your writing than for your acting." If it hadn't been for that sale, I think I might have remained an actor, but that really persuaded me. Since that time I've earned my living as a writer.

First I began writing for quite a few of the live shows. And then I got a very lucky break. One of the hour shows that I did was *The Sentry,* a Civil War piece. There was a motion picture company in Los Angeles called Hecht–Hill–Lancaster, the Lancaster being Burt Lancaster, and just by circumstance all three of the partners saw *The Sentry.* The next morning they got together, discovered they had seen the show and liked it, wondered who this guy John Gay was, and almost immediately brought me out to California. I stayed with them for about three years, writing feature films until the company dissolved.

The first script I wrote for them that was produced was called *Run Silent, Run Deep.* Then I did *Separate Tables,* where I rewrote a screenplay by the author of the play, Terence Rattigan, and shared screen credit with him. I was pretty much like a carpenter; I worked on just about whatever they had there. I got involved with all of the things they were doing, sometimes with credit, sometimes without. Then, eventually, I went over to MGM and wrote *The Courtship of Eddie's Father* and *The Four Horsemen of the Apocalypse.* Then *Soldier Blue* for Embassy and *Hallelujah Trail,* with John Sturges directing.

I was also writing for television at the time. My contract with Hecht–Hill–Lancaster was only for films and not for TV, so I did some *Playhouse 90*s. I wrote three of them. One was an original called *The Sound of Trumpets,* one was an adaptation called *Out of the Dust,* and then I did an original entitled *The Day Before Atlanta,* which was another Civil War play. Excuse me—I call them plays. But that's what live television was to me, because we rehearsed the shows as plays. This isn't true, of course, of today's filmed television.

There seems to have been a point in your career when you stopped writing theatrical motion pictures and concentrated exclusively on long-form television.

GAY: Well, I never consciously said that I was going to stop writing films. But there was a time when the motion picture industry went through a very difficult period. Then these long-form television films began appearing on the horizon, so I began working on them. And I liked them very much. When you're doing a feature film, you can be six months or more on just one project. You work on it and hope it gets done, and endless time goes by. Whereas I find that a television film doesn't take nearly as long. And I think that the work is just as good. I don't feel the quality suffers at all.

Most of the television movies that you've written are adaptations of stories or novels by others. Why adaptations rather than originals?

GAY: All of the shows I did in the live days were originals. So were two of my *Playhouse 90*s. And when I started out in the long form—by the way, I never worked on a series—I began by writing originals. But then it just happened that I was offered a number of adaptations. I think the first one I did was for a producer named Norman Rosemont, who specializes in filming the classics. He asked me to do *The Red Badge of Courage* by Stephen Crane, which I really enjoyed.

Then, too, economics entered into it. When I do an adaptation of something I really like, it takes me about half the time that I would spend working up an original story and writing the script. So if adaptations are there to be done, I do adaptations. In terms of original work, I'd rather write plays. Stage plays. I do them in my spare time.

When you're adapting a novel for television and you have the book as source material, do you find it necessary to write an extensive outline?

GAY: I don't know whether you'd call it extensive, but yes, absolutely. After I've read the book the first thing I do, whether it's 1500 pages of *Les Misérables* or 250 pages of something else, is write an outline that is essentially the way I see the story—the beginning, the middle, and the end, what it's about, and what the key elements are. I put all of those things in my outline and then I know where I am with that particular book.

I'm able to judge certain relevant bits of information from that outline. For example, is it a two-hour film, or would it be better as a three-hour or four-hour picture? Can it hold at that length? Should it be longer, shorter? When I count the number of pages in the outline, I also learn something else. I don't know why it is—it's the way I work and it's crazy—but I usually write four script pages to one page of outline. Therefore, when I complete the outline I know approximately just how long the screenplay is going to be. It's uncanny, but that's the way it happens. At that point I tell the producer that I think we have a two-hour, a three-hour, or whatever. Of course, the network may specify in advance the length of the film that they want, but I might come back to them and say that I just don't see it.

For instance, take a classic like *The Hunchback of Notre Dame*. It's really quite a fragile story. It's just a lovely sweet trio of people caught in a dilemma. To build that up doesn't really add anything. Stay with those three people for two hours and you come out very nicely, I think. At least that's how it seemed to me.

On the other hand, when I read *Les Misérables,* I realized that the story literally covered decades. I felt I really needed at least three hours to tell the story well, and that's the way it finally went on the air.

How do you deal with the age-old writer's problem of writing dialogue based on a classical text? Do you modernize or do you try to reproduce it more or less as is?

GAY: I know I'm certainly not going to have the characters speaking in a contemporary way, nor do I want the dialogue to be as archaic as it is in the book, so I pretty much go by instinct. I listen to it in my mind and then try to find something that will be a compromise, something understandable and dramatic that the audience can respond to. It's neither modern nor old-fashioned. I think it helps that I started out as an actor. I hear the dialogue, I feel it, and then I write it.

Do you ever have specific casting in mind when you write?

GAY: No. Not unless I'm told it's going to be for somebody in particular. Sometimes, when you're halfway through a script, you might say to yourself that so-and-so might be just marvelous in a given part. But then you can't get him or her out of your mind. And they wind up casting somebody else, anyway. I always find that my suggestions for casting are hardly ever listened to.

You've done several so-called docudramas, most notably a piece about Caryl Chessman that ends with a rather graphic depiction of his execution, and one which seemed to take a very strong position as to his innocence. Your other controversial film was The Bunker, *in which you were accused of presenting a sympathetic portrait of Adolf Hitler. What are your feelings about the docudrama form?*

GAY: I just try to be as responsible as I possibly can. I really do. In the case of the Caryl Chessman film, *Kill Me If You Can,* I went to see his lawyer up in Sacramento and spent two weeks with her. I listened to her, I read all of the Chessman books, I read the court testimony, and I came to my own conclusion that the man had been railroaded as far as a capital offense was concerned.

Keep in mind that there wasn't any murder involved in

that case. So it is true that I became convinced of his innocence, but it's also true that I was writing the story of Caryl Chessman, and Caryl Chessman believed in his own innocence. I didn't put words in his mouth, or if I did, they were very few. I was using *his* words. And if you listen to Caryl Chessman talking about himself, he constantly declared his innocence. My intention was to deal with him and his lawyer, what she felt about him, and their personal story. I did not go into that project to take a stand either for or against capital punishment.

Yet, when it was completed, it did seem like an anti–capital punishment piece—although when we showed it to a group of law-enforcement officers, they came out smiling. We said, "Did you like it?" And they said, "Give us a happy ending and we'll like it every time."

As for *The Bunker,* I started with the book; essentially I did a faithful adaptation. I also went to other sources for references about Hitler and those who were involved with him, but the only new material I brought in was information that would make it flow more easily. I know some people criticized it; I was apprehensive myself when I saw the show. But I think that Howard Rosenberg, for example— he's the TV critic for the *Los Angeles Times*—went overboard. He was so much against the show and the way he perceived its portrayal of Hitler that he didn't even like Tony Hopkins's performance. Which is a shame because it was a marvelous, wonderful performance. Hopkins got an Emmy for it. I just tried to adapt the book as well as I could. That's what I was there for.

Still, even assuming absolute fidelity to the original material, there are those who feel that the docudrama tends to falsify history.

GAY: It's not a documentary, it's a docu*drama.* And I don't think, as some do, that the form itself is a mistake. I think it can be a good thing. Take this television film I did, *Fatal Vision.* While I was working on it, I became completely convinced of Jeff MacDonald's guilt. Not only from reading the Joe McGinniss book, but also because of all of the people I talked to. When I think of those two little babies and his wife murdered, I think that a nation-wide television audience should have the opportunity to be exposed to the facts.

But the question remains as to whether a writer, with a potential audience of thirty to forty million people, has a right to come to conclusions about a real case and put those conclusions on the air.

GAY: I feel I dealt with the facts and let the audience draw their own conclusions. I relied heavily on the book. And Joe McGinniss, the author, actually lived with Jeff MacDonald. I can't think of a scene in the script that I made up on my own.

In addition, even though a book may be very well documented, I also like to speak to the people involved because I always get an insight in person. When I wrote the script for *Fatal Vision,* I got personal things I simply could not have gotten from the book.

I'm currently doing another docudrama called *Son,* and I spent some time with the author, Jack Olsen. But I also went to Spokane, where the story takes place, and I talked with the people involved up there, including the police.

Is it an uneasy relationship between the adaptor and the author of the original material?

GAY: No, not at all. At least not in my case. I've only done it two times, with Joe McGinniss and Jack Olsen, but both of them have been cooperative. Extremely so. And they both wrote very good books. So it wasn't one of those things where I had to go up to the author and say, "You know, I really have to make a lot of changes here." Also, they were very careful about documenting their stories—although the network legal departments go over everything with a fine-tooth comb.

TV movies seem to traffic a great deal in the so-called "disease-of-the-week" concept. Do you think it's become a cliché?

GAY: Well, I did a few of them myself. I did *A Private Battle*, which was the story of Cornelius Ryan, the man who wrote *The Longest Day*. The film was about his struggle against cancer. I do think there has been too much of that. It gets to be a formula. The main thing, regardless of what you're doing, is to be as truthful and as responsible to the material as you can, no matter what the form.

Getting back to historical dramas, I cannot tell you how difficult *Ivanhoe* was to adapt. It's just the most difficult book. But I tried to be faithful to it and keep it as dramatic as I possibly could. And I think I succeeded. If anyone saw that film, even if they didn't like it, at least they'd say, "Yes, there it is, he did the book; he didn't go off on some flight of his own imagination."

However, there are times when you're adapting when you absolutely must make changes. For instance, *The Hunchback of Notre Dame* was a particular problem because at the end of the book the girl chose a goat rather than her lover. A goat. Now we just couldn't have her choose this animal over this lovely poet. We just simply couldn't do it. So I changed the ending. But still, overall, I was faithful to the book. Far more faithful than the films they made of classics such as the *Hunchbacks* and the *Ivanhoes* in the thirties. In those days they just departed completely from the books and turned them into Hollywood scenarios.

Would you adapt a work that you didn't particularly respond to?

GAY: It isn't a matter that I wouldn't, it's that I couldn't. When producers send me material, I say, "Look, I'm not going to tell you whether this is good or bad, I'll just tell you whether I can do it or not." If I feel I can do it, then obviously I like it. But I can't do something that I don't like. I'm not any good at it. When something is offered to me, I choose what I respond to the most.

However, I can see material that's very good and yet still feel I'm not right for it. For example, a producer called me and said, "John, a network wants to do a show in which there's a blue-collar family and a white-collar family, and they both live in the same city, say Detroit. They want a lot of power business going on and an intermixing of the two families. Would you be interested?" And I said, "Let me ask you a question. Is what they really want a version of *Dallas* that they're going to call *Detroit*? Because if they do—and I don't denigrate *Dallas* in any way, it's very popular—then I can't write it. I don't know why, I wish I could, but I can't write *Dallas*. So ask them over there what the situation is."

He called me back the next day and said, "John, you were absolutely right. *Dallas* is exactly what they want, and I thank you for your honesty." I told him it wasn't honesty, I just couldn't do it.

Given the fact that the television writer has so little power, what kind of relationships have you established with producers and directors?

GAY: I started in live television, where we rehearsed the work as a play and the writer was very much a part of the process. He was there from day one, staying with the rehearsals and remaining from the beginning to the end. Now, unfortunately, it's a very different situation. The writer is no longer as closely involved. After the script is completed, you're called in and given rewrite notes. You get your first set of notes from the producer, your second set from the network, and your third from the director, or somebody's wife or cousin. So you do rewrites upon rewrites. But when that work is done, and everybody says yes, there's not much call for you to be around.

I try to suggest rehearsals, but I'm not always success-ful, although a director like Buzz Kulik likes to have at least a reading or two. The advantage of having a rehearsal, at least for me, is that I can hear it. And not until you hear it can you really tell whether it works or not. Even though I think I hear it in my head, it's more revealing when the dialogue is spoken through the personalities of the actors. Then, when you're on the floor, you can say, "I think I know what you can do here. Why don't we try this or that?" If there isn't a rehearsal period, or at least a reading, and they just go ahead and shoot, then you're left with whatever they decide to do.

In recent years I never have as many readings as I like, and very few rehearsals. I'm not usually invited to the set, because even if the director doesn't have an ego thing, there's always a little problem. I mean, there's the director and there's the writer, and then there's the actor saying, "Which way do I go?" And I can't keep my mouth shut, so I'll tell him. Once you've turned your material over to the director, you just have to hope he's in synch with what you've written, and that's that. As for your relationship with the producer, if you've worked with him before, you're naturally going to have more influence.

Also, it depends on whether or not you're an established writer with many credits. If you are, the producer is more likely to fight the networks for you. I think the writer's position depends on his experience and his qualifications. The same holds true for producers. Many don't have the same clout with the networks as established producers do. As a matter of fact—and I never listen to this because I always go by the material—sometimes your agent will tell you that a certain producer may not have enough clout to get a project on the air. And I always say that's tough, because if I'm really fond of the material, I'm going to do it.

Do you have a personal relationship with any executives at the networks?

GAY: Yes. I've done a lot of shows for CBS, and at the moment I seem to be doing a great deal of work for NBC, so I know a lot of people in the long-form departments of those networks.

For example, *Fatal Vision* was an in-house show. In other words, NBC was producing it, and I was very close to them. Usually an outside producer will bring a project to a network, and in those cases the writer and the producer like to present somewhat of a united front. You go into a meeting together, sit down with the long-form people after they've read the script, and they give you their notes. You either accept the notes, or you don't accept them, or you say you'll think about it. You try to be diplomatic; if you don't like their notes you don't look at them and say, "That's the stupidest thing I ever heard." You say, "Well, that's very interesting, but if you do that, how could you possibly do this?" That sort of thing. It goes on all the time.

Any desire to produce your work yourself?

GAY: No I haven't. Because what I really like to do is sit down at the typewriter. I find I don't want to get involved in the problems of production. I don't want to hold the actors' hands. I have enough problems of my own with the characters in the script. I realize that you have more creative control if you produce, but for me it just isn't worth it. I try to exercise control by coming to an understanding with the director and the producer, but I certainly don't want to perform those functions. It's very interesting for me, not having been involved with the actual production process, to go to see an assembly, or rough cut, or answer print.

What's your usual response?

GAY: I always find myself thinking three things as I watch the screen. Number one is: "How could they do that? It's terrible." This isn't a reaction to the entire film, just individual scenes as they go by. Number two is? "Hey, that's exactly what I had in mind." And Number three: "That scene is really something! I had no idea it was that good."

How much rewriting do you normally do before you deliver a script?

GAY: I do three rewrites before anyone ever sees it. I do a first, second, and third draft. When I write my second draft, I really get into it and get things the way I want them. When that's finished, I think everything's fine. And then I realize that there's still a great deal I want to do, so my third draft is a polish. It gives me the opportunity to have a last chance at every line. I never use a secretary. Then I hand it in. And the producers always infuriate me. If they just said that it needs work, it would be fine. But they say, "This is pretty good for a *first* draft," and it always gets me. I hate that line.

How elaborate are your stage directions?

GAY: Not elaborate at all. I don't write lengthy stage directions and I don't write in emotions for the actors to play: "laughing," "smiling," "embarrassed." I hardly put any of those in unless I feel it's absolutely necessary, usually because the actors might misinterpret a line.

I was complimented at a reading we had several years ago. The film was called *A Piano for Mrs. Cimino,* and it starred Bette Davis. I was amazed because in the middle of the reading she stopped and said, "Has everyone here noticed that Mr. Gay does not give us any directions as to how to say our lines? I wish to commend Mr. Gay."

I suppose I resented being told how to interpret dialogue when I was an actor. What I tend to do is use a lot of dots. If I want a sentence broken up, or a feeling that there should be a pause, I put in dots. If the actors want to run the dots together and ignore them, that's fine.

You adapted two famous mysteries for television movies, Dial M for Murder *and* Witness for the Prosecution. *Was your approach relatively the same for each piece?*

GAY: No. *Witness* was adapted from a screenplay by Billy Wilder and I.A.L. Diamond, not from the play by Agatha Christie. However, in the case of *Dial M for Murder*, I ignored the Hitchcock film and went back to the original play. Boris Sagal was the director of *Dial M*, and he and I sat down to look at the Hitchcock version. After about twenty minutes we both agreed that it was probably the worst film Hitchcock ever directed. I think the reason it wasn't terribly good was because it was shot in the 3-D process. So all of the sets had to be constructed in a certain way, and it just looked flat and uninteresting. I decided to stay away from the screenplay.

Witness, on the other hand, was a brilliant screenplay. Wilder and Diamond just did a brilliant job. For me it was a matter of fitting it to a television format and, most important, starting it in the most dramatic way possible. It makes no difference whether you're doing *Ivanhoe*, *A Tale of Two Cities*, or anything else; you still have to try to get that audience at the beginning. There are so many commercials that you want to envelope the audience in your story as quickly as you can. I don't look for cliffhangers or anything like that, but I do try to find something dramatic.

In *Witness for the Prosecution* I realized that the actual murder had never been shown, either in the play or in the screenplay. I felt it would be a dramatic way to involve the audience immediately. So I had the housekeeper come home and hear the old woman talking to a man in the room beyond. Murder, most foul!

You've done long forms of up to three hours in length. Have you ever written a miniseries?

GAY: Yes, and it remains my favorite of the things I've done, but it's unproduced. It's an eight-hour adaptation of *Around the World in 80 Days*, which I wrote for Fox and NBC.

Everyone knew it would have to cost a lot of money going in—you just can't do something like that without spending big bucks—but they gradually became very apprehensive about it. Aside from the expense, one of their concerns was that there was a great deal of emphasis on comedy. I don't think there's ever been a comedy miniseries. The people over at NBC say to me, "John, one of these days we're going to do it." We'll see.

How many plays have you written?

GAY: About four or five. Three of them have been produced. One, *Summer Voices,* is an autobiographical piece, and it was done by Oliver Hailey's group here in Los Angeles. Another is *Christophe,* produced by the Chelsea Theater Group in New York. The third, *Diversions and Delights,* is a one-man show about Oscar Wilde and starred Vincent Price. It toured every major city, then New York—then, when all of that was over, he took it around to colleges and universities. It succeeded far beyond my expectations.

I enjoy doing plays. There's obviously more freedom than there is in television, freedom in language and freedom in the time element involved. If it needs to be one act, it's one act. If it has to be three, it's three. When you do a television film, if it's two hours you know you have to come out within that exact time period. You can't ask for ten more minutes.

Not that there's anything wrong with the television long form. We take on all kinds of controversial issues on TV. It's rare that feature films deal with a subject of some substance anymore. There's a youth market out there— which is not the case on television—and you find yourself doing pictures about nerds at universities and things like that. Sure, television constricts you, particularly in language. But that was true of the films of the thirties and the forties. And frankly, I think some of this new freedom is appalling. I don't think it enhances the films at all.

If someone sells more than one script to television, he or she has to join the Writers Guild of America. You've been involved with Guild affairs in various capacities, most recently as vice-president. What are your feelings about it?

GAY: The Writers Guild is a union that provides numerous benefits that have been gained over many years of strikes and negotiations. Health benefits, pension benefits, minimum salary benefits, not to mention the monitoring of residual payments and credit arbitration services.*

There seems to be a lot of anti-union sentiment these days. I don't know why, but everyone is out for themselves. In this particular case all you have to do is look at the benefits offered, and you can't help but be a pro-Guild person. Before there was a Guild, management would eat you alive if you were a writer. The men who founded the Guild back in the thirties all but had their careers destroyed. They went for years without any work. But they persevered, and that's why we achieved what we have today.

My son is a writer—he's working on a series now for Universal—and he just joined. Because I'm involved in a lot of Guild activities, he's involved, too, and he appreciates the fact that there's a union there protecting him and his writing credits.

What kind of responsibilities does a television writer have?

GAY: Speaking for myself, I feel a strong responsibility to the material. As I said, I cannot accept a project that I don't like. But when I do accept something, I believe in it and try to do the best work I can. I love writing. That's why I'm not in production. I try to avoid things that are done just because they're commercial, or because a network thinks they're commercial. The networks are usually wrong in that respect, anyway.

There is one thing I do hold to, however, in terms of

---

*When a writing credit on a film or television show is in dispute, a panel selected from the Guild membership is called upon to arbitrate, and its determination is binding on all parties.

being commercial, and that's the idea that I'm lost if I don't have the audience in the first five minutes. If you don't get them quickly, then you may not have them for the rest of the story. So I feel that it's a major responsibility of mine to find a way to involve them immediately.

When I was writing live half-hours, a story editor named Charles Jackson—he's the fellow who wrote *The Lost Weekend*—once said to me, "John, you know what you're writing when you do a half-hour show? You're writing a one-act play." I agreed with him. Then he said, "But there's a major difference. What you're *really* writing is a three-act play—and you're doing the *third* act." He was absolutely correct. Because when you only have a half hour, you've got to become almost instantly involved. And that's also true of the longer forms. I moved into two-hour films, and finally three-hour and four-hour programs, and I still feel that my responsibility is to seize the audience quickly.

Do you have much interaction with younger writers?

GAY: I taught a course at UCLA, but I'm afraid I didn't like teaching, at least not teaching writing. One interesting thing I noticed was that when new writers start out, they'll write something and cling to it. They'll believe in it, think it's the most wonderful thing in the world, and they won't let it go. I tell them: "For God's sake move on to something else," even though it may well be as good as they think it is, because you just can't hang on to what you've written, as much as you love it. Maybe later, when you're established, maybe then you can take it out and sell it. But you must keep writing.

I find that now I can adapt a book and grasp what's essential in it far more easily than I could ten or fifteen years ago. I've gone through the process, and you just can't help but learn through experience. You've got to keep doing it. You've got to *keep* writing. It's the only way.

The Director
DAVID GREENE

David Greene was born in Manchester, England, in 1921. He came to the United States as an actor and quickly made the transition to director, occasionally writing and producing his own work. Greene has directed for live and taped television, both in New York and Los Angeles, and in recent years, he has concentrated on television movies and miniseries. His motion pictures include The Shuttered Room, Sebastian, Godspell, *and* Hard Country. *He has won four Emmy Awards for his work on* The People Next Door, Rich Man, Poor Man, Roots, *and* Friendly Fire.

What kind of education did you have?

GREENE: I went to a public school in London until I was fifteen. Then I saw a Tyrone Power movie where he was a newspaper reporter and he wore this wonderful hat and coat. I wanted to wear that hat and coat, so I went to a commercial school and studied shorthand and typing with a lot of girls destined to be secretaries. As soon as I was fluent in these mechanical skills, I walked up and down the streets of London where the newspaper offices are, looking to find an opening for a junior reporter. There weren't any vacancies, of course, but I eventually did find a spot on a local weekly paper. So at the age of fifteen and a half I became a police reporter, a sports reporter, and

I even did illustrations. I thought I was going to be a journalist.

Then I gave that up and put myself through art school. It was during World War II, and I paid for my classes by being a fire watcher on the roof of a bank. I had a bucket of sand and a shovel, and if a bomb fell on the roof, I was to shovel it up and put it in the bucket of sand. Fortunately, this particular roof was spared.

Somewhere in that mix you were an actor.

GREENE: Yes. Whenever I speak at film schools or universities, the question they always ask is, "How do you become director?" And, of course, the answer is—speaking for myself—that I did it through a whole series of accidents, mistakes, lies, and bluffs. I didn't realize I was training to be a director when I spent three or four years as a journalist on the streets. When I spent a year and a half at art school studying painting and composition, I didn't realize I was learning to be a director. And when I became an actor for ten years, I still didn't know I was learning to be a director. But once I started to direct, I realized that all of these experiences had equipped me to be a director, and indeed it felt like that was what I was born to do.

What took you from England to America?

GREENE: I was working on the stage in London, and on the BBC, and in the fifties Laurence Olivier and Vivien Leigh brought me to Broadway in their *Antony and Cleopatra*. When the company returned to Britain, I stayed on in New York playing parts on live TV. The U.S. seemed to like me, and I had begun to love the U.S.

I went to Canada, temporarily, I thought, to change my immigration status—I was in America as a visitor—but it was five years before I got back to New York. In Toronto I found myself in just the right place at the right time: They badly needed TV directing talent, and since my credits were great—the Old Vic company, Stratford-upon-Avon, London, and Broadway theater—and the other credits that sprang from my imagination even greater, they signed me to a contract with the Canadian Broadcasting Company. I'll always love Canada because they gave me a chance to show what I could do.

Finally I returned to New York with my precious green immigration card. Those were the days of live TV. I did most of the Golden Age dramas: *Studio One, The U.S. Steel Hour, Omnibus, Leonard Bernstein and the New York Philharmonic,* and then, when I moved to California, I directed *Playhouse 90.* But they didn't trust live-TV directors in the filmed-TV world. It was difficult to break in. Two men took a chance on me, Bill Sackheim and Bill Froug; they gave me a half-hour film to direct. After that I never wanted to go back to live TV again.

Although later you did, and you won your first Emmy for a live program.

GREENE: Yes, *The People Next Door.* It was remade as a feature film, which I also directed.

You did a number of episodes for The Defenders, *didn't you?*

GREENE: Yes, I was one of their regular directors, and I believe the only English director at that time working steadily in the U.S. What I used to do was design shots for every new lens as it was invented. I staged whole scenes in a style that would force me to use new camera techniques as I learned them. But I had to confine these experiments to the opening scene, or "teaser," because if I didn't, I'd invariably find myself behind schedule and have to race through the rest of the episode. I'd like to see a show-reel of those teasers today. They were fun.

You've directed a great deal of episodic television, but in recent years you've stayed almost exclusively within the long form. What are some of the differences between the two for a director?

GREENE: In episodic TV a director is concentrating on

just getting the work done, on covering the pages rather than actually interpreting the material. Time is so desperately limited. Actors have told me, in fact, that when they work on a series, they sometimes don't even get to know what the director looks like—he's always behind the lights somewhere. It's the producer who counts in the episodic field. Directors come and go, changing frequently, and the producer must impose the same style on all of them in order to maintain the character of the series from week to week. The director's job is to keep the whole thing rolling during the brief time he's handed the controls. He isn't required to come up with something special because that might take an extra a day or, God forbid, a day and a half!

The first step is always the script. You're offered many projects. How do you zero in on the one you want to do?

GREENE: When you read a script, you've got your very personal antennae fully extended, and all the little messages are coming in to you. Everything you've lived and all you believe in are at work. Sometimes you're hooked by a line or a stage direction on page one. It reveals the way the writer thinks, and you feel connected. Maybe you sense a life going on *beneath* the words. That turns me on at once. If it doesn't turn me on, I turn it down. I learned a long time ago that I can't do anything well unless I'm stimulated by it. It doesn't have to be profound, it just has to be something you respect, even if merely as a piece of viable entertainment.

Years ago I was out of work and applied for a job selling TV sets to the public. As it happened, it was a rotten brand, made up of seconds and parts from other sets. But we job applicants were given an intense lecture that started something like this: "You're going out to sell the finest TV set on the market today. If you don't believe that, you'd better quit now, because you'll never be able to sell it." I've remembered that. A director can't lend conviction to material he despises. He can't direct anything successfully if he's holding it at arm's length.

You know those big TV hits that you switch off immediately because they're so plastic and shallow? One reason they're successful is that they are done by directors who actually believe in them. When I did the original *Rich Man, Poor Man,* I didn't know it was supposed to be nighttime soap opera. To me it was good strong drama and the characters were thoroughly real. I think I imparted this conviction to the actors, and it came across to the audience. When I saw it on the air, I was almost shocked by the packaging—the *Reader's Digest* illustrations and the sentimental music. I suddenly realized I'd been out there doing Ibsen while the producers were thinking *Peyton Place.* It didn't matter because I'd looked up to the material, not down on it.

Once you've selected a script, what kind of relationship would you like to have with the writer?

GREENE: Obviously I'd like it to be a temporary love affair. But the facts of life are that by the time the writer meets the director, he's already partially exhausted. He's probably been working with the producer for a long time. Remember, producers can't employ a director until they've got financing, and they don't usually get that until they have a script of some kind. So the writer is put through rewrites until finally the network says, "Okay, it's a deal, now hire a director." By the time the director walks in with a lot of new ideas and changes in mind, he finds a writer who's very tired, maybe one who's already bored with his own subject and longs to move on to another assignment. Maybe one who for financial reasons *needs* to move on to another job. He looks at this fresh horse of a director with baleful eyes as if to say, "Give me a break, this producer's drained me."

This is particularly true if the producer is not a creative filmmaker, but rather a deal-maker who happens to have bought the rights to a desirable literary property. In such a situation the poor writer may have been given contradictory instructions for months, and he's worn out changing his story from Plan A to Plan B and then back to Plan A via Plan X. He just doesn't want to hear any more ideas. He wants out. Fortunately, there are always some writers who almost throw their arms around you as if to say, "Thank God you've come. Now we're going to start heading in the final direction."

You've made a number of two-hour television films for your own company, properties you've acquired yourself. What are the ramifications for you as a director when you wear the other two hats of producer and owner?

GREENE: You're able to be there at the beginning. Usually your own idea *is* the beginning, and the directing process starts at once. Writers like it because they feel they're heading in the proper direction right from the start, since the man they're working with is going to put it on the screen.

For me there's a huge advantage too. Much of a director's work is intuitive, not intellectual. You do something in a particular way because it seems "right," that's all. But you've learned to trust those flashes of feeling. You don't question the emotion, you just try to get it across to the audience. Can you imagine how tedious it is to try to explain in words the importance of an image that, to you, conveys more about the story than a page of dialogue? If you're also the producer, you don't have to spend your time justifying the choices that you make. It's liberating to be able to go with your own instincts and then be content to live or die by them.

How do you approach casting?

GREENE: I like to work with a casting director whose casting judgments seem to echo mine, someone who goes to the little theaters and looks for new actors not yet known to TV. The networks want "names" in the principal parts, but for the other roles your casting director will bring in a group of hopefuls and you read them and read them and, if necessary, read them again. You make mistakes. Sometimes an actor gives a wonderful reading, but when you get him in front of a camera, that's it, he doesn't have anything more. Having been an actor myself, I die a thousand deaths for all of them at readings. They enter a room and find between five and fifteen people sitting around, and there's one empty chair that they're going to sit in. There's the director, the writer, the producer, the associate this and the associate that, the casting director, network people—you name it.

If you know the actor/actress, you can try to help: "Hi, hear you've just had a baby." Or, "You were great in that show last week." Otherwise it's "What have you done recently?" or "I like that dress." You try not to notice their hands trembling as they turn the pages of their scripts. You haven't got time to really put them at their ease—you've got to get on with it; there's a line forming outside. I'm glad I gave up acting years ago.

What do you look for in a director of photography?

GREENE: Rapport. Someone whose head is in the same place as mine. Someone with the same outlook on even such things as politics and art. I don't want to sound pretentious, but photography has something to do with how a person responds to life. If a man is honest, his work will be honest, it's as simple as that. Of course, skill is needed, and technical sophistication, and the ability to vary style in accordance with the material, but honesty is number one. Some cinematographers don't have it. They use tricky lighting that pretties up the picture without conveying the mood or atmosphere of the place being photographed. Every place looks like Hollywood, faces are bathed in light—from where? This artificiality comes from a dishonest approach.

When you're fully cast and your crew is in place, what kind of preparation do you do?

GREENE: It depends on the material. For example, take some of the long-form docudramas I've directed, *The Trial of Lee Harvey Oswald, Friendly Fire, Fatal Vision,* true stories requiring a great deal of reading, research. In the case of *Fatal Vision* I knew that the murderer, Jeffrey MacDonald, was in jail and would be watching the film, and I wanted to be sure I was being fair to him. I wanted to really know the evidence. So I went home every night and read huge stacks of transcripts of the trials and the hearings. I also talked to a number of people who knew him at various stages in his life, from his time in high school to his conviction for murdering his family. Before directing *Friendly Fire,* I drove around Iowa for days, talking to Iowans, soaking up the way the farmlands looked, the way the corn grew. If you can't film it there, you need to know the look and taste and smell of it in order to reproduce it elsewhere.

One of the great things about being a director is that you find yourself immersed in areas of living and thinking you previously knew little or nothing about. What did I know about farm life in the heartland of America before I did *Friendly Fire?* What did I know about village life in Africa two hundred years ago before I did *Roots?* What did I know about the circumstances surrounding the assassination of President Kennedy before I staged it, precisely and meticulously according to the evidence, at the actual spot in Dealey Plaza in Dallas for *The Trial of Lee Harvey Oswald?* I read a lot, I went to all of the places Oswald went that day, and I had an assistant fire a gun from the sixth-floor window of the Texas Book Depository while I stood in the plaza below and listened to the deceptive echoes of the gunshot.

When you arrive on the set for the first day of filming, do you leave any room for improvisation, for what some directors call "happy accidents"?

GREENE: In television you can't improvise much, because the clock is ticking away, and you know that every tick represents money being spent. The first thing that's expected of you is a high degree of efficiency—and, in fact, many directors are employed for that ability alone. So it isn't appropriate for you to sit around thinking. There are fifty or more highly paid technicians waiting to be told what to do next. But I do improvise, and I think most good directors do. It just has to be kept to a minimum because of the time element.

What kind of homework do you do the night before you shoot a scene?

GREENE: I look for certain things in the script. First, I notice the order in which characters speak, i.e. Joan, then Bill answers her, then George interrupts, then Joan, Bill, Joan, Bill, George. I begin to feel that the shots would be economical and expressive if Joan and Bill were together, and George was in a separate shot. Joan and Bill are together, George is the outsider. Because of the relationships, and the order in which the characters speak, an economy can be effected by staging them like that. This is an oversimplification, of course, but it's one way to look at a scene prior to staging it. It gives you notions about who should be standing near who, and who should be passing in front of someone at a particular moment in the dialogue.

Another important thing to observe is the dynamics of the scene, the rise and fall of action and emotion. For instance, here's a static scene, two or three people sitting in a coffee shop talking. It's okay, because it follows the chase scene, but what about the scene coming up? It's a man talking to his brother on the phone. Got to do something about that! The movie will come to a halt and turn into a talk show. It would improve if the brothers could meet eye-to-eye, where eye contact or the avoidance of eye contact could help express their inner thoughts. Better still, perhaps I could persuade the writer and the producer—although hardly the night before shooting; it would have to be well in advance—to let me stage it in a park, with a soccer game in the background. One brother could get accidentally hit by a stray ball, and the reaction of the other brother to this piece of physical action might convey as much as a page of dialogue in the original phone-call scene. Each brother would have something to play with or against.

When I come to the set, I have a concept about what is of primary importance in the scene, as well as what is secondary and therefore should not be overemphasized—that is, unless I want to deliberately obscure the primary by overemphasizing the secondary, but that's another story. I might have an idea that the pace quickens and the energy builds to the top of page so-and-so, and then at its peak the door bursts open. I have a very vague feeling that they have their arms around each other on the sofa at the start, and at the bottom of the page their quarrel has begun and they separate.

How do you convey these feelings to the actors?
GREENE: At first I let them mumble through the scene a few times, free to follow their own instincts. I hope they will find the same things I've discovered in the scene, and while they're moving around saying their lines, I might kind of nudge them into the positions I've imagined. I also might hint at the emotional shape I hope to achieve for the scene. In a feature film this might go on for a half hour or even longer, but in television you can only let it happen for five or ten minutes, no more. Then I have to take a hand. "Closer together." Or, "How about breaking apart? Her remark infuriated you but don't let her know it." I feed them thoughts that will inevitably lead to the staging pattern that I began to perceive the night before and that's been sharpening itself in my mind as I watch them finding their way through the dialogue and the emotions.

I'm working on many levels at once: story, photographic possibilities, mood, editing, style, patterns of energy in the eventual film, places where music will play a part, etc. Most actors are responsive to the gentlest suggestions. I try not to say, "I want you to cross to the window." Instead, I might say, "What if you crossed to the window here? How would that be?" Now, a director may have nine important reasons for an actor to go to the window at that point in the scene. Unfortunately, sometimes you run into an actor who has a neurotic problem with what he sees as an authority figure—the director—and who just can't take suggestions from without. Then it becomes very difficult, because you have to give him all of your nine reasons, and many times he won't buy any of them.

At moments like this the levels I'm thinking about go right out the window—the window he won't cross to. The only thing a director can do with someone like that is follow him around with the camera as if it's a follow spot in vaudeville—which is probably what the idiot wanted in the first place.

Since you were an actor yourself, it would seem you'd be particularly sensitive to the actor's needs.

GREENE: I believe I am. Actors are human beings and therefore subject to all kinds of psychological vagaries, just like the rest of us. But they're the ones who have to stick their faces in front of millions of people, and as a consequence they're sometimes scared stiff. They need tender loving care. And occasionally they need a kick in the ass.

I believe the director's job is to feed them, nourish them with ideas. Each actor needs different things from the director. This one needs support, this one needs to work at it harder, this one needs to have his imagination stimulated because he's always done merely the first thing he's thought of, this one needs help in letting go. If an actor needs it—and believe me, some of them do—I can have a big discussion with him just before a love scene about what he had for breakfast that morning.

Then there are actors who are ready to work immediately. They know their lines and want to know the results you hope for, then off they go to find out for themselves how to achieve those results. Other actors enjoy the search for the result more than actually getting there. For them acting is self-therapy, and the process is never-ending. This is fine in the theater, where you have weeks of rehearsal before you have to reach the result, but it's not good in film and it's agony in television.

How do you feel when actors take liberties with the dialogue?

GREENE: I don't have much time for anyone who doesn't bother to memorize the author's words exactly. Some actors like to play it loose and pretend they're making it up as they go along, unaware that the writer, if he's good, labored painstakingly over every "and" and "but." This is simply ignorance, not to say insufferable arrogance. Actors aren't writers, and the lines they "invent" are usually utterly banal or else something they've remembered from a movie they've seen recently. I never work with people like that a second time.

Your method of staging frequently requires very precise movements in terms of the relationship between the actors and the camera. Do you find that some actors feel restricted by this?

GREENE: I try to convey movement to an actor in actor's terms. I never tell him merely to hit a mark here or a mark there. Instead I try to give him inner motivations for making moves and arriving at positions. I wouldn't say, for example, "Don't lean back because you'll get out of the shot." What I might do is tell him that he's getting eager in the scene and that he should lean forward to convey that eagerness to the other character. I prevent camera operators from instructing actors about positions. I want the operator to tell me if there's a problem, and then I'll translate the message in terms the actor can use.

You have a reputation for being a visual director. Do you give more emphasis to the visual aspects of the material as opposed to the literary content?

GREENE: It's interesting about directors, because very few of them have everything. All of us have a weak area. Many directors—and I'm talking about successful directors— just work with the actors and leave the "look," the photography, to someone else. Others are obsessed with the visual realization of their ideas and try to cast actors who don't need help. There's no right way.

Painters work differently too. Cézanne always painted on top of an old painting, whereas Matisse had to start with a clean, new canvas. It doesn't matter how you do it, as long as the results are worthwhile. But it does make me sad when I see nonvisual directors working in, say, other cultures and revealing no awareness of the totally different aesthetic surrounding them. They come up with the same over-the-shoulder shots and close-ups they'd do in Hollywood. There might be a magnificent and unique piece of architecture, and all you can see is part of the door.

You've specialized in both miniseries and two-hour TV movies. What are some of the differences?

GREENE: Well, with a miniseries there's more of it, of course. The script is so damn heavy, you can't carry it around—you've got to put it in several folders. As the director, you have an enormous number of pages to shoot. An enormous number. It's almost unthinkable. You need stamina and concentration and energy—for weeks and months at a time. You never have a day off. In the time it would take to film a feature movie you make the equivalent of half a dozen! You can never slow down. You get up at five in the morning and shoot seven, eight, nine pages a day, which is just like episodic TV. And all the while you strive to prevent it from looking as if it's been manufactured on an assembly line.

You have to be a little mad. Correction, you have to be completely mad. On top of the quantity of the work there's the detail. In a miniseries, wardrobe and makeup is very important because in many of them the audience watches period changes and actors grow older. In *Rich Man, Poor Man*, I had actors in their late twenties who began by playing high school students and ended up as forty-year-olds.

How much of Roots *did you do?*

GREENE: I directed the first three hours, and I helped to plan the series and cast it.

Roots *is arguably the most famous of all miniseries. How did you feel about doing it?*

GREENE: I was honored. They asked me to do it simply because I was just about the only director at that time who had handled a miniseries. I felt a black director should have done it, but they told me there wasn't one who had experience with something that long.

Unfortunately nobody knew it was going to be one of the most successful TV programs of all time, and so money was very, very short. It had to be done at high speed. We constructed an African village in Savannah, Georgia, and I would have liked to have the actors move into the straw huts and let the village find a life of its own for a few days. I would have had somebody from a university teach us about life in Africa two hundred years ago. Instead of that, at eight o'clock the first morning I faced a crowd of black kids recruited from gas stations or high schools in the neighborhood—kids who had never been in a film before—and I had the task of teaching them to be African villagers. All of this while the camera crew was standing around waiting for the first shot, and the producer was tapping his foot.

Because of the time element, I don't consider *Roots* one of my best achievements as a director. Luckily the subject matter was so fascinating that no one cared about the quality of my work.

Other than your sense of obligation to accuracy when you were doing Fatal Vision, *what were your other problems with that particular docudrama?*

GREENE: The main problem with *Fatal Vision* was simply this: How are you going to show on television a man murdering his wife and two little girls? I didn't want to turn a real event into one of those horror-shockers. I knew at once that I had to avoid jazzing it up with melodramatic camera angles and scary music. So I made what, to me, was my most important directorial decision. I decided that in the murder scene I wouldn't try to involve the audience, which is what a director normally attempts to do. Instead I would *distance* them from it. The facts of the case were so indescribably horrible that they would speak for themselves without emphasis from me. So I shot the scene in an almost detached way. No music. No heavy breathing. No sound of blows landing. No child screaming—you could read one of the little girl's lips when she yelled "Daddy," but the sound track was mercifully silent. I think this was the right way to do it, and I'm proud of the result.

You seem to pay a lot of attention to the use of music in your films.

GREENE: Yes, I do. Some producers don't handle music with confidence and don't understand the contribution it can make. For instance, music doesn't have to underline what is already amply expressed on the screen. It should provide *another* element, one that might otherwise be lacking.

Years ago I wrote and directed one of the early hospital shows. When the rough cut was shown to prospective advertisers, some of these cynics were seen to cry. "My God," they said, "there isn't even any music yet!" Now the producer—I wasn't there—drummed it into the composer's head that it was a moving scene—he said everyone will cry, the advertisers cried, I want the audience to cry, I cried. So the composer wrote music to make you sob by. But the picture was *already* doing that. What the music might have *added* was the mood of a deserted hospital corridor at two A.M., or the loneliness of a nurses' station. Instead the music's emotional overkill alienated the audience, and tears dried up quickly. If the director has already put it on the screen, the composer should play something else. It's the same with comedy. If you have a funny film, you don't want the composer to write funny music. The composer should provide emotions that aren't already on the screen.

What about the use of sound?

GREENE: The sound track should be musical, too. I take great liberties with the sound track. In *World War III*, a four-hour piece I directed for NBC, I found that the sound of wind became tedious, since much of the story took place in a blizzard. So I mixed in some windy sounds from a synthesizer. Nobody knew, but it made the wind kind of melodious. It conveyed cold, but it didn't get on your nerves.

Then you're not particularly interested in logic when you add sound to a film?

GREENE: I'm interested in emotional impact, and sometimes one uses illogical means to achieve it. You might want to have the creaking of branches in the trees, and you hope the audience won't notice that the leaves aren't even stirring. I mean, look at the problems you run into when you film in Los Angeles. Let's say it's supposed to be Christmas, yet the trees are all blooming and it's quite obviously spring. But if you're convincing enough—if you have the sound of sleigh bells and the actors all wear muffs—it's amazing what you can get away with. Most people aren't listening carefully when they watch a film, so you can slip sound messages into their brains without them being aware of it. That's an important thing to know.

Any other important things that you can pass on to a soon-to-be director?

GREENE: Many, but in particular the fact that you should never stop thinking about the pace. Actors tend to view the scene they're doing as the whole picture. It isn't. If you let them overload it with pregnant pauses, it will sink of its own weight. I always tell actors, "This scene is merely a transition to the next one." I even exaggerate it to press home the point: "There are no periods in this scene, only commas. It has to keep moving."

I suggest that directors should speed-read the entire script at least once or twice a week when they're shooting. That way you get to notice the river-flow of energy that must link what you've already shot with what you're going to shoot. Despite all this, when I view the editor's leisurely rough cut, I always feel suicidal. I always think, "Where on earth was the director, allowing them to talk so *slowly*!" However, after a couple of weeks of tightening with my editor, confidence returns and the darned thing begins to resemble the crisp, attention-holding piece of work I'd tried to make. Usually, that is.

PART THREE
SUPPORT STRUCTURE

PREFACE

The network. The supplier. The agent.

American television viewers are dependent for almost all of what they see on the interaction among these three entities. They are the major players in the game, and the writers, producers, actors, and directors must wait until accommodations are finalized and deals are struck—until, in essence, the money is spoken for. Only then, with license fees agreed upon, deal points negotiated, and lawyers and accountants satisfied with the bottom line, does the actual creative work begin.

Fortunately, neither the networks, the suppliers, nor the talent agencies operate out of total self-interest; each has restraints and responsibilities. The agent must answer to the client, and though the agent-client relationship is almost always contractual, there are circumstances under which it can be terminated if disenchantment sets in for either party. The supplier usually has to answer to its stockholders. And the networks not only have stockholders and the government to contend with but also a fickle public.*

What is amazing to the casual observer of the television industry is the ever-changing variety of interlocking patterns—

*At this writing ABC is about to be absorbed by Capital Cities Communications, and RCA, the parent company of NBC, intends to merge with General Electric. Thus two of the three networks will also be responsible to their new owners.

like a daisy chain gone mad—that bind network, supplier, and agents to each other, as well as to the creative community. Moreover, the roles can be interchangeable: Agents have become suppliers, for example, as have former network executives. Suppliers become network executives, and former writers and producers run the television divisions of major studios. There is even the case of a former agent (Victoria Principal) who forsook the agency business to resume her acting career in a continuing role on *Dallas*.

It is a matter of wonderment that there aren't perpetual accusations of conflict of interest. Yet by and large the system works—at least to the satisfaction of most of those involved.

Still, it is amusing to contemplate the dynamics of a meeting in which Fred Silverman—who, at one time or another, controlled the programming choices of all three networks—tries to sell a new series to one of his former subordinates. Or the experience, shared by an increasing number of writers, of "pitching" a project to one's former agent, who has now become a buyer.

Whether or not the public interest is served by this Byzantine arrangement is a moot point, but as those in the industry are fond of pointing out, the viewer votes with his fingers on the dial, and the entire web of contacts, connections, and mutualities of interest falls by the wayside when the Nielsens cease to pass muster.

Normally the networks and the agencies tend to be of a conservative bent, opting for the status quo, and it is up to the suppliers and their creative personnel to rock the boat. *All in the Family* owes much of its success to the intransigence of Norman Lear, who threatened, cajoled, and stonewalled the CBS censors during the early days of the show. Steven Bochco and Michael Kozoll demanded—and won—unusual latitude on *Hill Street Blues* and, as a result, expanded the borders of the television series. And Steven Spielberg was guaranteed a forty-four-episode order *in advance* for his *Amazing Tales,* an unheard-of commitment at a time of short orders and quick cancellations. He also kept the series under wraps for months before NBC was permitted to view any of the material.

It's almost axiomatic that the more diversification that is built into the structure of commercial television, the better it will be. New ideas, flowing from as many sources as possible, are clearly beneficial, but they can only flourish unencumbered in an open marketplace. Unfortunately television, at least for the present, is more or less a closed shop. There are only three networks and barely a handful of major talent agencies (William Morris, CAA, and ICM) who have client lists of sufficient strength-in-depth to give them leverage enough to change the landscape.

As for the suppliers, many of the independents are in jeopardy, not only from escalating costs but also because the networks are seeking to supplant them by finding ways to increase in-house production and thus cut as large a slice as possible of the lucrative syndication market.

Even so, the major studio suppliers are still a force to be reckoned with. The networks know that Columbia (a subsidiary of the Coca-Cola Company), Paramount (a division of Gulf & Western), Universal, and the others are going to be in business for the long haul and that they are a reliable source of product. They have the production facilities and—perhaps more important—the cash reserves to withstand the obligatory deficits.

The majors have also been wise enough to "lock in" talent, offering long- and short-term, exclusive and nonexclusive contracts to actors, writers, producers, and directors. When a supplier attempts to sell a new series to a network, it comes to the meeting armed with a batch of these "auspices," thus assuring the (always nervous) network executives of creative continuity and gilding the package with recognizable names who bear that most magical of virtues, "track records."

Naturally the deals that have made all of this possible have been negotiated by the final member of the triad, the agent, who receives commissions or packaging fees in return.

It's an old joke that agents, suppliers, and networks are both antagonists and collaborators, friends and enemies—depending on what time of day it is. Each needs the other as they maneuver for a slice of the electronic pie, and at any given moment it is difficult to tell the pilot fish from the shark.

They do have one thing in common however: They exist so that stories can be told in the dark. The fact that they are not storytellers themselves never seems to give them pause as they decide what will or will not sell, who is in demand and who is passé, and, ultimately, what will assault the eyes and ears of the nation.

Like Everest, they are very much *there,* sometimes a help and often a hindrance, and if one chooses to be in television, one will eventually have to do business with them. As a frazzled writer observed after a particularly harrowing network meeting, "The problem for all of us is that we like to paint ceilings and they own the church."

The Agent
BILL HABER

Bill Haber was born in Santa Monica, California, and attended a number of universities before graduating from UCLA with degrees in Political Science and English. After working for the William Morris Agency he and four of his associates formed their own company in 1975, the Creative Artists Agency. Since then, CAA has become one of the largest agencies in the entertainment industry, representing some of television's most successful writers, producers, actors, and directors. As one of the founding partners, Haber specializes in TV movies and miniseries, as well as the packaging of weekly comedy and dramatic programs.

How did you become an agent?

HABER: I grew up here in Tinsel Town, and although I had no family background in the entertainment industry, it always held a great attraction for me. Also, I suppose you could say that fate was involved. Only one time in its long history did the William Morris Agency run a classified ad. It ran for one day. And only once in my life did I ever read the classified ads. That was the same day. The ad read, "Agent/Trainee." It sounded interesting, so I called them, went through a series of interviews, and got the job.

At fifty dollars a week it was a gamble for me, since I was married and had children, but I knew it was a business where gambling was expected. I didn't know exactly what an agent did, but I wanted to be a part of the entertainment world. I started in the mail room delivering mail, became a legal secretary, then an assistant. The Vietnam War was just getting serious, and several of the younger agents were drafted. I woke up one morning to suddenly find myself in a sink-or-swim situation as an agent in television talent, where I represented actors, actresses, and directors.

What kind of services does an agency perform for its clients?

HABER: There are different kinds of agents, and each one of them performs unique functions. But every talent and literary agency basically procures employment, provides career guidance, negotiates deals, and serves as a combination father-confessor and psychiatrist.

You and several of your fellow agents left William Morris and founded your own agency. Did you have any particular philosophy that set you apart from the other agencies of the time?

HABER: We had two philosophies that we wanted to use as a new foundation. One was that we would never make more money than our clients, which is a real possibility in the TV packaging area. The other was that our clients were more important than we were. In effect, we wanted to be in partnership with our clients. Our concept was that they owned ninety percent of the company and we owned ten percent. We felt we could be flexible in terms of the packaging commission we charged as long as there was a certain equitable floor. Flexibility was very important to us. If there were times when our clients wouldn't make large sums of money, then we wouldn't make large sums of money.

There was a memorable meeting at the William Morris office—it served as a catalyst for our leaving—when we asked whether we should continue to take a ten-percent packaging commission regardless of the deficits on a production. The head of the agency told us emphatically that the commission would be changed over his dead body. It made us all realize that we were going to have to leave there in order to make revisions in what were then the standard operating procedures.

What exactly is packaging?

HABER: To begin with, the term "packaging" is something that no one has ever defined properly, and I don't particularly like it. I ask our people to try not to use it except as shorthand or with friends. I prefer the term "sales representation." In effect, it means that instead of selling a single piece of material or creative talent—a writer, a script, a director, or an actor—you sell a total product. I like to say that it's really no different from selling a Cadillac. If I were selling a Cadillac to you, I'd sell you everything that makes that car work. I'd show you the engine, the interior, the bodywork, and you'd buy the car as a whole. I wouldn't just sell you the tires.

Some companies are in the tire business and aren't interested in the final, completed product. They do a wonderful business and there's a need for them. But an agent who represents the sale of a TV series will be selling a project that has been put together in advance and includes many of the creative elements. For this service he will make what is called a packaging commission. It will be a specified percentage of the license fee, be it 10 percent, 6 percent, 5 percent, 3 percent, or whatever. If the license fee happens to be $400,000, and the agent is getting 5 percent, then he will get $20,000 for each episode that's produced. If the agent has clients involved with the production, as he almost certainly will on a package, he cannot commission their individual fees. He can only commission, for lack of another term, the package itself.

It's possible to earn a packaging fee for a project that doesn't contain any of the agency's clients, but this is rare. It's far more likely that the agent will be involved with at least one element somewhere in the mix. It may be as small as a newspaper article. It may be just the writer. Often it's just the lead actor. Obviously it makes life easier for the parties involved when the agent represents a substantial number of the elements, but it's also true that he often puts himself in a packaging position simply by virtue of his many years of experience and his valuable relationships. It's not difficult to get a no from a network, but the price of the infrequent yes comes justifiably high.

Have there been any major changes in the agency business in recent years, as it applies to television?

HABER: Agenting has splintered a great deal. There are now smaller television packaging agencies. Everyone has realized that it's possible for one or two men to package television effectively, and that's certainly a change. In the past only a few of the major agencies involved themselves with packaging, or for that matter felt qualified. But now others have learned to function on their own and represent TV series.

There's also a developing flexibility. Agents are realizing that we're all in a cooperative enterprise, and there should be a little give-and-take. This is a continuing trend, and over the long haul it will benefit both agents and clients.

Other than that, I really don't think the agency business has changed very much. An agent, by definition, is an intermediary for his client, and I don't believe that can ever change.

What does the agent who represents a package do during the annual selling season in New York, when the networks decide which series they're going to buy and which ones they're going to renew?

HABER: "Selling season" is another term I don't understand. Actually, it should be called the "buying season." The truth is that the three networks order whatever it is they wish to put on the air, and nobody influences them.

All of those people who are in New York spending massive amounts of money at 21 are accomplishing very little except expanding their waistlines—or their egos.

However, just because you can't influence the networks *during* the buying season doesn't mean you can't influence the networks. The time to do that is *before* they go to New York, when you help to persuade them to make a pilot, when you attempt to assure them of your client's ability to deliver a splendid series should it be ordered.

But when they're actually setting the schedule, I don't believe there's much you can do. The bell has rung and you're really not allowed in the ring. The main functions of an agent at that time are to be part of the team that wins or fails, and to be a source of information for his clients. The client has a right to know what's going on before anyone else knows, to be told if there's anything he can do—and I've seen it only happen twice in twenty years—to affect a decision if it's on the fence.

A few buying seasons ago I was walking a fine line between an order and a cancellation on a series I liked called *Hagen* for 20th Century–Fox TV. The ratings were marginal, but I believed I had convinced some of the more influential CBS executives to go with the show for one more year. Only Bill Paley, who still really programmed the network at that time, was balking. On the crucial night before the schedule was to be set, providence placed me behind him at a Broadway play. I felt I had to do something. During the intermission I turned to a companion next to me and in the loudest possible voice I said, "Did you see *Hagen* this week? I think it's CBS's finest show and I simply adore Chad Everett. I hope it runs forever." Paley leaned slightly back and to the left, and I could tell I had finally pushed the show over the hump. That night I toasted myself as TV's cleverest influence-peddler. Two days later the champagne went flat: *Hagen* had been canceled. So much for influencing the networks during the buying season.

You may often be asked to submit material that you don't particularly like. How do you reconcile your personal tastes with the needs of your clients?

HABER: There's an old down-country agent's aphorism: "We sell 'em, we don't smell 'em." We try not to judge the material that our clients give to us. We do make sure that whatever it is will meet the standards requirements of the networks, or that it hasn't already been done, but there's nothing that can't be submitted.

It *is* a mistake to submit material that we know will be rejected, and when we feel that's the case, we try to persuade the client to change his or her mind. But if they ask us, then as their employees we'll do as they wish. The enthusiasm level may not always ring bells, but the material will be submitted.

How is the television department of a large talent agency structured?

HABER: There are usually two divisions in the TV area, a Television Talent and Literary Division, and the Packaging Division. The first division has the function of procuring employment and negotiating for writers, actors, and directors who work in television. It also occasionally sells articles and material. The Packaging Division utilizes the clients of the agency in order to put packages together to sell as a whole to the networks. Each division of the television department will have a staff meeting once a week. The divisions meet separately once and together once, which means that there will be three meetings a week. They're held early in the morning when everybody is fresh. One of the major purposes of these meetings is the exchange of information.

Occasionally there will also be a night meeting of the Packaging Division where the agents try to come up with ideas they think will work as television series. They'll bring newspaper and magazine articles to the meeting, as well as various concepts for television movies or series. If something lights a spark, it will be given to the clients.

Also, at a major agency the television agents will attend the Motion Picture Department meetings, and someone from the Motion Picture Department will always attend meetings held by the Television Department. There is an exchange of material from the two areas. Often a book submitted in the feature area will work more effectively for television.

Is there such thing as a typical day in your business?

HABER: One of the things that's interesting about being a television agent is that you don't have typical days. When you go to work, there will always be surprises. Obviously you have certain constants. For example, if it's pilot season, most of your life will be involved with the execution and then the sale of pilots and the negotiation of pilot deals. If it's not the pilot season, then, after the many meetings I mentioned, you'll constantly be on the phone with your clients. If anything happened to America's highly sophisticated phone system, show business would grind to a stop.

You'll usually have a lunch date with a client—a producer, writer, or director—to discuss an idea they want you to take to a network. Or else you'll have lunch with someone from a network. The lifeblood of the television agenting business is network relationships. Your afternoons are often spent in network meetings where you will submit the product that's been discussed in the mornings. Nights are frequently taken up with business dinners or screenings.

Some agents, the ones who represent actors and actresses, will spend a great deal of time with various casting directors. It's important for an agent to know what the network is looking for at any given moment. Also, it's equally important for the agent, based on his knowledge of the medium, to point the client in the most productive direction.

An agent that I was working with received an hour-length television concept about a police officer who worked in the San Fernando Valley. When he read the material, he suggested to the writer, Ted Flicker, that as an hour show it might be competing with *Columbo*, but as a half-hour comedy it would have a chance. Ted Flicker agreed, and then the agent put him together with a producer, Danny Arnold. The two of them worked out the half-hour version, went to ABC, and sold a half-hour comedy pilot that led to the *Barney Miller* series. So in that particular case an agent changed the course of a show based on his knowledge of network needs. The clients are happily still taking the money to the bank, even though the agent has long since left the agency business.

What is the difference between an agent and a personal manager?

HABER: Under California law a personal manager cannot solicit employment for his client, although that is currently being debated in the state legislature. Obviously, soliciting employment is one of the agent's major functions. The manager's job is to provide constant and careful career guidance. He's able to do this on a more intimate level because he usually has far fewer clients than an agent at a major agency.

More often than not, the manager has actors as his clients, although there's a growing trend for managers to handle writers. Not directors or producers, but writers. I think this is because an increasing number of writers feel they need career guidance on an extremely personalized basis.

How do entertainment lawyers fit into the equation?

HABER: They usually have little involvement with procuring employment or career guidance, though many of them have close ties to their clients. Sometimes they'll work in concert with the agents on negotiations and legal work on contracts.

Most major agencies have legal departments, but their

franchise with the guilds and unions enjoins them from practicing law. It's interesting to note that many of the most successful agents have come out of law school. The legal profession is a very fertile spawning ground for all areas of the industry.

What qualifications are useful for someone who wants to be an agent?

HABER: Agents should be well schooled and well read. They should have the widest possible background in arts and letters, and they should know something about the entertainment industry. When I interview a potential employee, I like to see what kind of educational background he has, what kind of degree he graduated with. I like to see how he'd function in a literary world.

The agency business is a literary business. It's based on concepts, scripts, material, writers, and historical moments. If a writer pitches a miniseries about Charles de Gaulle, it helps if the agent knows it's not an airport. When ABC spends fifty million dollars on a Civil War project, there has to be an understanding of why that event was so important. Much of television comes directly from today's headlines. An agent should not only want to influence the American psyche, he has to be influenced *by* it. The narrower a person is, the narrower his skills become. An accountant who spends his life only adding up figures would not, in my opinion, make a good agent. An agent should be a generalist, and then, as he learns the business, he can begin to specialize. But the more you know about the world—assuming you also have the ability to communicate your perceptions—the better an agent you'll be.

How does someone become an agent?

HABER: All of the major agencies have extensive training programs. If you're interested in the agency business, the first thing to do is submit a résumé to whomever in the personnel department is in charge of trainees. If you're at all qualified—that is, if you have a college degree or if you've had some relationship with the industry or a related industry that would lead us to believe you could succeed in the agency business, then you will get an interview. But be advised that you have to be prepared for a long haul. If you're accepted as a trainee, you will work in a mail room for as long as two years, working twenty hours a day for very little money. And by very little money I mean the lowest pay scale of any job in our industry.

After the mail room you'll be put on a desk in a particular area functioning as a secretary-assistant to an agent. That can last for as long as two years. You may work at a television desk for six months, then a literary area, then in motion pictures. You'll be changed around until you're well rounded and have an idea of where you want to specialize. Then you'll become an assistant in a department.

At that point you'll be considered a junior agent, although the term "junior agent" is a phrase I'd like to see eliminated. You're either an agent or not, there's no middle ground. You'll assist other agents in an area, and as you become more senior, you'll begin to have your own areas and handle your own buyers and your own studios. This process can take as long as five years.

There is, of course, another approach entirely. You can begin at one of the smaller agencies, of which there are now more than two hundred franchised by the Screen Actors Guild alone. You'd go to work immediately as an assistant to an agent, and I would assume that if they think you have potential, you'd become an agent within a year. Obviously there isn't the same kind of extensive training background, but for some it beats delivering scripts to Burbank for two years.

Is it difficult for women to become agents?

HABER: At this moment it's probably easier for women than it is for men. At our agency, right now, it's fairly evenly distributed at fifty-fifty.

What about blacks?

HABER: There are several agencies that only have black agents and represent black clients. At CAA, at the moment, four of our twenty trainees are black. As with many businesses, we're constantly on the lookout for an ethnic mix.

Does being an agent prepare someone for other positions in the entertainment industry?

HABER: If you want to be a producer or an executive producer, I think it's a good background. A producer is involved with the packaging of a project, very much like a packaging agent. Historically, many successful producers have been agents. So have several of today's studio heads. Naturally, any corporation is unhappy when an important piece of manpower uses it as a stepping-stone to something else. But there isn't a company in the world that can keep someone who really wants to leave.

On the simplest level, what does an agent do to get a writer client a job in episodic television?

HABER: First, the agent will know that a certain series has openings for twelve scripts. It's his job to have that information. Secondly, he'll submit his client for one of those openings. The producer will often ask the agent for a sample of the writer's material, and the agent will provide it. Once it's been read, the agent will set up a meeting. This is usually done if the producers don't know the writer, or if he's relatively new. If the writer is well known, however, then there won't be a meeting. Instead there'll be an understanding between the agent and the producer that the writer will be committed to do an episode. A deal will be made.

The deals on episodic television are very easy because they're scale deals. They're all exactly the same for every series. There's a certain price for a half hour, there's a certain price for an hour.

Once the deal is made, the writer will go in, he and the

producer will agree on a story, the writer will begin to write, and contracts will come out. The agent will review them and decide if they're acceptable—he'll make any necessary revisions—and then they'll be sent to the client's attorney, if he has one, or else to the client directly.

You currently represent Aaron Spelling. Since he's exclusive to ABC and has close personal relationships with many of its executives, why does he need the services of an agent?

HABER: Aaron devotes his time to reviewing and sometimes rewriting material, screening dailies, and working on the cuts of episodes or pilots or television movies. It's incredibly time-consuming. He's one of the few company heads who began as a writer and is still intimately involved creatively.

When you have five to seven hours of series on the air, plus dozens of hours of long-form television as well as theatrical motion pictures, you're extremely preoccupied. But you still have a constant need for material. We give Aaron a continuing flow of material, as well as writers to meet for new series and movie ideas. He also has intermediaries to speak with the network so he doesn't have to do it every day on every level. It permits him to be free for the creative functions that he performs best.

Once a week there's a Spelling staff meeting. We frequently participate in those meetings, and at one time or another all of the material that comes in will be discussed, whether it comes from us or from other agencies. The final decisions as to what to do with the material and the form it will eventually take is made by Aaron. And, of course, he creates several series himself every year. But we try to provide him with as much outside material—and support—as possible.

Is it essential for a television writer or director to be based in Los Angeles?

HABER: I think it's helpful, although more for a director

than a writer. A director has to be here for meetings, for preproduction, for location scouts. It's possible for a writer to live outside Los Angeles, providing there are easy communications by phone and an easy way to get here within a few hours.

Is CAA involved with the cable business?

HABER: All of the major agencies have cable departments, and they all service the major cable companies just as they do the networks. Even though cable's impact seems to have lessened in the past few years, we will continue to perform services in this area for our clients.

All of the large agencies also have videocassette departments. For example, we just made a deal for a client to produce and star in a cassette teaching tap dancing, and that cassette has great financial potential for all of us. I think the cassette business will get more and more important. The cable business, after a period of time, will grow, but certainly not with the explosive expansion we all anticipated. This entire area really isn't as arcane as it appears. Agencies supply software for the new hardware media. The broadcasting method is unimportant. In a sales world the salesman knows he has a buyer and what that buyer needs. The approach is the same.

The one question everyone who is trying to break in asks is: How do I get an agent?

HABER: I've always found that the easiest way to do it is through someone you know who already has an agent. That's not as difficult as it sounds if you're in California— and that's one reason to base yourself here, at least in the beginning—because someone you know will be in the entertainment industry. If they have an agent, they can arrange for you to meet him. If they don't have an agent, then they probably know someone who does. This industry has many agents, so eventually you're going to meet somebody who knows at least one of them. Once you've spoken with an agent, even if she or he won't represent you, he or she can recommend someone who might.

Let's say you live in Ohio and you want to write for television. Can you send a script to a major agency and ask them to read the material with an eye toward representing you?

HABER: Unfortunately, there are legal problems. As we all know, there have been a dozen suits against MCA, instituted by any writer who's created a skinny, loose-skinned alien that knows how to dial a phone. No good agent accepts unsolicited material without a signed release from the writer. Even with a release it's not a wise thing to do. The material should come in through somebody who has some contact, no matter how small or how distant, with the entertainment industry, be it a theater owner or someone who knows someone who writes a column for a local paper. I don't know of any agent who will receive and read unsolicited material without that kind of contact.

Having said that, there is another way. Many of the universities in this country have creative writing programs, and they've worked out arrangements with some of the agencies. For instance, CAA has a relationship with most of the universities in California. If they think some of their students' material is suitable for us, we've agreed to review it.

Do you watch television, go to the movies, or see much theater?

HABER: Being familiar with the industry's product, all of it, is an absolute requirement for an agent. I see every film that's made by a major studio and the more serious independents. I see at least one episode of every television series. I try to know every book that's on the national best-seller list, or at least read coverage of it if I haven't read the book itself, so that I have a feeling for what's selling. I try to know the most important novelists in the world at any given time and what their next book is going to be.

Theater in Los Angeles is still relatively nonexistent, although there's more than most people think. Still, there's not the same tendency to go to the theater here as there is in New York. And as for ballet, classical music, or opera, you try to keep current, but when you're in the agency business, you don't really have as much time as you'd like.

What criticisms do you have of the television industry as it exists today?

HABER: It's been wonderful to me for two decades, so there's not a lot I'd like to see changed. I do have a couple of pet peeves. First, I'm not fond of agents in the business who are more interested in themselves than their clients. Agents are intermediaries only, not principals. An agent cannot have an ego. And I strongly criticize those agents who would prefer to sell themselves when they go into a meeting, rather than their clients. You can usually spot them when you see them. They are looking to better themselves in the industry in terms of other jobs. When they begin to get too high a profile, they should no longer be agents.

As for my criticism of television itself, I think it's a business that probably doesn't take as many chances as it should. It's also a business that doesn't let the producers produce. A network will go out and spend hundreds of thousands of dollars for the best talent in the world and then, ironically, it will not leave that talent alone to produce the product. The networks claim that they're now starting to change this long-standing habit, but we'll all believe it when we see it.

Do you see any major changes ahead in the structure of network television?

HABER: I think it's possible there will be an attempt by some of the large companies who own a number of stations to put together the equivalent of a fourth network. But I suspect the networks as they are now, and as they operate now, won't change much over the next few decades. Audiences will come and go, the skyline of antennae will become fiberglass dishes, and agents will emerge with ambitions to change the face of television. But I'm fairly sure that someone sitting alone in Kansas, in the year 2010 will still be watching the flickering image of rerun #342 of *I Love Lucy*.

The Supplier:
The Studio

BARBARA CORDAY

Barbara Corday was born in New York in 1944. After a career in public relations she turned to television writing in partnership with Barbara Avedon. The two collaborated on scripts for a number of series, as well as pilots, and served as executive story consultants on Fish, Grandpa Goes to Washington, Turnabout, *and* Executive Suite. *They are perhaps best-known for creating the television series* Cagney and Lacey. *Corday joined ABC in 1979 as Director of Comedy Series Development and was named Vice-President, Comedy Series Development, a year later. In 1982, she became a producer at Columbia-TV and then, in 1984, was appointed President of Columbia Pictures Television. She is married to Barney Rosenzweig, the executive producer of* Cagney and Lacey.

Is it true that you come from a show-business family?
CORDAY: Yes. My mother was a vaudeville singer and comedienne—known in some circles as the poor man's Fanny Brice. My father wrote special material for acts, and during the war he wrote radio shows. Later he became a pop songwriter until the advent of rock and roll in the mid-fifties, which put him and everybody else in the Brill Building out of business. After that he spent most of his life writing jingles for television commercials.

As for me, I didn't go to college. Since I could neither sing nor dance—I called my production company Can't Sing, Can't Dance Productions—I got a job as a receptionist at a small theatrical agency in New York. From there I went into public relations. For eight years, on both coasts, I did PR work promoting restaurants, nightclubs, things like that.

How did you become a television writer?

CORDAY: There's a simple answer to that, and her name is Barbara Avedon. During the Vietnam War I volunteered my services as a publicist to an organization called Another Mother for Peace. Barbara Avedon and Donna Reed were the chairpersons. I knew very little about the political scene before that, and I got very swept up in it. We were quite active; we even went lobbying in Washington.

Barbara and I became good friends. She was a television writer, doing mostly comedy, but she had given up working for several years during the war. Many of us were involved with Another Mother for Peace part-time, but she totally devoted herself to it. She had an infant son and a tremendous personal concern about the war.

At one point I went to her with an idea that my father had come up with. He had written an unpublished novel, and I asked her to read it to see if she thought it could be the basis for a television series. I didn't think it was a great novel, but I did think it had series potential. She agreed with me. And she said the only way she'd get involved was if we did it together. We began collaborating part-time on a presentation, and gradually it became a full-time partnership. I quit my job in public relations in 1972.

Besides writing comedy, we wanted to do dramatic shows. And God bless Sam Adams, one of our agents at the time. There was a series at Universal called *Sons and Daughters*. It was a high-school show. Sam decided somehow that because the show was about teenagers, and because we were women, clearly we were just right for it.

Amazingly, he sold us to Universal on the basis that as women comedy writers we'd be perfect to understand the teenage mind. Also, women were a commodity that everyone wanted at that time. You had to have women writers.

We went in and met Barney Rosenzweig, the producer. He was fired three weeks later. But during those three weeks I asked him out, and we've been together ever since. Also, Barbara and I did several episodes for the series, so it was a very lucky show for me, aside from being our first venture into TV drama.

Why did you leave free-lance writing to become an executive at ABC?

CORDAY: What was happening at that moment in my life, which was in 1979, was that Barbara was not terribly interested in producing, in going to an office every day, or in any aspect of television other than writing. What she really loves to do is write. She's older than I am, and it became apparent at a certain point that she only wanted to work about six months a year, write some scripts, and go on vacation. I, being newer at it, was very interested in spreading out and doing more. Barbara had had a great deal of success in her life, but I was just at the beginning, and some of the offers we were getting appealed to me.

I was also very aware that going out there alone and getting a job as a writer, then coming home to my room and closing the door, was not something I really wanted to do, particularly since I had spent eight years in a happy collaboration. I did not want to sit by myself and write. There's also the fact that when one member of a team goes it alone, people will always say, "Well, we don't know how good she'll be without her partner, and we'd better read something she's written." I was convinced that's what I would be facing. If I wasn't Avedon and Corday, who was I?

So when I was offered a job by ABC, it seemed to be incredibly fortuitous. I could go into what, in theory, was a creative situation, I could make a name for myself as an individual, and I could come out on the other side and go back into producing or writing with a different kind of experience behind me. And that's exactly what happened.

At the time I had no idea of the visibility and the cachet that comes with working at a network. I really didn't fully appreciate it. After three years at ABC I had more offers than I knew what to do with. Everybody wanted to make me a producer. Everybody wanted to pay me lots of money to come to their studios and make shows for them, in spite of the fact that I had demonstrated absolutely no ability whatsoever in that area.

Speaking as a studio executive now, I think we all believe that the most recent person to come out of a network must have some idea of what the networks want, and so we hire that person. I may be stretching it a little, but I really do believe there's a bit of that attitude at work. In my case there was the added ingredient that I had actually written, which is something a lot of network executives haven't done. So I had a little bonus going for me. Not only were they buying an executive who might have more knowledge than the average person off the street, but I actually knew what a script was and I actually knew how to type.

Having become a producer at Columbia, why did you then change horses and move into your current position?

CORDAY: Because I hated what I was doing. I hated every day of it. I have discovered finally at forty that I am not a loner. I was spoiled by my three years at ABC where, as difficult as it was and as demanding as the job was, there were people who were a lot of fun to be with. We were always in and out of each other's offices all day long. I arrived at Columbia as an independent producer, and if my mother hadn't called me every day that first week, I don't know what I would have done. I mean, there was nobody to talk to. All of the stuff about "Come to the studio, it'll be terrific, here's all this money," and I arrive at my office and I'm suddenly expected to start something from scratch. The idea is to wake up in the morning, come to work, and get something going.

It became apparent to me that although I think of myself as being something of a self-starter, and although I'm not afraid of hard work, I didn't much like a year of being alone, trying to generate activity. And all to get to a moment—the two or three weeks of actually making a pilot—when I suddenly had a hundred people working for me and everything was a lot of fun. And then, of course, the pilot doesn't sell and the show doesn't get on the air, and it's back to another eight months of sitting alone and working by myself. I think it takes a very special personality to be able to do that year after year.

What are your responsibilities as the president of a major studio's television division? Is it anything like producing?

CORDAY: Very much so, but instead of producing a show you're producing a studio. It's finding the best possible people in all areas and putting them together with each other, with other studio executives, with other writers, producers, directors, and with the networks. It's orchestrating, if you will. I'm the one who goes out and tries to talk some wonderful producer or writer into coming here. I'm the one who goes to an agent and tries to make a deal with an actor to marry to that producer or writer. People will come in and tell me why they need another $40,000 to do a stunt. It's a complete potpourri. I mean, I can be doing anything during the day from signing an executive's expense account to being at the network meeting on a series deal. I cross over all the lines.

For example, I've spent hours sitting with writers just to work out a pitch. The end result of all of this is to try to get television series on the air and keep them there. As with some of the other studios, Columbia has a television group, which includes the distribution, syndication, and acquisition divisions. Herman Rush is the president of the television group, and because of his background as an agent, he's a fabulous businessman and a very creative deal-maker. He pretty much leaves me alone to handle production and anything relating to production—the business affairs, the physical production of pilots and series, and the creative side. So the buck stops with me in terms of these things.

I'm not involved at all in syndication and distribution. It's totally out of my area. The exception to this is when we do movies and series directly for first-run syndication. We're currently doing twenty-two new episodes, for instance, of an old series called *What's Happening*. It completed its run several years ago and we had sixty-five episodes. The twenty-two new episodes will be added to that package, which will almost geometrically increase the value of the original sixty-five. So I'm in charge of getting those twenty-two episodes made, which will go immediately to our distribution people. They'll never be seen on a network, but they'll be included within the syndication package of the original show. The point of this is that there are a lot of new things going on that I'm learning about. It's a constant educational process for me.

How are you staffed?

CORDAY: I have fourteen departments that report directly to me. To give an incomplete list there's Production, Post-Production, Tape Production, Music, Drama Development, Comedy Development, Current, Daytime, Off-Network, Movies and Miniseries, and Publicity and Advertising. Each of those departments has a vice-president and is staffed by either one, two, or occasionally three people. It varies. I've just promoted a young man named Steve Berman to be my Senior VP of Creative Affairs. I've taken a full year to fill that position because I didn't know what the job was going to be until I had done it myself.

Are you closely involved with series already on the air?

CORDAY: I no longer read every script of every show, which is what I tried to do my first year. Now I'll read the first six scripts of a new series. And if our Current people have a problem with something, I'll go to a meeting or whatever. In terms of ongoing shows my involvement is mostly with budgets and production decisions, such as, Are we going to Tucson to make a particular episode or are we going to do *Crazy Like a Fox* in Las Vegas? Also, an actor might want more money, and I'll have to meet with the network to deal with it. These are the kinds of things I do with series already on the air, but I don't really get into the individual scripts and the creative side. However, I *am* deeply involved with the pilots for new series.

During the selling season are you part of the exodus to New York?

CORDAY: Yes. I spent two weeks in New York this year. I've been there often—this was my sixth year—as either a network executive or a producer, and on this recent trip I discovered, much to my surprise, that I had a lot of work to do. The networks actually did call and ask us a lot of questions about the shows that we had up for sale. In one case I was asked to prepare a memo about how we'd deal with certain aspects of a series if they bought it. I went to a number of meetings, and I was involved with several actors who were going to be appearing at various network functions. It was a very, very busy period. I really didn't expect it to be, because having been there in other capacities it always seemed to me that the studio people were just there to have a good time.

Can you be an effective salesperson for something that you don't like?

CORDAY: Everyone has a personal line they draw, and I really don't think I would have an easy time going out and selling something that offended me. I'd probably turn it over to somebody else or just let it take its own course. I don't know. I have my own biases and predilections toward certain kinds of material, although obviously, in my job, I have to be eclectic. But it's hard for me to believe—since I'm responsible for bringing most of the producers here, and since I'm involved to at least some degree in the development process—that we'd get to a point where we'd have a project that really offended me.

Unless, of course, the network brought it to you.

CORDAY: Up till now I haven't had to face that situation.

Does the fact that you have a daughter influence you in your work?

CORDAY: It influences me every day. I have four daughters, actually, including my husband's three, and it affects everything I do. I'm almost never in a meeting where there isn't some pertinence to the fact that I have a daughter or a child or a teenager. I'm very aware that it's another eye that I have on the world. I have a forty-year-old eye, and having a seventeen-year-old eye in the house is very helpful because it can make me look at something differently. I do feel a responsibility. I mean, I saw a movie the other night, and if someone had brought it to me, I wouldn't have been able to make it.

You're the first woman ever to hold this kind of position in the television industry. What are some of the ramifications of that?

CORDAY: I think the fact that I'm in this job has been helpful to other women. I get an awful lot of mail from women saying we love seeing you there, we think it's great, it gives us a feeling that we can get ahead. The people who work for me can speak for themselves, but I do think that I take the time to create an atmosphere that is friendlier, homier, and more familial than I encountered in the places I worked where men were in charge.

It's rare for me to come out of a meeting with someone

without knowing a little something about their personal life. It's rare for me to run into somebody in the hall without asking how their kid is or how they enjoyed their weekend. The same response comes from them to me. A lot is being written about this difference in atmosphere in corporate America today—they're discovering that women have added a human element to the business community. I believe that's something I've established here.

One frustration that perhaps emerges, because I'm a woman, is that I find myself this season with five or six shows going on the air, none of which has a female in the lead role. I'm distressed about that. I'm thrilled that I was able to have a good selling season, but I'd feel a lot better if one of those shows had a female lead.

Any criticisms of the industry?

CORDAY: I have a hard time blaming everything on the networks, although I criticize them as much as anybody else. But I read a lot of material, and sometimes I think we censor ourselves. I've been out there myself, and I can't tell you how many times, as writers, that Barbara and I would say to ourselves, "Oh, they'll never buy this, they'll never buy that." The networks contribute to the problem, but we are our own censors. On the other hand, I think it's startling that we're all able to do what we do. The fact that there are twenty-two hours per network of first-run prime time that is well produced, good-looking, makes sense, some of which make you laugh and some of which make you cry—the fact that this is on every single week is extraordinary. But I do wish we were stretching a little more. Why does everything have to be like something else?

Cagney and Lacey *wasn't like everything else.*

CORDAY: Sometimes things can happen if you try hard enough. It took us seven years to get *Cagney and Lacey* on the air. And if it weren't for Barney—and I say this knowing that he's my husband and therefore it can be taken with a grain of salt—but if it weren't for Barney and his perseverance, the show would have died a long time ago. It also wouldn't have gotten on in the first place.

We wrote it in 1974 as a theatrical feature. Several years later, when Barney was trying to peddle it as a television movie, I ran into the former president of the film company where we had originally written the screenplay. I said to him, "Barney just had a meeting at CBS and he thinks he might be able to sell *Cagney and Lacey* as a TV movie." And this man said to me, "Are you kidding? Are you guys still trying to sell that thing? Why don't you stop and go on to something else?"

Well, if everybody had that attitude, then things would never happen. The whole world was telling us that we'd never get it on. Everyone was telling us it wouldn't sell. In fact—and I mean this literally—everyone in town had turned us down. The project had been rejected by all three networks as a series and by two networks as a TV movie. And the last person we went to, in the movie department of the third network, said yes. So we actually got it made. And when it got a 43 share, they called us and asked if we could turn it into a series. We were hysterical. That brings me to another criticism I have about this business. Everyone is always saying "Next!" "Next" is not always the right attitude in terms of accomplishing something.

Did anything happen that you didn't expect when you moved into your present position?

CORDAY: Yes. The volume of work. Once you actually do it, no job is quite what it seems to be from the outside. That's something I discovered when I went to work at ABC. But when I came here, I really had no idea of the enormity of the workload. I can clean off my desk every night and the next morning there will be eight inches of paper on it. If I'm gone for three days, it takes me three weeks to get out from under the stuff that accumulates. I think the reason that people like Herman Rush never take a vacation is not because they're workaholics but because they're afraid of what's going to be waiting for them when they get back. The sheer volume of material. The fourteen departments waiting for decisions.

People are in and out of here all day long. When people tell me they called me yesterday and I didn't call back, and what's the matter, don't I return my phone calls, I feel terrible about it. I still have enough Jewish guilt to be put away by something like that. They just don't realize the number of telephone calls that come into my office every day, the number of pieces of mail, the strangers who write saying that they know I'm really busy, but could I just read their script.

Do you do any reading for pleasure?

CORDAY: Yes. Usually when I'm on vacation, or on weekends, or whenever I have chunks of time. I just bought John Irving's book, *The Cider House Rules*. I'm going to take it with me on a trip next week. I also got *The Discoverers,* by Daniel Boorstin. I recently had to go to Florida to visit my dad, who's ill, and I knew I was going to have two very long plane trips within three days, so I took along Michael Korda's *Queenie* because I knew it was going to be trashy and terrific. I also love the theater. I don't go as much as I should in L.A., but I do go when I'm out of town. I go in New York, I go in London. I love good drama, I love comedies. I don't enjoy musicals as much as I used to.

Do you watch any television?

CORDAY: I generally watch at least one or two episodes of every new television series. I watch as many pilots as I can. If I can't catch them on the air, I borrow them from people. But in terms of watching television for pleasure, I do very little of that.

Do you have any time for a personal life?

CORDAY: It may have something to do with being a woman, but I *make* time for a personal life. I mean, my kid came to the office this morning, and we sat here for twenty minutes, and we talked, and I shut the door. Even if it's nine o'clock at night I'll meet my husband someplace for dinner and we'll spend a couple of hours by ourselves. It may be only two or three times a week, but we do it because that's what's important to me. You just make a personal life. You just say "This is it."

Obviously your job, in spite of the negatives, has its rewards.

CORDAY: The reward for me is the action. I love it. I love it. One day, three or four months ago, I was in the middle of pilot season and I was a crazy person. It was my first season in this job, and I wanted so much to do good work. And my husband sort of looked at me and said, "God help you, you love the action, don't you?" And I started to laugh, even though I was tired, because it was true. Yes, I love it. I am having the best time I've ever had in my life.

The Supplier:
The Independent
AARON SPELLING

Aaron Spelling was born in Dallas, Texas, in 1929, and attended Southern Methodist University on an Army scholarship. After working as a theater director, an actor, and a free-lance TV writer, he has become one of the most successful and prolific production entities in television. He has been involved, either by himself or in partnership with others, with such series as Mod Squad, Starsky and Hutch, Family, S.W.A.T., Charlie's Angels, Love Boat, Fantasy Island, Hotel, Dynasty, *and* Hollywood Beat. *Spelling has also produced movies for television, miniseries, and* Mr. Mom, *a theatrical feature. In recent years he has been under exclusive contract to ABC.*

What did you major in at SMU?

SPELLING: Journalism. But I also did some writing and directing of one-act plays while I was there, even won some awards. After I graduated I directed little theater in Dallas, including a play for Margo Jones.

By then I thought I was a big director, so when I was offered a job directing a revival that was supposedly headed for Broadway, I got on a bus and went to New York. It turned out that they were going to do *Tobacco Road* with an all-black cast. It was the most vulgar, demeaning thing I've ever seen, so I said no. I stayed in New York, pretty much destitute, for about a year and a half, and then I caught a bus for Los Angeles.

To work in the entertainment industry?

SPELLING: No. My first big job in L.A. was at Western Airlines as a reservationist. Fortunately, I met a man named George McCall. He was married to Ada Leonard and they had a show on KTTV called *Ada Leonard and Her All-Girl Orchestra.* George was intrigued with me and offered me a job as a band boy.

Well, that put me back in show business. A band boy is someone who carries instruments on tours. From that I worked my way up to being a recruiter. The program was like an amateur show, with all-girl contestants, so I found myself going to tap-dancing schools, baton-twirling schools, accordian schools, and vocal schools.

Then some of the kids in the mail room at KTTV heard of a one-act play contest. So in my skinny, Texan, Orson-Wellesian fashion I announced that I was going to write one. I did—it was called *Thorns in the Road*—and it won the contest. Then we got the idea of doing a three-act play. I had directed Garson Kanin's *Live Wire* in Dallas, and I thought it would be just right for the mail-room kids. Since there weren't enough of them to fill all of the parts, I combined some of the characters.

We opened it over a bus station in a theater that seated forty-five people. One of the actors—he's now a judge in Los Angeles—approached the *L.A. Times,* so they sent in their drama critic and we got this glowing review. For me it was particularly good: I was the new young George Abbott. And then, on closing night, a very distinguished-looking man walked into the theater and said, "I would like to see your play." I tried to sell him a ticket, but he swept right past me. I didn't have the guts to stop him because I had never seen a man wear a cape before. He had a cape around his shoulders, and a big hat, and after the show he said he wanted to meet Aaron Spelling. I introduced myself and he said, "I would like to move your play to my theater. My name is Preston Sturges."

Well, of course, he was an idol of mine. And he owned

a theater-restaurant on Sunset Boulevard. So we moved over there, everyone joined Equity, and we all made fifty-five bucks a week. Garson Kanin came to see the dress rehearsal. He was furious that I had combined some of his characters, and Preston told him my reason was that we didn't have enough people for the cast. After the performance Kanin came to see me. He said, "You know what? Now I know why my play didn't work on Broadway." Which I thought was marvelous, because he really did have too many characters. You couldn't focus in on anybody.

Aside from directing little theater, you also began getting work as an actor on television.

SPELLING: It started one night when a man came to see me backstage. He said he didn't need directors but that he wanted to do something for me. He had met my wife at the time, Carolyn Jones, who was in the play. He asked me if I had ever acted. I told him, "Yeah, I toured with the Lunts in Europe." And he said, "Well, good," and that he wanted me to do his show. I thought he was kidding. But he was Jack Webb, and the next day I got a script from him for *Dragnet*.

Over the next two years I did seventeen episodes. The truth is, I wasn't really that interested in acting; I had always wanted to write. Jack allowed me to visit the set, and I learned things like fade out and fade in, dissolves, and straight cuts. And then I did something that I wish young writers would do today—I'd sit down, see a show, and write a complete script. Then I'd submit the script to the producer of that show.

Don't you feel that today's young writers are willing to do the same?

SPELLING: No. And it bugs me. They come in, they've never written anything, and they tell you an idea. Then, to show you an example of their work, they promise to write a script on spec. I tell them I can't ask them to do that, it's against the rules of the Writers Guild, but they say they're going to do it anyway. And when they deliver the script— this is for an hour show—it's only twenty pages long. It bothers me that they don't seem to know their craft.

What was your first professional sale?

SPELLING: While I was acting I heard about a new series called *The Jane Wyman Theater*. I knew the producer because I had worked for him as an actor, so I brought in a story. Lo and behold he bought it. It was called *Twenty Dollar Bribe,* and I was the happiest human being in the world. But by the time I got home my agent called and said they only wanted the story; they would not let me do the teleplay. Well, I needed the money desperately, and a sale is a sale, so I sold it to them.

About three weeks later I got a call from Jane Wyman. She was there in the producer's office when I had sold him the story, and now she wanted to know what the hell I had done to my script. I told her I didn't write the script. The producer, it appears, had taken off the writer's name and left mine. So she said, "Go write your script." This was on a Friday, and I was so excited that on Monday morning I came in with my script. A week later they started shooting it.

How did you get an agent?

SPELLING: I had already been working with an actor's agent, but he didn't know anything about writers. I have to give my former wife credit. When she was nominated for an Academy Award, she left her smaller agent and went to the William Morris Agency. She made it a condition that they sign me as a writer. They did, and they sent me over to a new series called *The Zane Grey Theater* to meet with the producer, whose name was Hal Hudson. I told him three stories, and although he didn't buy any of them, he assumed I knew about the West because I came from Texas. But from a Jewish family in Dallas you don't ride a lot of horses, let me tell you that.

The important thing is that as I left his office—I swear this is true, and it's the way careers get started sometimes—I saw Abe Lastfogel, from the Morris office, and Sam Weisboard, from the Morris office, and Stan Kamen, also from the Morris office. They were standing there with Dick Powell. And he was saying, "I'm not going to do it!" They kept telling him that he had a contract, that there was a deal. And he said, "I'm not going to do a series where I have to stand there and tell them what the show is about!" I realized that he was supposed to be the host of *The Zane Grey Theater*—and not very happy about what they wanted him to do.

As I drove home I got an idea. I called Stan Kamen at the Morris agency and told him I had heard they were having problems with the *Zane Grey* host spots and that I had an approach. He said, "The first damn thing you should learn in this business is not to eavesdrop." Well, I was mortified. So I shut up. But the next day he called me back and asked what I had. When I told him my idea, he asked me to put it on paper and he'd set up a meeting for the next day. I said I couldn't get it on paper that quickly. What I didn't tell him, of course, was that I knew very little about the West and had to get to a library. So he said we'd make it Wednesday.

On Wednesday I walked into Dick Powell's office, which was the biggest office I had ever seen. I felt like a condemned man. By the time I got to his desk I was perspiring. I told him that I didn't know what scripts he'd be doing, but if, for example, the show featured a Conestoga wagon, then he should actually have one of them on the set. He could come out in Western clothes and explain exactly what it was. Or if he was doing a show about Boot Hill, he could read some of the actual epitaphs on Boot Hill tombstones. Powell didn't say much, and then Abe Lastfogel, who was there, asked me to read one of the epitaphs out loud. And that was the thing that did it.

I said, "Now, Dick—Mr. Powell—those epitaphs were

very colorful and sometimes told a man's whole life story. Like this one: 'Stole a cow that wasn't his'n. And was hung before he got to prison.' " Dick roared. Because the one thing he kept saying was that he wanted humor. Well, I was signed to do the host spots at a hundred dollars each. I went to the library like a good little boy and my writing career was launched. After all, here I was making a hundred dollars, and since we did thirty-nine *Zane Grey Theaters* that year, I made thirty-nine hundred dollars. The main thing was that I qualified for unemployment.

Did you write any of the actual scripts?

SPELLING: Dick Powell asked me if I had ever considered writing a *Zane Grey*. I said I had submitted a few stories. He asked me which one I liked the most, and I said "Crying Need for Water." He asked if I had it on paper, and I said sure. He told me he wanted to see it, and literally the next day he called me and said, "I like this, I spoke to Hal Hudson, let's do it." That year I wrote seventeen *Zane Grey Theaters*.

How did you become a producer?

SPELLING: A man named Marty Manulis saw one of my shows. He was doing *Playhouse 90,* and since they had never done a Western, he asked me to write one for him. I wrote a script called *The Last Man,* and John Frankenheimer directed it. It was one of the pleasantest experiences of my life, because here was a director who did not allow the actors to change a word. If there was a problem, if a scene wasn't playing, they would bring me in. I was at every rehearsal, and John and I would talk about it. Also, *he* didn't change a word, which pleased me even more, because directors do as much rewriting as actors.

Then, a few days after it was aired, Stan Kamen sold it to 20th Century–Fox as a theatrical movie. I met with them and they said, "All we want you to do is expand it, don't change it, we like it, just give it some air." So I reported to 20th Century–Fox. It was fantastic. I had a drive-on pass, a parking spot, and an office. I also had an eighty-year-old secretary who I later found out was keeping tabs on me. They did that with new writers, to make sure you're there and working.

Well, I wanted to make a good impression on the producer, so I had started over the weekend, and on my first day I walked into his office and gave him thirty pages. First lesson I learned. He said, "Dammit, don't you ever hand in more than two pages a day. I'm on a weekly!"

So I was miserable, really bored, doing only two pages a day. I spoke with Dick Powell and told him about it. Dick had a company called Four Star Productions. They had a character named Johnny Ringo that they thought could be the basis for a television series, and Dick asked me if I'd like to write the pilot. I said yeah. And here's the fantastic part, and it's true—while I was handing in my two pages a day at Fox I wrote the *Johnny Ringo* pilot, we shot it, and we sold it. At that point Dick asked me to come with him. But I didn't want to produce.

Obviously you changed your mind.

SPELLING: The thing that did it was a script I had written for Westinghouse called *The Night the Phone Rang*. I really loved it. I had written it for a man I met at Dick's house named Edward G. Robinson, who was an idol to me. It was about a little Italian plumber, and it was very important that it have a quiet sensitivity and an Italian feeling. Well, they lost Edward G. Robinson for five thousand dollars. I won't mention the actor they used, but he was a very good Irish actor doing Italian with the worst accent you ever heard. When I saw it on TV, I literally went into the bathroom and regurgitated.

My wife said, "You're never going to write anything again that you don't produce." And I went back to Dick Powell and asked if he still wanted me to produce *Johnny Ringo,* and he said yes. Then, miracle of miracles, I produced six series at Four Star, including *The Dick Powell Theater.*

How long were you there?

SPELLING: Ten years. I was very happy; I didn't want anything else. I was getting royalties on things—I didn't know what ownership meant—and I had a guarantee of $100,000 a year. I would have been willing to sign a twenty-year contract. And then Dick passed away. Without him, I don't know, I could not write or think or create. It became a whole different company. It was just over for me.

You entered into two major partnerships, first with Danny Thomas, then with Leonard Goldberg. Why didn't you go out on your own?

SPELLING: At first I did. After I left Four Star I was signed to be the head of television for United Artists. I got on a train, went to New York, and met with all of the UA people. I told them I had some great ideas. I wanted to bring in some of the writers I had known at Four Star—no producers—and eventually everybody would produce their own things. I got back on the train, and by the time I arrived in Los Angeles, United Artists had gone out of the television business. True story.

Well, I was desperate. Even though UA owed me money, I didn't know what to do. Then I walked into a restaurant one night and this loud voice screamed, "I want you!" I thought somebody was going to kill me, but it was Danny Thomas. He said he had just talked to Abe Lastfogel, he knew the United Artists deal was over, and that he wanted me to be his partner. It was just like that. I went into partnership with Danny for three years. After that I decided I didn't want a partner. I loved Danny and he was nice to me, but I wanted to see whether I could do it on my own. So for seven years it was just Aaron Spelling Productions.

Finally, one day I said to myself, "I don't have anybody to talk to." I felt I needed a sounding board. I had worked with Len Goldberg for years and years; while I was at Four

Star he was my contact at ABC and we got along very well. So I asked him to come in and we formed Spelling–Goldberg. When that ended, I started Aaron Spelling Productions again. Doug Cramer and Duke Vincent own pieces, but it's not like a partnership. I don't think I could ever do that again. I had two good experiences with Danny and Len, but there comes a time when you need your privacy as much as you need a sounding board.

With a half dozen or more hours of programming on the air, how do you manage to handle the work load?

SPELLING: I get a great deal of help from Doug and Duke. On the first few years of *Love Boat,* for instance, I worked very hard on it. I started out reading every outline, because if the outline is good, there's no chance the script won't work. But after that I didn't think there was any need for me. Doug took it over and did a magnificent job.

I usually pay very close attention for the first few years. On *Dynasty* I saw every day of dailies, and I still see rough cuts. What I enjoy now, now that I'm not a writer, is working with film. I think that editing is a sensational process. It can also protect the words. I don't like directors who are showing you the wall when writers have written great lines. And I demand a lot of coverage.

As for casting, I'm totally involved. I don't think it's fair to put that kind of pressure on the producer-writers. By the way, I don't have producers. I have *writer*-producers. I don't want any producer who isn't a writer. Because I don't care whether you're doing a slick, trashy show or if you're doing *Family,* it's all in the material. When we cast—even the bit parts—we've developed a system that works quite well. The writer-producers and the directors will interview maybe twenty or thirty actors, and then they'll bring in the top three people whom they like. And I'll say, "Guys, I really think we should go with number two instead of number three." And sometimes they'll talk me out of it. They'll tell me their reasons and they'll be right.

Casting is instinct. And the most important thing for an actor to have is likability. Barbara Stanwyck has it, and Angela Lansbury. John Forsythe has marvelous likability. Linda Evans? How can you hate Linda Evans? A lot of these people have become my friends over the years, so I know who I can get and who I can't get. Why should my writer-producers worry when I can shortcut the process? So I do casting personally. Obviously in pilots. Especially the leads.

Do you get involved with the hiring of directors?

SPELLING: Absolutely. On every show—every show but *Love Boat*, because we now have a group of directors who has done it many times. At the moment we're setting a list of directors for *The Colbys*, a spin-off from *Dynasty*, and Esther Shapiro, Doug Cramer, and I are sitting down and making selections.

I think it's very important who your first three or four directors are, because they set the feeling for the show. I like directors, I really do. The ones I dislike are those who don't give a damn about the series, who are showing off their talents and not showcasing the scripts and the actors. That's one of the reasons I like to select directors. You can tell if they're right after they do one episode.

Do you personally select the writers?

SPELLING: No. With writers it's a totally different situation. All I ask is that if I don't know the writer, I want to see something that he's written so that I can read it. If it's a new writer, and they think he's fresh and seems to have it, then by all means use him. The only thing I warn them about is that if the outline isn't good, then don't think it's going to get better.

Do you do any rewriting yourself?

SPELLING: Oh, yes. I love working with dialogue. I hate structure. But I enjoy making the dialogue better. By the way, every time I get a first draft, I make myself write down the date. And if I don't return it within two days, with my notes, I feel guity as hell. If I have to read it at three o'clock in the morning, I'll read it at three o'clock in the morning. I won't keep writers waiting. I remember that when I used to hand in a script, it would be weeks before I got it back. You just die.

Do you work on weekends?
SPELLING: No. I devote Saturdays and Sundays to my kids. I usually come into the office at nine in the morning and leave at eight at night. Some nights it's eight-thirty and I have to apologize to my family. But I will not stay here any later because if I miss kissing my kids good night, I'm just dead for the day.

In the trade there is what's known as the Aaron Spelling Look, or the Aaron Spelling Approach. It usually connotes a casting philosophy that tends toward a mix of young, attractive actors and well-known older movie stars. It also involves a certain style of lighting, which some critics feel gives your films a "flat" look, and an overemphasis on establishing shots.
SPELLING: I'm guilty of one of those charges. I have used too many exterior establishing shots. But we're cutting down on those. Although there are reasons for them. I like to use music to lead the audience into an act, and I like it to go out before the dialogue starts. Anything to protect the dialogue. The establishing shots give the music something to play over.

Also, I don't like to come out of a commercial without music. You never know in advance what the commercial's going to be, and sometimes, even though your act has begun, the audience thinks they're still watching the commercial. Maybe establishing shots are old-fashioned now, but I read a book once where the head man at CBS had a line about showing them where the bathroom is, and I think, especially in a new show, that it's very important.

On *Dynasty* I like to see that house because it's a character. The beauty of it, the immensity of it. And on *Hotel* I think the establishing shots kind of get you in the mood of San Francisco. But, as I said, we're cutting down on them.

As for our approach to lighting, it's not flat. We do in-depth lighting, which actually takes more time. It's a bright, very rich look. If I'm going to spend money to have real flowers on the far wall, I want to see them. If there's going to be a green dress, I want to bring out the green. Also, when you think about some of our more successful shows—*Love Boat* and *Fantasy Island* and *Charlie's Angels* and *Dynasty* and *Hotel*—you'll realize that they're all glamour shows. All of our cinematographers are people who can light women beautifully. You wouldn't want that kind of look on *Hill Street Blues,* and we didn't use it on *McGruder and Loud.*

In fact, I'll tell you a funny story. We did a film called *Dark Mansions.* And when I saw the first day's dailies, I went crazy. I said, "What have you done? This should be mood and shadows and you've got it all pumped up and bright!" And the people from the lab said, "We're giving you the Aaron Spelling Look." They literally said they were giving me the Aaron Spelling Look, as if I were a third person.

What are your feelings about the use of music?

SPELLING: I think that if you have a great theme, then you should use it with many variations. *Dynasty* has a marvelous theme. When you hear that music, you know the show is on the air. That's very important, because you're not in a theater, you're at home. You could be talking to someone on the phone or you could be in the kitchen—but when you hear the theme, you rush in to see the show.

We're going to use a different kind of music on a series we're doing called *Hollywood Beat.* It's going to have today's sound, and I know we're going to be criticized for it. People will say we're ripping off *Miami Vice*. Well, it didn't start with *Miami Vice*. There were pictures around before that like *Flashdance*. And if you're going to do a series where your leads are twenty-six or twenty-seven, and you're on the air at eight o'clock at night, you can't very well play Rachmaninoff. You're not going to do country-and-western for *Hollywood Beat*. You're going to play the music of today, the music that young people listen to.*

Another aspect of the Spelling Approach is that you seem to gravitate toward stories with strong emotional appeal and you embrace a very positive, upbeat view of life.

SPELLING: I'm an incurable romantic, I really am. If there's anything that I've given to television, it's to bring hope to people, and fantasy. I guess it's because I grew up in such poverty. The movies were my escape from the ghetto; I could lose myself in them. I mean, Ginger Rogers and Fred Astaire saved my life.

There's so much terror in the world right now. Every newspaper talks about impending doom. I don't know how kids can grow up today, wondering if there's going to be a tomorrow. I'm concerned about that. You've got to release the pressure valve and say that there's hope, that there's goodness in man. Some critics may think that's syrupy. Well, I'm sorry.

How do you release your own pressure valve? Do you go to the theater, read, watch movies?

SPELLING: Whenever we're in New York, we make a steady diet of theater. We also go here in Los Angeles, although not as often as I'd like because I prefer to spend my free evenings with our children. Right now they only really understand musicals, so we take them to every

---

Hollywood Beat was not a success. It was canceled before it completed its first season.

musical that comes to town. On Saturday nights we show a film at our house. Two films. We start at six-thirty with a picture for the children, although they're getting harder and harder to find. We've gone back to get some of the old Disney films like *Bambi* and *Snow White*. The classics. Then we see a second movie. As for reading, I try, I try. I love reading about Hollywood's bygone era. And once in a while I'll read a book like *Day One*. As much as it frightens me, I'll read it.

Millions of people spend many hours every week watching your shows. Do you feel you have any kind of public responsibility?

SPELLING: Of course. You'd have to be inhumane not to. My thoughts on that have changed since I've had children. I would never, ever, ever do a violent show like *S.W.A.T.* or *Strike Force* again. I now see things through the eyes of my children, especially the twelve-year-old girl who is so ready to be molded.

I've become very concerned over the last two years by how much drinking I see on my own shows. I'm cutting down on it. I also want to do more shows, not about the chase to catch the drug dealer, but about the victims of drugs and the families of the victims of drugs.

I'm also going to do four two-hour live presentations of really good theater. Originals. Originals that say something. I do feel a little guilty that I haven't given enough back. And I want to prove to myself that I can still do films like *Best Little Girl in the World,* which was about anorexia, and *Family.*

What do you think about television critics?

SPELLING: They're the sore spot of my life. I think they stamp you. Whatever I do, they say it's from the man who gave you *Charlie's Angels* and *S.W.A.T.* They never mention that I did *Family.* Norman Lear once said something to me that helped a lot. He said that if he had done *Family,* he would have won six Emmys.

Do you think critics resent the fact that you specialize in broadly based popular entertainment.

SPELLING: I suppose they don't feel that's good enough. But we're in something called the entertainment business, and I see nothing wrong with popular entertainment. Take Steven Spielberg, who I think is a young genius, and George Lucas, who I think is a young genius. They do great popcorn entertainment and the critics love it. But when you do it on television, for some reason you're damned for it.

I must say that I regard ninety percent of the critics who write about television as frustrated writers. They're also frustrated critics because they put themselves in such a strange position—they don't see the medium as they should through the eyes of an audience. Frankly, I'd rather be loved by sixty million people in the audience than by six hundred critics. I was even attacked when I did a feature film called *Mr. Mom*. They said, well, this shows you, he should stick to television. They called it a little television movie. Then, after it had grossed about fifty-five million dollars, they decided, in retrospect, that *Mr. Mom* was working because of Michael Keaton and Teri Garr. Never once did they mention the writer and me, never once did they mention the fact that the writer came to me, I didn't go to a studio, I put up my own money, we developed the idea, and he wrote what I thought was a lovely script. I did it when my agents said it couldn't be done, I took it away from Paramount because they wanted the wrong director on it. But none of this was ever mentioned.

So I don't like critics. I find them to be unfair, and I think they've been really unfair to me. I don't want to be compared to *The Execution of Private Slovik*. I don't want to be compared to a series that may really be doing something special. What I *do* want to be compared with are other series in the same genre I'm doing. If I do a police show, compare me to other police shows. If I do a show like *Dynasty*, compare me to the other serials. That's all I ask. And I think that's fair. I don't want to be picked on just because of my success.

Even with the critical abuse there must be compensations other than the money.

SPELLING: Oh, yes. It's absolutely wonderful when I go into a department store to buy something, or when I'm in New York, or when I went to England, and people come up to me and ask if I'm Aaron Spelling. I gotta tell you, that gives me a lot. The fact that they recognize me and know my face, that they're interested enough to know a producer, means that maybe I've given them something in their lives. And that helps a lot, it really does. I'm not a megalomaniac, I don't throw pages from my typewriter at the end of my shows, but gosh that's good, that I've been able to enter other people's lives.

When we were in London we received a letter from a woman who said she was a fan of my series, and could I come to Liverpool because she was dying to meet me. I was so impressed by the letter, it was so articulate, that I wrote back and said we couldn't come to Liverpool, but that I'd be more than glad to pay for her ticket to London so we could meet. She refused to do that. Instead she came at her own expense. She wore the sweetest little lace dress that you knew had just been bought. She was thirty-nine years old, a mother of two, and I can't tell you what it meant to me. I can't tell you.

The Network
BRANDON TARTIKOFF

Brandon Tartikoff was born in New York City in 1949 and graduated with honors from Yale University in 1970. After working as the Director of Advertising and Promotion, first at WTHH-TV in New Haven, and then at WLS-TV, the ABC-owned station in Chicago, he joined the ABC-TV network as Manager, Dramatic Development. Tartikoff moved to NBC as Director, Comedy Programs, and then held the post of Vice-President, Programs, West Coast. In 1980, he was named President, NBC Entertainment, becoming the youngest division president in the network's history. During his tenure he has been involved with such television series as Hill Street Blues, Cheers, St. Elsewhere, The A-Team, The Cosby Show, *and* Miami Vice. *In December 1980, the United States Jaycees named him one of the Ten Outstanding Young Men of America.*

Did you have any particular career in mind when you went to Yale?

TARTIKOFF: I knew I wanted to do something that involved writing. During high school I had been the editor of the yearbook and the school paper and the literary magazine, so writing seemed to be my forte. My original major in college was Economics—at least until the New York Jets–Baltimore Colts Super Bowl. The day after the game I had my Economics final, but I had spent my study time watching Joe Namath beat the Colts, so I flunked the Economics exam and decided to become an English major.

At the time I had a suspicion that television would be an interesting field, although Yale had absolutely no courses in either journalism or communications. They had only one film course, which I took in my sophomore year, so I used to go to New York and audit film courses at NYU.

I graduated the same year that the three networks were severely hurt by the removal of cigarette advertising from the airwaves. Hundreds of millions of dollars no longer flowed into network coffers, and quite a few jobs were eliminated. My initial plan had been to go to New York and assault the three networks. I thought I'd get a job as a page, but the loss of cigarette advertising took care of that. I had a girlfriend in New Haven, and I was finishing a novel, so I stayed there and eventually got a job at a local advertising agency. I started in the mail room running packages to trains, and later I worked my way up to copywriter.

Had you tried to get a job in television first?

TARTIKOFF: Yes, when I was a senior. There was one local television station in New Haven. I took them a class project I had written, a parody of soap opera. I had been involved with some of the actors at the Yale Dramat, so I went to this local station and I said, "Boy, am I going to make your day. I've got these terrific actors, I've got this script, and we can put on this show once a week for your station. All we need is a living room set."

The local program director looked at me, shook his head, and told me that I didn't understand how the business worked. He said they were a local station and they didn't put on their own shows; they either ran network programs or they bought syndicated shows. He said that what I had written was for me and my friends, and that's not who watched television.

Then he gave me a piece of advice. He asked if I had an Instamatic camera and I said I did. He said, "Why don't you go down to New York, go to the Port Authority Bus Terminal, and take pictures of the first hundred people who get off the busses? Take those pictures, blow them up to eight-by-ten glossies, and wherever you go to work in television, put those photographs up on the wall somewhere. And every time you have to make a decision, look at those pictures and ask yourself, will *they* like it?" If I did that, he said, I'd be very successful in the business.

This took place in 1970. And the irony is that in 1975 Norman Lear produced a soap opera parody called *Mary Hartman, Mary Hartman,* and it went on to become somewhat of a success in syndication, playing for local stations exactly like the one I had tried to sell my idea to. It was essentially the same concept. And the program director left the station a year later—not because he didn't buy my show. The promotion director was moved into his job, and it created a vacancy. I left the ad agency and took the job, so there I was at the local station because the guy who didn't like my idea was gone. If there's a moral to any of this, it's eluded me.

After your apprenticeship and the years during which you were a protégé of Fred Silverman's both at ABC and NBC, you've gone on to become the President of NBC Entertainment. Is everything you do aimed at getting highly rated TV series on the air?

TARTIKOFF: Not everything. Mostly everything. My basic job is to provide a certain level of profits for my division, and my division includes virtually all programming the network turns out, with the exception of news and sports. It's the Saturday morning cartoon shows, it's the game shows, soap operas, late night—*The Tonight Show, David Letterman, Saturday Night Live*—and, of course, prime time. NBC guarantees RCA, its parent corporation, certain profits every year, and I'm obliged to deliver those profits. The higher the ratings of my shows, the greater the profits NBC enjoys. That's the crassest way of looking at my job.

If I had to be black and white about it, I'd say that eighty percent of my function is to compete against CBS and ABC to win every time period. The other twenty percent is what I call the Second Agenda, which really started when Grant Tinker walked in the door. This involves what we can do to further the medium, to improve it. It's everything from the Television Academy Hall of Fame to the occasional movie for television that we produce not because it will get a 40 share—we know it won't—but because it deserves to be put on the air. Plus an occasional television series that you know will probably not be successful but whose creative auspices are impeccable enough to risk the long shot. I'd rather take a chance doing six or eight episodes of a superbly crafted show than do six to eight episodes of another cop with another gun going after another criminal.

What kind of staff reports to you?

TARTIKOFF: I have a head of Movies and Miniseries. I've got a man in charge of Talent and Casting who comes up with the people who are going to be in everything from Movies of the Week to dramatic television series to situation comedies to the new cast members of *Saturday Night Live*. The head of Daytime reports to me. The head of Advertising and Promotion reports to me—these are the people who make all the promos and commercials for upcoming shows. The head of Late-Night Programming reports to me, as does the head of Saturday morning cartoon shows. I also have a Program Planning person who works with me on scheduling—what goes on this Sunday at eight, what goes on three weeks from now—so that the viewer won't be sitting home some Friday evening and NBC comes up with a slide that says: "Read a good book, folks, because we don't have anything to show you tonight."

I also have a person who handles all of the new pilots for comedy and drama series, as well as the maintenance of the episodes of ongoing series. And I have someone in charge of Specials and Variety. We're the lone network that is still trying to keep the flame going for variety. And that's about it.

We don't have a sprawling kind of organizational chart, with hundreds and hundreds of people. The programming people, the ones who work in the Entertainment Division on the actual shows, as opposed to the auxiliary people who make sure the film comes in and commercials are integrated into the program, number less than a hundred.

Trace an idea, from the buyer's point of view, from its inception to its commitment as a series.

TARTIKOFF: First it should be understood that there are usually two ways ideas come in. In one case someone will meet with you and tell you he or she has a wonderful idea. You listen to it, you're getting it cold, and you think to yourself: How can this idea help me? Is it going to solve my problem Friday at eight, is it going to solve my problem Wednesday at nine? If not, at least is it so overwhelmingly wonderful that I don't want it to go to ABC or CBS? It may not fit in with what's being developed or what we currently have on the air, but you don't want it to come back and bite you. Better to have it on your shelf than someone else's airwaves. So you listen, you judge it, and you either buy it or you don't.

The second situation is when the idea originates here at the network. This approach began when Fred Silverman was at NBC and we were in third place. In those days producers would much rather have their shows go on CBS or ABC because there would be a better chance for success. They wouldn't have to face *Charlie's Angels, Happy Days,* or *M*A*S*H.* They wouldn't be scheduled against the juggernauts. If they went to NBC, given the fact that networks usually program new series in failed time periods, they'd get an order for thirteen episodes, they'd run up the same deficits as they would elsewhere, and there was a good chance they'd be scheduled in a killer time period. But if they went to the other two networks, their show might actually follow *Three's Company* on ABC, or *Dallas* on CBS.

To counteract these disadvantages, to make ourselves more appealing, we tried to generate ideas that we thought were applicable to our schedule. Then we'd go to the producers we wanted to be in business with—the suppliers who weren't exactly jumping into their cars to drive over here to Burbank with their firstborn—and offer them these home-grown ideas. In return for taking the raw elements of our rough concepts, they would have a chance to make more than thirteen episodes. Thirteen episodes was the standard deal at CBS and ABC, but we held out the possibility of twenty-two episodes, or even getting to a second year. The lone stipulation was that the producers execute the agreed-upon concept and that they do a good show. Not a show that got good ratings. Just a good show.

We began backing up this philosophy by renewing *Hill Street* and *Cheers* and *St. Elsewhere,* even though they hadn't earned their marks in the Nielsens. We tried to send a strong and clear message to the creative community that there was an alternative to the prevailing mass hysteria, that creative people didn't have to be treated badly, and that we were offering a kind of safe place where people could do good work. If they wouldn't bring us their ideas, we'd give them ours. We didn't present anything fully developed. Usually it was a notion, a germ. And we had an advantage over the supplier—we had total access and a total understanding of the demographics we were attracting, so we could create shows for a certain kind of audience: eighteen to forty-nine, youthful—

In other words, yuppies.
TARTIKOFF: Yes. Or as we refer to it here, the *Y* word. To give an example of the network-originated idea, let's

take the case of *Miami Vice,* where we started with a very vague notion and embarked on it on two fronts. First, we wanted to take *Hill Street Blues,* which was a pure cop show, and *Starsky and Hutch,* which was a relationship show, a buddy show, and blend them. Second, we wanted to somehow utilize music videos.

When MTV was just hitting its stride, and it was making its presence felt in *Time* magazine and elsewhere, I said to my staff that I thought we should take a crash course and try to understand what it was all about. I suggested we all spend some time watching an hour of MTV every night. So we became couch potatoes for a week. One video in particular interested us, Randy Newman's "I Love L.A." This was long before Nike made it their commercial.

When you develop something, you know that for every three pilots you make in a given genre, only one of them will be good enough to schedule. So we went to several different sources. We played the Randy Newman video for David Chase, a writer who had worked on *The Rockford Files.* I said to him, "You know how Randy Newman drives around in that big Buick in 'I Love L.A.'? What I'd like is a detective who wears Hawaiian shirts, and he runs around L.A. in an old car, and instead of cutting the show the way Aaron Spelling used to cut *Starsky and Hutch,* let's cut the action sequences, the jeopardy scenes, like videos. And we'll get original music." David Chase got excited, and he went after the rights to the Police song, "Every Breath You Take." He said that would be his main title, and he wrote four different episodic scripts about a character called Jaguar. The scripts were very obtuse and very dark and we chose not to make them.

At the same time we went to another source, Universal Studios. We said to them, "You guys have the best lot in town for production, and we're interested in doing something that's hot and contemporary, with a video feel." We asked for a hard police show. Much different from the

David Chase idea, which was a character detective piece. We said that if *Hill Street* was the cop show of the late seventies, what would the cop show of the eighties be? How could we take *Hill Street* fifteen degrees further to the left?

On *Hill Street* we'd been playing around for years with the idea of spinning off Hill and Renko into their own series—the Michael Warren, Charlie Haid characters. Tony Yerkovitch, a writer from *Hill Street,* had just made a deal with Universal, so we said, "Hey, why don't you expose this idea to Yerkovitch? God knows he can write Hill and Renko, and we'll just add the video element to it." So it started out with the black guy and the white guy—the Hill and Renko image—and the video aspect. It was called *MTV Cops.*

Yerkovitch said he loved the idea and wanted to do it. But he wanted to set it in Florida. He was sick of shooting the same L.A. corners, and Florida was open territory. The idea then became known as *Dade County Fastlane.* Michael Mann, who had left television to direct feature films, was brought into the project and became executive producer. That's how *Miami Vice* was initiated.

Even though the first germ of the idea came from us, there was never a moment in time when someone from the network said, "Let's give it a distinct look, with only some of the colors that are on the palette, let's do it all in pastels." No part of the collective network brain could ever have articulated something like that, nor could we have come up with the idea of having the leads wear the latest Armani clothes or giving them a Ferrari even though there are no vice cops anywhere driving Ferraris. The words of Tony Yerkovitch and the vision of Michael Mann are what made the show a success.

How do business considerations influence you when you're deciding whether or not to program a new series?

TARTIKOFF: There are two constituencies that we have to get behind us when we come up with a schedule: the advertising agencies and the affiliates. We have to make sure we have the kind of shows that people on Madison Avenue in New York and Michigan Avenue in Chicago feel will provide a compatible, comfortable medium for their commercials. If the shows are offensive, if they're morally outrageous, if they're too violent or too sexy, we could be getting 28 ratings, but our sales department would be selling them at half sponsorship. So, obviously, we have to please the advertisers.

As for the affiliates, they're our points of distribution, and our national ratings are based on having a full distribution system. We have two hundred and four of them at last count. If we do a situation comedy about a Jerry Falwell type and his three nasty kids, and if people in the Sun Belt don't like it, they're going to write to their local station and perhaps even challenge the license of the station owner. So the affiliates look at our programs on two levels. One is content. Are we giving them something we feel is suitable to run on their airwaves? Secondly, they look at the show from a competitive point of view—does it have a snowball's chance in hell in that time period; i.e., will it succeed?

Ideally I want a show that will have advertisers lined up around the block—there's a waiting list to get into *Miami Vice* now, and *Cosby* and *Family Ties*—and even though this is a pretty big country, with different regions and different tastes, I hope to get ninety-nine percent representation of our affiliates.

Isn't it true that some of the affiliates, for a variety of reasons, choose not to carry the network feed on occasion?

TARTIKOFF: Yes. A local station knows we're offering *x* amount of dollars, but the station owner may say, "Look, I'm going to spend my own money and go out and buy *Solid Gold,* or I'll buy my own movie, and I'll preempt your program on that night because I'll get a hundred percent of all the money that comes in. Besides, I think your show is only going to get a sixteen share, and I can get a sixteen share with a local movie.''

So I know that on any given day I'm going to lose two or three stations. And if I cancel a particular program in a tough time period, I have to hope that the stations don't lose confidence in my ability as a programmer and start going out and buying shows to supplant the network shows—or switching to another network entirely. The converse of that is that if there's a given affiliate, let's say in Pennsylvania, who constantly preempts the network for Billy Graham specials, for baseball games, for every Operation Prime Time miniseries that comes down the pike, then at some point we might look at the situation and decide we're better off without that particular station. We'll forget about Channel X in that market and see if we can bribe Channel Y to take us.

What happens during selling season in New York? Does the fact that the suppliers are present make a difference to you?

TARTIKOFF: There used to be a day and age—it was before my time—when the networks were primarily run out of New York and the heads of programming were located there. In those days people could actually sell shows on the spot, make them up, take the buyers to 21 and get them drunk, and do some arm-twisting. That no longer happens, but there's still a pilgrimage east. I suppose the suppliers want to be closer to the moment when they get the yes or no. They even bribe secretaries to see what planes we'll be on. They're like groupies. I guess some dinosaur habits die hard.

Don't you see most of your pilots before you leave Los Angeles?

TARTIKOFF: Yes. Every year we make about thirty pilots for our prime-time schedule, and we probably look at about eighty to eighty-five percent of them here in Burbank. We go back to New York for about five days. We always announce in New York—the major agencies are still based there, so that's where we make our initial presentation of the new fall schedule.

In New York we see the remaining ten to fifteen percent of the product, either because it's come in late or else we've asked to see it in a revised form. We look at the shows, or re-look at them, and we bring in other network constituencies beside the programming department. We bring in the head of Sales. We bring in the head of Affiliate Relations, who might tell us that if we move a popular show to a new time period, the stations will be in an uproar. We bring in the corporate Standards people, who make sure we're aware of the social reaction we might experience from special-interest groups for a given program.

There's also the fact that we're not setting our schedule in a vacuum—the other two networks are doing the same thing. So we start to get intelligence. We trade information with various suppliers. A guy calls up to ask how we like his show, and we say that before we tell him, we want to know what's going on at ABC and CBS. We begin to hear enough things from enough sources so that we can start to form a police artist's sketch of our competitors' fall line-ups. We obviously want to avoid putting a certain show on our schedule Friday night at nine when ABC is programming a similar vehicle in the same slot.

Finally, we're getting research information. We cable-test all of our pilots in five different markets across the country. Real people in real homes with real television sets watch the programs that were just made. Our research department, which has been running these kinds of tests for the last fifteen years, will give us norms as to how well the shows tested. We begin to get a sense of our reactions versus the results of the test audience. Sometimes these reactions coincide—they hate it and we hate it. Sometimes, like *The Cosby Show*, we loved it and the test audience loved it. That makes the decision very easy.

But we don't always agree among ourselves. When we saw *Miami Vice,* half of the programming department thought it was terrific and half didn't understand it. The Doubting Thomases were very nervous about it; basically, they thought the two leads weren't particularly good. The testing was abysmal. In fact, it was the last show that we scheduled. But when I see a show that I think could be a breakthrough, I get a little chill down my spine and I say to myself, "God, this thing is really daring and different." At that point you have to say, "Screw the testing, we're putting it on, anyway." Those are the same words that Fred Silverman uttered—a little less cleaned up—when he saw *Hill Street Blues* in the spring of 1979.

Since you have such enormous influence, what are the checks, if any, on you and your personal preferences?

TARTIKOFF: I have my own checks on myself. I've been in this job for quite some time now, and I'm much better at figuring out what appeals to Brandon Tartikoff the person and what appeals to Brandon Tartikoff the programmer.

I probably have more esoteric tastes than the average television viewer. I'll go to see *Amadeus* and pay my five dollars and fifty cents, but when the salesman from Orion comes and asks me to buy it for the network, I'll say no, because it's going to get a twenty-two share. I don't have to buy a twenty-two share; I have a hundred films on the shelf that can get a twenty-two share. So it becomes almost a private battle.

I'm sure there were other programmers at other times whose tastes were much closer to the average viewer's. I once worked for someone who used to laugh exactly when the laugh track laughed on situation comedies. When I go to a comedy taping, sometimes I'll laugh where the track will laugh, but there will be other times when I may be the only one laughing because there'll be a joke that might be a little out of the reach of most of the audience. I remember in the pilot of *Cheers* there was a John Donne joke.

Another potential conflict arises because, like most people, there are some things that I'm personally very attached to, both politically and emotionally. Several years ago a project was brought to me based on a book called *O Jerusalem*. It was a six-hour script developed for another network. I'm Jewish and I'm concerned about and interested in the health of Israel. It was a very powerful story. But as a programmer I had to ask myself if it was something that would get a thirty share or better, if it would justify the millions of dollars that it would cost. Now I wasn't just saying that if it didn't get a thirty share I wouldn't put it on. There are times when something is so good, so worthy, that you have to make it. But when I looked at the slate of what we were doing in the miniseries area, I saw that we had a project called *Evergreen* and we also had *Wallenberg*. So, in the relative scheme of things we were not ignoring this theme or this particular group of people. I finally decided that it would be unfair for me to impose my personal viewpoint, and I turned it down. I still think about it. Obviously I'm still thinking about it today, many years later, so it was not an easy decision.

Do you see a continuation of the TV movie and the miniseries?

TARTIKOFF: Absolutely. They're very strong and important forms. I think what will happen is that the networks may not do as many of them, but the ones they do will be more worthwhile.

Right now, anytime a network gets into trouble, it removes a night of series and throws on a night of movies. You go to the head of your movie division and say, "Give me sixteen more movies." But there aren't sixteen good scripts lying around, so you end up making films just to fill time periods—and that results in very uninspired pictures. People look at them and say, "Why should I watch the ninth movie about a female vampire?"

One thing that TV movies can do, by the way, that can't

be done in theatrical features, is the socially themed subject. We have ninety-nine-percent distribution around the country, and if you want to get America focused on a particular subject—*The Day After, Adam,* and a film we just did about AIDS, called *An Early Frost*—there's no better way to do it than through a television movie together with some sort of discussion program, or else having the local stations tie it in with their eleven o'clock news special reports. The cable companies can't do this kind of event because they don't have the distribution. And motion pictures have such a long gestation period, sometimes two or three years, that if the subject is current, it will be long out-of-date by the time the movie is released.

What's your attitude toward the press? Help or hindrance?

TARTIKOFF: The press has certainly been favorable to NBC. I'm probably the only network person who will say this. CBS thinks the press is in our camp, and ABC is very nervous about the print media. In our darkest, darkest days the press was skewering us for our *Supertrains,* but when we came up with a *Hill Street Blues,* they really got behind it. They also got behind some of the series that have become the cornerstones of our resurgence, our success, if you will—*Cheers, St. Elsewhere*—even the shows that didn't last five years but started with us, such as *Fame.*

That's not to say that journalists can make a show a hit. I learned that the hard way. In the fall of 1983, NBC put on nine new shows, and all nine were canceled by the end of the year. Five of them enjoyed critical acclaim from the TV writers and the general press, shows like *The Yellow Rose, For Love and Honor,* and *Bay City Blues.* But the press couldn't save them. What they *can* do is take something that's borderline and give it a boost.

Along with the praise they also gang up on shows they don't like. The A-Team, *for example.*

TARTIKOFF: If *The A-Team* is so cartoony and junky, as the critics seem to think, if it's so easy to do, then why don't ABC and CBS copy it and get their thirty-four shares? God knows they have no qualms about copying our shows—there are two copies of *Miami Vice* coming up and three of *Bill Cosby*. The reason they don't copy it is because it's very sophisticated and intricate. It has a lot of comedy, tremendous characterization that the young audience loves, and it's far from easy to do, or others would have done it.

As to the fact that it isn't getting critical acclaim, I don't do my program schedule for the press. When I met with them this past June, they started in on me about a series called *Misfits of Science*. And I said, "Hey, wait a second, this show wasn't created for you. We have some things we think you'll like, Steven Spielberg's *Amazing Stories* and *Golden Girls*, but we're not naive enough to think that everything we do will get great reviews from *The New York Times*." We didn't get reviews for *Knight Rider* or *The A-Team*, but the audience watches, and they keep the lights burning here in Burbank.

I've always contended that the *Hill Street*s and the *Cheers*—call them sophisticated shows or urbane-quality type programs—actually start to compete with each other, and not with the other series they run against on CBS and ABC. In certain households the viewer is saying, "I don't want to be stuck at home every night of the week to watch a television show, so I'll just pick one. Maybe I like *St. Elsewhere* better than *Hill Street* at this moment in time, so I'll stay home on Wednesday and accept dinner invitations on Thursdays." Hard-core action-adventure viewers, on the other hand, will mass-consume *The A-Team*, they'll watch *Knight Rider*, they'll watch *The Fall Guy*, they'll watch *Magnum*. It's like you can't give them enough, although God knows we've tried.

Have your attitudes about your work changed since you became a parent?

TARTIKOFF: Yes. I used to fashion myself a responsible broadcaster, but I can honestly say I'm more aware and more responsible now that I have a child on my lap as I watch the tube. The television set is sending out images, and I'm more aware now of what this little person is making of them.

My social conscience in this regard goes beyond delegating our standards to the areas of the company that are supposed to be worried about those things. I personally turned down *The Guyana Tragedy*. It went on CBS and did very well. I had absolutely no interest in *The Atlanta Child Murders* when that was being peddled around. I just feel that there are some things that you should not do just to get a rating point.

Hopefully we have enough creative juices to find more than one way to skin the thirty-five share cat so that you don't have to run out and do the San Ysidro McDonald's massacre for your Saturday Night Movie. Someone might do it, and you might have to swallow deeply and run against it on a given night, but I'd rather have that happen and be able to live with myself. The worst thing is when you put on a show you've had reservations about, and then you read the papers the next day and learn that three teenagers in Alabama emulated something terrible in that particular movie.

You've been criticized for being fixated on youth, on programming for the young audience. What's your response?

TARTIKOFF: Well, if you live by youth, you die by youth. Because when you seek out the young audience, you're entering into a pact with a certain kind of Nielsen devil. On the one hand, these people are the most mobile, the least set in their ways, and the most vulnerable to an advertiser's message. When that advertiser comes up with new commercial telling them to drink Pepsi instead of Coke, and he hits the eighteen- to thirty-four-year-old audience, there's a good shot he'll make an impact on them. My mother will see that some commercial for Pepsi-Cola and she'll say, "I'm sorry, I've been drinking Coca-

Cola since I was twelve, and I will go to my grave drinking Coca-Cola. You could have Steven Spielberg direct that Pepsi commercial, I don't care, I'm drinking Coca-Cola.'' So the advantage to the advertiser is the openness of the young.

On the other hand, they're the most fickle viewers. Once you get them to watch *Miami Vice*, for instance, you have to realize that unless you keep the series hot and change it every year, the first people who are going to leave are the first people who came to the show. They're first in the door and first out. *The A-Team* used to get a forty share. Now it's a thirty-four share. The viewers who left were probably the teenagers who were initially fascinated by Mr. T. They're the trendy viewers, and they get tired quickly.

My model for the ideal network is based on aspects of CBS and ABC at different moments of their history. I'd like us to have the mantle that CBS used to wear because they programmed shows like *The Mary Tyler Moore Show*, *All in the Family*, *M*A*S*H*, and *The Defenders*. When people thought of class, they thought of CBS. I'd also like the youth image that ABC connoted in the mid-seventies, when it was the personification of rock and roll television. So I'm trying to find a happy medium, all puns intended. If that means at some point we happen to like a show that doesn't particularly appeal to a young audience, we'll do it, anyway. The stars of *Golden Girls*, for instance, are all over fifty.

Although you've scheduled it for Saturday nights when your usual young audience isn't home.

TARTIKOFF: I just think that's the right night for it. We're not doing terribly well on Saturday nights, so maybe altering our usual strategy will help. But to conclude this point about my so-called fixation with youth, it really has to do with what I feel most comfortable programming. My personality and this network have curiously merged in a way so that now we've become the favorite network for two disparate groups: yuppies and nine-year-old boys. The yuppies watch the *Cheers,* the *Hill Streets,* and the *St. Elsewheres.* The nine-year-old boys watch the *Diff'rent Strokes,* the *Silver Spoons,* the *Knight Riders,* whatever.

There's a nine-year-old boy trapped in my body who's trying to get out, and it's easier for me to develop shows for that boy than it is to develop things for an audience between thirty-five and fifty-four. To decide what this latter group will like is a bit more of a reach for me as a programmer. I mean, I can come up with a *Misfits of Science* by saying to myself, if I were a nine-year-old boy, I'd ride over people on my bicycle just to get home in time to watch that show. But obviously, if you only attract nine-year-old boys, you'll end up with a nice, rip-roaring fifteen share. The trick is getting the nine-year-old boys plus everyone else.

What changes do you see coming up in American television?

TARTIKOFF: I suppose there will be a day when there are more than three networks. Probably four or five. But the odds are that NBC, CBS, and ABC will still get the majority of the viewing audience—hopefully in that order.

When people crystal-ball the future, they tend to get hung up on the so-called new technologies and the new competitive media. But the network share of the audience depends on how well the networks do their jobs. Put another way, whoever comes up with the hits will not only survive but thrive.

So far cable, with all its ballyhoo, has not come up with a hit. If HBO, instead of NBC, had gone to Tony Yerkovitch and Michael Mann, and whispered the magic words, "MTV Cops," and if *Miami Vice* was on HBO, I guarantee you their subscription rates would have skyrocketed—assuming, of course, that HBO could have afforded such a high-ticket show. Eventually there will be a hit on cable or on an independent station network—ad hoc or otherwise—and it will unfavorably impact the networks' share of audience on a particular night. But if the TV audience continues to grow, and it should, and if the networks come up with some hits of their own or develop some new forms of television, the "majors" will weather this increased competition.

However, I think the traditional forms will still be with us. There's always an audience for a compelling drama like *Cagney and Lacey* or an adventure show like *Magnum, P.I.* There will be comedy, because since the cave dwellers, we've always enjoyed a good laugh. What *will* change, and this is a change for the better, will be the quality of the content you'll be seeing, because what will fall by the wayside are what former NBC Programming Chief Paul Klein used to call The Least Objectionable Programs.

When you've got a Zap Box in your house, and the average number of channels in the typical household is somewhere in the twenty-five to thirty range, you've got much more control and many more choices. Networks can no longer hammock a weak show between two hits and count on it doing well. And there's no guarantee that just because a marginal program has a strong lead-in, it will hold on to most of the audience. Lucille Ball said that television changed with the invention of the remote control device. As soon as a guy doesn't have to get up from his chair to switch the channel, television becomes a new ball game. Viewer inertia, which supported many an uninspired show, has given way to viewer impatience.

But I do see a rainbow on the horizon, because as the share points among the networks start to decrease, you won't have to hit a thirty share to keep your show on the air. You won't always have to come up with programs that have such enormous mass appeal. Broadcasting won't become "narrowcasting," but a network may find that a twenty-two or a twenty-three share means it's got a winner on its hands.

Interestingly, shows such as *Cheers, Hill Street,* and *St. Elsewhere* are the least affected by increasing competition and the increase in the number of channels; they actually get higher ratings in cable households than they do in overall television households. They're the most cable-resistant. And they hit the best demographics, so advertisers are willing to pay a premium. Perhaps these kinds of shows are the wave of the future.

What are the positives and the negatives of your job?
TARTIKOFF: The best part is that you have the keys to the biggest toy store in the world. A network is a great laboratory to experiment in and fool with the beakers. When I wake up in the morning with an idea, I don't have to worry about who I can sell it to. I just have to decide which one of my departments can put it to best use. Every day there's a great creative adrenaline rush, and you have the ability to implement your own ideas.

There's also a tremendous variety to the work itself. I enjoy the eclectic approach, and I'm able to go from a meeting on *The Smurfs* to a meeting on Johnny Carson's contract, to a pitch on a miniseries that won't be broadcast for four years, to a meeting about what's going to happen between Sam and Diane next season on *Cheers.* You almost never get bored.

The downside is that television is a monster that constantly has to be fed. The monster eats for fourteen and a half hours every weekday, and it most certainly eats its young. As a programmer, you constantly have to be plugging up the holes in your schedule. You're always worrying about whether or not a show is running out of gas. Remember the old joke about the fact that a woman gives birth every seven seconds, and if only we could find that woman, we could stop the population explosion? Well, there's always a star walking off one of your shows. And you're going to hear about it. And have to deal with it. The main negative of this job is that there's never any downtime.

Now, probably a lot of that is brought on by my own competitiveness. I'm constantly on the lookout for the next great idea. And the canvas that I paint on is so large that almost everything applies to my work. If I see a commercial and there's an interesting actor I'll write down: Prell commercial, call casting tomorrow, find out who the blond guy is, is he a lox, can he put three sentences together, could he be a detective? When I go to the movies with my wife, I'm always asking myself if there's some kind of dynamic at work in the film that can be translated to a television series.

Then, of course, wherever you go there are always people—from the valet guys who park your car at restaurants to guys on the jogging track—who will say, do you have a minute, has anybody pitched you this story or that concept? So you're constantly being hit on—thirty to forty times a day, three hundred sixty-five times a year. In my half dozen years in this job I've handled more pitches than Johnny Bench did in his career.

When you're home—if you're not out with friends or at a screening—somewhere between eight and eleven the television set will be on for at least ninety minutes, because you realize that you should really spot-check *Kate and Allie,* or see if the subject matter of a CBS movie is going to conflict with something you might be doing. There's really no downtime at all. It's the only job in America where, when you finish up for the day, you leave your office and get home just as your work goes on display for the entire country—as well as your competitors.

AFTERWORD

Each summer, and sometimes during the school term, groups of students arrive in Los Angeles with their professors, disport themselves in local motels or university dorms, and spend a week or so attending sitcom tapings and visiting soundstages, dubbing rooms, editing cubicles, and other places where lurks that *rara avis*, the TV professional.

These young people are usually from college-level or graduate-school communications courses, and they come (as Robert Papazian noted in his interview) to learn the difference between classroom theory and its application in an actual work environment.

We have been asked on occasion to lecture such groups, and we are not alone. Others in the television industry (including some of the people in this book) make themselves available for question-and-answer sessions, imparting whatever kernels of wisdom they can dredge up, attempting both to inspire and forewarn, to avoid sounding too cynical while at the same time trying to ground the neophyte in some kind of practical reality.

A year or so ago, as one particular class was preparing to return to a Southern university, we asked one of its professors what had most impressed—or interested—his charges. "The fact," he answered, "that all of the people who spoke to them were so nice, so intelligent, and so well intentioned."

Implicit in this remark, or so we felt, was surprise that

all of these nice, intelligent, well-intentioned people turned out, in the main, so much mediocre work.

Perhaps that was just our interpretation, but as we interviewed our colleagues for this book, we, too, were struck by their enthusiasm, their basic decency, and their sense of social responsibility. Yet we doubt that many of them, in their more reflective moments, are entirely satisfied with the current state of their medium. Even Barbara Corday, who professed to be astonished by the quality of programming given the number of on-air hours to fill, complained about the rampant imitation and the tendency to self-censorship.

The head of a major studio once told us, "The primary purpose of American television, as it's presently constituted, is to deliver an audience to an advertiser at the lowest cost per thousand. Quality, style, content—these are all matters of subjective taste, and they are important only as they relate to the rise and fall of the ratings, which are the yardstick by which television time is sold."

Clearly the ramifications of this view—an economic need to be popular in the broadcast sense—have a deadening effect on those within the system who endeavor to take their work seriously and seek to be creative.

There is also the vexing matter of the television audience. Stephen Kandel speaks of the steelworker who would rather watch *Lady Blue* than *Death of a Salesman,* and it should be noted that even *Hill Street Blues,* with all of its success, has never been as popular as many series of lesser artistic merit.

Audiences, it's been said, get what they deserve, and television has a long history of catering (some would say pandering) to its viewers. Critics are endlessly frustrated by the disparity between what they respond to and what the average viewer watches. In self-defense—and to avoid stating baldly that many in the vast TV audience aren't particularly bright and get exactly what they want—these critics have constructed elaborate explanations: The ratings are wrong; people simply can't be watching this trash. TV has brainwashed the entire country into an acceptance of the banal; left to their own devices, without a daily electronic reinforcement of pap, viewers would opt for Shakespeare and PBS. The audience is never given a choice; it's *all* bad, and therefore Americans are driven into selecting the least objectionable programs.

For the most part these are rationalizations. It would appear that what many viewers want from television, as opposed to what others *want* them to want, is to quote Stephen Kandel, "relatively painless entertainment." TV may have created these expectations; in that sense the critics may be right. Yet regardless of the reason, the fact of their existence is a major constraint for those of us who work in the medium.

Some of the failings are our own. Confronted by network restrictions, by our day-to-day nuts-and-bolts problems, and by what some of us perceive as the indifference of our audience ("Why would anyone watch something like *that,* for God's sake?") we all too often settle for second best in our work. We remind ourselves that we are only in the "entertainment" business, and we seldom aspire to a broader definition of that word.

Still, it is not against the law for us to do things that are worth watching. Even if we accept that our role is essentially to entertain, there is always the tantalizing possibility that we can create *quality* entertainment.

A situation comedy can be mindless, or it can be *M*A*S*H* or *Cheers* or *The Cosby Show*. A police series can be car chases and Uzis or *Hill Street Blues*. A private detective opus can be an insult to the intelligence, or it can be *The Rockford Files*. If, as they keep telling us, our job is to fashion genre pieces for mass consumption, there's no reason why we can't make *good* genre pieces.

We are all, of course, painfully aware of the obstacles that stand in the way of even such a limited goal. Steven Bochco speaks of censorship. John Gay mourns the lack of rehearsal time. Gary Goldberg is only comfortable working for one of the three networks. Angela Lansbury remembers being stunned by the paucity of preparation in episodic TV. Stephen Kandel feels that there's not much room in the medium for relatively serious drama. And Brandon Tartikoff keeps his eye on the numbers, knowing that a motion picture he enjoyed in a theater, which won critical praise and a batch of Academy Awards, will only deliver a 22 share on the small screen.

And yet, somehow, the *Hill Street*s and *All in the Family*s and *St. Elsewhere*s get made. And somewhere in the Movie of the Week mix, along with this month's third variation of the rape or alcoholism story, and next month's film on wife abuse or child abuse or parent abuse or dog and cat abuse, we still get the literate sensitivity of a *Do You Remember Love?*, which dealt with Alzheimer's disease compassionately and artistically, avoiding the usual clichés of the "disease-of-the-week" programmers.

Granted, these are exceptions. So were *The Defenders*, *The Naked City*, *Mr. Peepers*, *East Side, West Side*, and *Playhouse 90*. But the fact that such anomalies exist at all, given the givens discussed in these pages, is a cause for at least cautious optimism.

Most of these bright moments, and others like them, are a result of dumb luck, talent, perseverance, and a kind of guerrilla warfare against the system by writers, producers, actors, and directors. They are also a tribute to the unpredictability of the audience; however maligned, it will respond on occasion to some of the better efforts in numbers sufficient to keep quality programming on the air—at least for a while.

This is scarcely a reason for dancing in the streets, but it is unrealistic to expect radical changes in an industry whose methods of operation generate enormous profits and have therefore become virtually set in stone. The best we can hope for in the immediate future are incremental improvements and more enlightened conduct on both sides of the screen.

We might also comfort ourselves with the possibility that as newcomers enter the field—including, perhaps, some of those students who journey to Los Angeles each summer to observe a process they wish to join—at least a few of them will go against the grain, becoming mavericks, gadflys, and saboteurs instead of servants of the status quo.

INDEX

About the Authors

Richard Levinson and William Link were born in Philadelphia and began writing together in junior high school. Both men attended the University of Pennsylvania where they wrote film criticism for the campus newspaper and collaborated on Penn's "Mask and Wig" musicals.

Since then, they have done much to change the face of American television. They created and/or developed over a dozen series (including *Columbo, Mannix,* and *Murder, She Wrote*) and pioneered in the television movie field with such ground-breaking films as *My Sweet Charlie, That Certain Summer, The Execution of Private Slovik,* and *Crisis at Central High.* They have been honored for their work with the Paddy Chayefsky Laurel Award for TV Writing Achievement, two Emmys, two Golden Globes, the Writers Guild of America Award, the Peabody, the Christopher Medal, the NAACP Image Award, four Edgars from the Mystery Writers of America, and prizes from film festivals in this country and abroad.

Their book for the Broadway musical *Merlin* was nominated for a Tony, and their plays *Prescription: Murder* and *Guilty Conscience* have been widely produced. In 1983, the Museum of Broadcasting held a month-long exhibition/retrospective of their work. They are the authors of a novel, *Fineman;* a psychological thriller, *The Playhouse;* and *Stay Tuned,* a memoir of their careers in television.